"Snappy, funny, charming."
—*New York Times* bestselling author Carly Phillips

"A trademark blend of comedy and heart."
—*Publishers Weekly*

"A funny and thrilling ride!"
— Romance Reviews Today

"Extremely sexy . . . over-the-top . . . sparkling."
— *Rendezvous*

"A whole new dimension in laughter. A big . . . bravo!"
— A Romance Review

WILD
About the
WRANGLER

A Sexy Texans Novel

Vicki Lewis Thompson

A SIGNET ECLIPSE BOOK

SIGNET ECLIPSE
Published by New American Library,
an imprint of Penguin Random House LLC
375 Hudson Street, New York, New York 10014

This book is an original publication of New American Library.

First Printing, November 2015

Penguin
Random
House

For my daughter Audrey, because I think this might be her favorite book so far.

Acknowledgments

As always, I'm grateful for my editor Claire Zion's unfailing enthusiasm for my books and my assistant Audrey Sharpe's valuable and calming presence in my life. I'm also thrilled to be working with agent Jenny Bent and her efficient team. And finally, kudos to the art department for a gorgeous cover!

PROLOGUE

Anastasia waited until everyone was sound asleep before she crawled out of bed. Mommy said horses were dirty and smelly and no little girl of hers was ever getting on one.

Oh, yes, she was.

Her new stepsister, Georgie, got to ride her very own horse named Prince. Anastasia's new daddy had a horse, too, and Georgie got to ride with him. It wasn't fair.

Riding didn't look hard. You didn't even need a saddle. Georgie sometimes climbed right up on Prince and rode off like girls in the movies.

And Georgie had a whip. Her daddy—well, Anastasia's daddy now, too—had taught Georgie to do tricks with it. Mommy said no little girl of hers would be doing tricks with a whip, either. Georgie got to do all the fun stuff.

Quiet as a mouse, Anastasia went downstairs and out the back door. Maybe she should have put on shoes. Lots of rocks out here. Ouchy. But it wasn't cold.

She had to shove real hard to slide the piece of wood out of the way so she could open the barn door. She left it open because she'd be coming out again. On Prince. Her heart jumped around like a frog in her chest.

A yard light helped her see what she was doing. The stall wasn't easy to get open, either. But she finally got it.

She reached up, took hold of Prince's mane and tugged. "Come on, Prince." He came right out, almost knocking her over. "Stop!"

He stopped, and she dragged a stool close to him. Getting on wasn't so easy, either. And once she was sitting on his back, she was surprised to see how high off the ground she was. His back was wide and kind of slippery.

Holding his mane, she kicked his sides. "Go!"

He walked out of the barn and into the meadow. Her tummy turned somersaults. She was riding! But not very fast. She kicked him again, harder. "Go, go, go!"

He did, and it was yucky. She bounced and bounced. "Stop!"

But he only went faster! This wasn't fun at all! Crying and screaming, she tried to hold on, but his neck was too big. She couldn't reach around it.

She yelled as loud as she could. "Noooooo!"

Just like that, he stopped and she was in the air. When she landed a second later, she hit the ground hard, too hard. She couldn't breathe. Her chest hurt.

Oh, no. He was coming. The horse blew through his nose and his hooves were huge.

"No!" She tried to scoot back. "No! Noooooo!"

She scrambled backward and screamed until her throat hurt. He finally went away. She sat and shivered, afraid to make a noise, afraid to move as her heart thumped really loud.

After a long time, she heard Georgie calling. She tried to answer, but it was a tiny sound. Her throat hurt so bad. Georgie called again, and she made another squeaky noise.

Then she saw the flashlight bobbing along. But she heard something that made her whole body shake. Hoofbeats. She made herself get up even though she ached all over.

The bobbing light came closer. She saw Georgie riding her daddy's horse and leading Prince with a whip around his neck.

She backed away. But running was no use. She sucked in all the air she could. "No horses!"

It wasn't loud. But Georgie stopped. Then she climbed down. Holding the flashlight, she came over. "Oh, Anastasia. What were you thinking?"

"No horses," she whispered.

Georgie brushed dirt and pieces of grass away from her face. Then she ran her hands over her arms and legs. "You seem to be in one piece, but you're in big trouble, kid."

She imagined her mommy's face, red and mad. "D-don't tell."

Georgie wiped away her tears with the tail of her shirt. "Shh. Don't cry. I won't tell, but we have to head back before somebody else wakes up. You can ride with me. Come on."

"No!" She stumbled backward.

"Come on. You have to get back somehow. I need to put these horses away and clean you up."

"I'll walk."

"Just let me boost you up on—"

"No!"

Georgie sighed. "All right. Here's the flashlight. Me and the horses will lead you home. I'll go slow."

She nodded and took the flashlight.

"But someday you'll have to get back on a horse, Anastasia. It's what people do when they fall off."

She looked at the two giant horses standing in the meadow and shivered. "No," she whispered. "Never."

CHAPTER 1

Present day

"Mac, you must be craving that cold beer." Travis hurried to keep up as they walked down Bickford's main street after another successful trail ride. "You haven't moved this fast since the time Vince snuck a tarantula into your shower."

"And let the record show I haven't forgiven him for that." But Mac modified his pace. Yeah, he was looking forward to sipping a cold one at Sadie's Saloon, but he was more focused on showing Anastasia the new pictures on his phone.

He'd snapped some beauties of the wild stallion and his herd on the overnight trail ride this weekend and Anastasia would go nuts over them. But he didn't want Travis to know that was why he'd unconsciously lengthened his stride. Knowing Travis, he'd read too much into it.

Anastasia Bickford was just a friend, and that's the way it would always stay. In the short time he'd lived here, they'd established the kind of relationship where they could talk about anything. Anastasia was a talented artist, and with a creative mind like hers, the topics were never dull.

"I like to savor my walk down Main Street after a trail ride," Travis said. "Makes me feel like a hero." He tipped his hat to a resident who walked by and called out a greeting. "People are grateful to us, Mac. I mean, just look at the difference we've made in this town." He gestured toward the colorful storefronts and the bustling tourist trade.

"Just remember, Vince got the ball rolling, not us."

"Yeah, but we keep it rolling."

"True." Mac did take satisfaction in that as he gazed at the revitalized town. They were having a mild fall season, not much rain and not a hint of snow. Mac's denim jacket kept him plenty warm in the evenings, and during the day he was in his shirtsleeves. Perfect weather for trail rides.

Most shop windows displayed a poster version of Anastasia's painting advertising Wild Horse Canyon Adventures. It was a great image, but then Anastasia was a great artist. The poster featured a majestic gray stallion against a blue Texas Panhandle sky.

Mac couldn't believe how much things had changed in Bickford in the last six months. He, Travis, and Vince had come to town then for a reunion, thinking they'd relive the fun times they'd had while working at a nearby guest ranch. They'd arrived to find stores boarded up and the town on the verge of collapse. After the guest ranch closed, the local economy had tanked, but Vince had saved the day with his brainstorm to offer trail rides into the canyon to see wild horses and their legendary leader, the Ghost.

"The way I look at it," Travis said, "we guide the trail rides, right?"

"Right."

"And according to those online surveys Anastasia sends out, customer satisfaction is high."

"So she says." He got a kick out of Anastasia's excitement over those surveys. He also suspected she deleted the negative ones.

"Which means we're doing a helluva job and I'm gonna claim some credit. Hello, ladies." He touched the brim of his hat as they passed a couple of tourists laden down with shopping bags. "You oughta come on the trail ride," he called after them. "I lead it!"

"Then we just might, cowboy!" one of them called back.

Mac shook his head. The actual trail boss was the one bringing up the rear, which would be Mac, but Travis did love to flirt.

"See? I just drummed up more business by being my usual outgoing self. You and I are vital to the success of this venture."

"You certainly are. You should get a sandwich board and a bullhorn."

"Nope. Doesn't fit my cool-dude image. But speaking of sandwiches, I'm hungry." Travis paused at the entrance to Bickford's refurbished ice-cream shop with its red-and-white-striped decor. "I have a hankering for a hot fudge sundae with extra fudge and nuts. Let's do it."

"You go right ahead. I'd rather have a cold beer."

"We'll have both. We'll drink beer after we finish the sundaes."

Mac grimaced.

"You're such a finicky eater, Mac Foster. Go ahead to Sadie's. I'll catch up with you after I have my primo sundae."

"Suits me."

"But don't start the darts tournament until I get there."

"Wouldn't dream of it." In the late afternoons, they'd formed the habit of playing darts with Anastasia and anyone else who was interested. "I'll just drink until you get there."

"Perfect. I'll be sharp and you'll be sloshed."

"As if that would keep me from beating you, amigo." Mac grinned and continued on to Sadie's. He was just as glad Travis had decided to stop for ice cream. Talking to Anastasia about the pictures would be easier without Travis hanging over his shoulder making comments and doing his usual flirting. Travis wouldn't ask her out, though, for the same reason he wouldn't.

Anastasia was Georgie Bickford's little sis, and Georgie was officially in charge of Wild Horse Canyon Adventures. Vince had dreamed up the idea but he hadn't wanted to run the thing. He hadn't even planned on sticking around to see how the business worked out, but that was before he'd fallen for Georgie.

So Georgie ran the operation, but Vince had become the official spokesperson for the venture, the one who handled the media. Surprisingly, there was media. A wild stallion and his band had turned out to be a story that had captured national attention.

In fact, Vince was in Houston this weekend talking to an animal-advocacy group, and a film crew from Dallas would arrive in three weeks to shoot a documentary. Bickford residents were busting their buttons with civic pride. Nothing this big had ever happened here. Dwarfed by Amarillo to the north and Lubbock to the south, the town had always been small potatoes, even when the guest ranch had been operating.

Mac was happy for everyone, especially Anastasia. She deserved recognition for her work, and the documentary would help give her that. Sure, she had some art in a local gallery in Amarillo, thanks to Georgie's prodding, but that wasn't nearly enough exposure. With her talent, she should be famous.

Opening the street door to the saloon, Mac looked straight over to the corner where she'd set up shop. Georgie had urged her to rent a storefront and create an actual studio, but so far Anastasia hadn't made that happen. She seemed to prefer the familiar atmosphere of Sadie's.

Maybe that wasn't such a bad idea. Lots of people came in here and her work hung all over the walls with For Sale tags on it. Ever since the trail rides had taken off, she'd sold plenty of her watercolors depicting the town and, of course, the Ghost. Plus she did charcoal portraits, and she'd picked up a lot of business sitting in a corner of the saloon with her sketch pad at the ready.

She was sketching someone right now, in fact. Mac smiled when he saw Ida Harrington sitting at Anastasia's table having her portrait done.

Some people might laugh at a ninetysomething woman who colored her hair bright red and wore jeans and vests decorated with bling. Mac thought Ida was terrific. She'd moved to Bickford after her wealthy husband died and left her a pile of money. She could have given it to the town when the residents were in so much trouble, but she said it would just be throwing it to the wind if they didn't have a plan. Once Vince had suggested the trail rides, she'd underwritten the bulk of the expenses to get the business started.

Because Mac didn't want to interrupt Ida's portrait sitting, he walked over to the bar and ordered a beer.

Ike Plunkett had been the bartender when Mac had been a wrangler at the guest ranch, and Ike had hung on through the economic downturn. He was probably only in his forties, but had started losing his hair early. That, plus his wire-framed glasses, made him look brainy.

But it was his welcoming smile that brought customers into Sadie's, and he flashed it now. "The conquering heroes return. Where's Travis?"

Mac slid onto a stool. "Eating ice cream. And don't tell Travis he's a conquering hero. He's already out of control on that subject. I keep trying to convince him that we're just regular working guys."

"Not to a lot of people around here." Ike set a foaming glass in front of him. "You're like knights in shining armor."

"More like tarnished armor." Mac reached for his wallet.

"Put that away. This one's on the house, like always."

Mac gazed at him in frustration. "I know the saloon's doing better, but you still have to make a living."

"I make a good one, thanks to Wild Horse Canyon Adventures. Steve and Myra are doing handsprings over the number of hotel reservations that came in this week."

Mac grinned at the image of Steve and Myra Jenson, both middle-aged and stocky, doing handsprings. They'd bought the Bickford Hotel and the attached saloon years ago when business was booming. They'd weathered the bad years, and now business was good again. They deserved to reap the rewards.

"I'm glad everyone's happy," he said, "but I still think I should pay for my beer."

"Don't tell me." Ike swiped a bar rag over the polished mahogany surface that had been the resting place for drinks for more than a century. "Steve gave me my orders. You'll have to take it up with him."

"Maybe I will." Mac sipped his beer and licked the foam from his lip. He liked it here in Bickford. He liked it so well he'd bought a fixer-upper east of town and was gradually getting it the way he wanted. First house ever. That was probably a sign he was growing up.

"Hey, handsome." Ida appeared at his elbow. "Where's Travis?"

"Eating ice cream."

"How wholesome of him."

"He plans to follow the hot fudge sundae with his usual quota of beer."

Ida wrinkled her nose. "That's disgusting. Did you tell him that's disgusting?"

"More or less. But he's a big boy."

"You don't have to tell me. All three of you are pure eye candy."

Mac's face heated. "Cut it out, Ida."

"Not on your life. Age has its privileges. Anyway, I'm done if you want to go over and chat with Anastasia."

"Can I see your picture, first?"

"I was hoping you'd ask." Ida opened the folder Anastasia mounted the portraits in to protect them.

Six months ago she'd sketched Mac and had simply handed him the sheet of paper. These days the presentation was far more elegant. He'd had her sketch of him framed, but he still didn't know what to do with it. Hanging it up in his house seemed conceited.

He looked at Anastasia's vision of Ida, and it was perfect. Anastasia had caught the woman's irreverence and sparkle, plus an underlying wisdom that some people missed because Ida was so outrageous. She didn't appear young in the portrait, but not ancient, either. More like ageless, and certainly someone you'd want to know.

Mac glanced at Ida. "It's you."

"I *know*. That girl has some kind of magic. I've had her do my portrait six times, and this is the best. She just keeps getting better. When I croak, I want this in the paper with my obituary, not some studio shot when I was a kid of fifty."

"I hope you're not planning on croaking anytime soon."

"God, no. Too much going on. They want me to be in the documentary, and eventually Vince will marry Georgie, and I can't miss *that.*"

Vince laughed. "You certainly can't. None of us can. I'd crawl through quicksand to see Vince Durant finally get hitched. He was so sure it wouldn't ever happen."

"He was at that, foolish boy." Ida smiled. "But I knew." Her thick glasses magnified the curiosity in her gaze. "When are you going to admit you have a thing for Anastasia?"

He gulped. "Excuse me?"

"You can't fool an old lady, Mac Foster. FYI, she likes you, too."

"I know she does." He tried to steady his racing pulse. Not a good conversation to have right before he walked over to her table. "We're good friends."

"I don't mean she likes you. I mean she *likes* you." Ida waggled her plucked eyebrows.

Mac was determined to make light of it, despite the way his libido reacted to that comment. "You're a romantic, Ida. You want everybody paired up. But I can't date Anastasia. It's way too complicated."

"Bullshit."

He cracked up. Couldn't help it. Hearing a woman her age using the word *bullshit* was plain hysterical. She was the type, though. Ida didn't pull her punches.

"Go ahead and laugh all you want, but that's another reason for me to stick around. I want to see how you and Anastasia turn out."

Still chuckling, Mac gazed at her. "I'm happy to provide the motivation for you to stick around, no matter how misguided that motivation might be. But I have to tell you, I'm not dating her. End of story."

Ida looked into his eyes for a moment longer. "You are completely clueless, just like your friend Vince was."

Then she stood on tiptoe, kissed his cheek, and left the saloon.

He wasn't sure if he'd just been blessed or cursed. But Ida knew things. You couldn't live on this planet for almost a century and not get pretty damn good at reading people and situations.

For the first time he questioned the wisdom of being so chummy with Anastasia. Maybe he shouldn't show her the pictures he'd taken, after all. She had a whole bunch on her computer already. These were nice, but if Ida was right and Anastasia *liked* him, then deliberately spending time with her wouldn't do either of them any favors.

Georgie was super protective when it came to her sister, or rather her stepsister. Georgie's mom had died when she was a toddler and later on her dad had remarried a woman with two girls—Anastasia, the younger one, and Charmaine, the older one. Charmaine lived in Dallas while she hunted for a wealthy husband, something her greedy mother hoped for.

It would have been a classic Cinderella story except that Charmaine and Anastasia weren't ugly stepsisters by any stretch. Charmaine was a sweetheart who mostly just wanted to please her momma, although she also liked the finer things in life and wasn't opposed to marrying a rich guy.

Anastasia had told him point blank that she'd rather die than marry for wealth or prestige. She'd told her mother that, too, but Evelyn kept hoping Anastasia would fall in love with some well-heeled tourist passing through Bickford. The chances of that had improved exponentially in the past few months.

Mac took another swallow of his beer. He wished Ida hadn't told him that Anastasia had a crush on him. Ida could be wrong, of course, or she could be up to her usual shenanigans. She might think if she planted that idea in his head, he'd be driven to act on it.

Well, he wasn't going to. He'd already taken a trip down the aisle only to discover he wasn't good at marriage. Nobody in Bickford knew about that episode except Vince and Travis. He'd been divorced for a couple of years, now, and figured that would be his permanent designation.

He chose to date women who didn't want anything more than a fun time. That wasn't Anastasia. She deserved a forever guy who was good at this relationship business and would make her happy.

But he didn't want to be unfriendly, either. Now that Ida had left, Anastasia sat alone at her corner table, her hand moving rapidly over the sketch pad propped against her bent knee. From this angle he could see the intense concentration on her pretty face but not what she was drawing.

But since she wasn't looking at him, he could sneak a look at her, always a pleasure. He supposed some people would call her a brunette, but he didn't think that was nearly enough of a description. Her hair, which she mostly wore in a ponytail, like today, was about six different colors of brown, ranging from dark to light. The variations in her hair fascinated him.

But after a second or two, he turned back to his glass of beer so nobody would get the wrong idea. He probably didn't have to worry, though. None of the customers sitting at the tables or at the bar were local and they all seemed to be involved in their own conversations.

He glanced over at her again and she happened to look up right at that moment. Her instant smile of delight made his chest hurt. Did she have a crush? He hoped not. That would cause problems for both of them.

But now that they'd made eye contact, he had to go over and say hi. If he didn't, she'd think something was wrong. So he smiled back, picked up his half-full beer glass and walked over to her table.

He'd ask about her work. That was always a safe topic and he really was interested. He loved seeing what kinds of pictures she came up with. "I noticed you over here furiously drawing something. What is it?"

She laughed and turned the sketch pad around.

There he was, sitting on a barstool looking thoughtful as he sipped his beer. Yikes. Maybe Ida had a point. "Hey, I recognize that guy. He sure could use a haircut."

"Nah, it looks better long. And it's way more fun to draw than really short hair." She turned the pad around and studied the sketch. "You seemed to be thinking so hard. I hope you didn't have any issues on the trail this weekend."

"Nope." He remained standing because if he sat down, he'd get into a longer conversation with her. It never failed. They always could find something to talk about, but now that he was worried she had a crush, he ought to minimize the amount of time he spent with her. "In fact, the ride went well."

"Good." She added a few strokes of charcoal to his portrait before glancing up again. "Got any good pictures of the Ghost for me?"

"Um, yeah, now that you mention it." Her eyes also fascinated him. It probably said *hazel* on her driver's license, but he couldn't decide what color they were. Depending on the light or what she wore, they could look green, brown, gold, or a blend of those colors.

Although he'd decided not to show her the pictures, he couldn't look into those eyes and lie. For some reason she trusted him and he never wanted that to change, which was another reason not to get involved. If she trusted him with her heart, he might mess up, and that would be terrible.

He opened his picture app, scrolled to the bottom, and handed her the phone.

She sucked in a breath. "Mac, these are stupendous! I'm surprised you didn't show them to me when you first walked in."

"You were with Ida."

"She wouldn't have cared. And it's not like I go into a trance when I draw. You've watched me. I chat and make jokes the whole time. Oh, *this one.*" She turned the screen toward him. "Text them all to me, but this is the one I'll do first. Head up, mane blowing in the wind, looking every inch the leader. I love it."

Happiness flooded through him. He'd known she'd react this way. When he'd checked out the shots early this morning, he'd been excited to get back here and show them to her. He almost hadn't done it after what Ida had said, and that would have been a damn shame.

Maybe Ida was mistaking Anastasia's natural enthusiasm for a crush. He'd heard her gush over the half barrels of flowers that lined the sidewalks as if she'd never seen flowers before. Now she was wild about the horse pictures on his phone.

That was just her way. She might have spoken to Ida about him with an edge of anticipation in her voice. It didn't have to mean anything except that she was glad they were friends and he brought her pictures of the Ghost nearly every weekend.

"As long as I have your phone, do you care if I just text them to myself?"

"No, go ahead. I took them—" He caught himself before he said *for you.* That might be a little too pointed, so he finished with "for people who hadn't been out there yet." Damn. He never used to watch what he said before. That had been half the fun of being around her.

Her thumbs moved rapidly over the screen. "That's something I'd like to talk to you about. Do you have a minute to sit down?"

"Sure." He hadn't meant to, but what could it hurt? She'd said a minute, not an hour. He pulled out a chair and set his beer on the table.

After she finished sending the pictures to herself, she handed his phone back. "I have a big favor to ask."

"What's that?"

She closed her sketch pad and tucked it inside the messenger bag she always carried. Then she looked straight at him. "I need to learn how to ride a horse."

That startled the heck out of him. "You don't already know?"

"I don't." She lowered her voice. "They scare me."

"Wow. I had no idea. I just assumed . . . I don't know what I assumed." But now that she'd brought it up, he realized that she'd never suggested going out to see the Ghost herself, and the only way to do that was on horseback.

She kept her voice down and leaned toward him. "I've been afraid of them since I was little, but it didn't really matter until now. I'm starting to feel like a fraud because I'm getting known for drawing a horse I've never seen."

"No one would ever guess. The pictures are perfect." He could tell she didn't want any of this to become common knowledge. Considering how easily she'd always told him things, it wasn't surprising that she'd tell him this and know he'd keep quiet about it.

"Maybe I'm fooling people, but when the film crew arrives, they'll be asking questions, and I don't want to admit I've never seen this horse. So if you'd be willing to teach me to ride, then I could— "

"Why not ask Georgie?" Instinctively he knew that teaching her to ride was not a good idea. He wasn't sure whether there was a crush involved or not, but now that Ida had mentioned the possibility, it was permanently planted in his brain.

Until now, they'd seen a fair amount of each other, but usually here at Sadie's with other people around. Riding lessons would mean scheduled private time on a regular basis, and if they had any chemistry . . . well, he didn't want to test it.

"Georgie would baby me. She wouldn't mean to, but I'm her little sister and she can't help being overprotective. You and I are the kind of friends who tell it like it is. You'd push me out of my comfort zone so I can get past this irrational fear. I know it's a big favor, but . . . you're the only person I really trust to help me."

"Hey, Mac and Anastasia!" Travis picked that moment to bounce in on a sugar high and hail them from halfway across the saloon. "Who's up for a game of darts?"

"Be right there!" Mac called back. Then he turned to Anastasia. "Look, I'm not sure if—"

"*Please* say yes."

When it came down to it, he didn't really have a choice. Disappointing her wasn't an option. He looked into those incredible eyes and knew he was about to make a huge mistake. "Okay. I'll do it."

CHAPTER 2

Anastasia gladly joined Mac and Travis for their weekly game of darts, although she wasn't fully engaged in it. Instead she was busy congratulating herself on achieving her main objective for the day. After thinking about it all weekend, she'd decided to ask Mac for lessons when he appeared at Sadie's after the trail ride.

He always came in for a beer and showed her his pictures, so the plan had seemed foolproof. Except today he'd broken his usual pattern. He'd come in for the beer, but then he'd stayed at the bar instead of walking over to her table.

She could understand why he might not want to interrupt Ida's portrait session. He could have, but she appreciated the respect he'd always shown for her work. When he hadn't come over after Ida had left, though, she'd wondered what was going on.

He'd known Ida was gone because she'd made a point of talking to him on her way out the door. That wasn't unusual. Ida never missed a chance to interact with any of the three cowboys who'd changed Bickford's fate for the better.

But once Ida had walked out of the saloon, Anastasia

had expected Mac to come over to her table. Instead he'd sat there sipping his beer and pondering . . . something. She'd given him a chance to say what he'd been thinking about, but he hadn't risen to the bait.

That was okay. When he wanted to talk about it, he would. While he'd stayed at the bar lost in thought, she'd made good use of her time.

Consequently she had another charcoal sketch of her favorite cowboy to add to her portfolio. Because she'd created a fair amount of portraits featuring Mac, he probably thought she was besotted. She was, in a way, because sketching his portrait months ago had jump-started her urge to draw again.

But she wasn't in the mood for romance. She was too busy with her art and her blossoming career. She'd learned in art school that love affairs could be distracting and even fatal to her creativity.

She was older and wiser, now, and probably wouldn't let herself get derailed again, but why take the chance? Mac's friendship was one of the joys of her life, so turning the excellent friendship into an affair made no sense, especially because he was also the perfect choice to deal with her phobia concerning horses.

She'd heard him talk about working with greenhorns on the trail rides, and he had the attitude she was looking for in a riding teacher. He had empathy for beginners. He'd be tough but not mean, insistent but never a bully. She was desperate to see the Ghost in person and he'd agreed to help her.

The documentary had been the inciting factor, but she'd been agonizing over the problem for months. Her strong sense of artistic integrity wouldn't let her build a reputation on a lie. Other artists might disagree, but drawing the Ghost without ever seeing him in the flesh felt deceptive. She couldn't keep doing it.

"Bull's-eye!" Travis won the current round and performed an elaborate victory dance. Then he halted in front of Anastasia. "Mac's giving our darts tournament his all, but if you'll excuse my saying so, you're giving maybe your two-thirds, maybe even your half. Definitely not your all."

"Sorry. I have some things on my mind."

His eyes widened in mock horror. "More important than this?"

He made her laugh, as he always did. When all three men had come to town six months ago, Bickford's population had been mostly composed of senior citizens. Vince had fixated on Georgie, which had left Mac and Travis for Anastasia, the only other eligible woman in town. She hadn't been sure which one captivated her more.

She'd flirted with both of them, but now she knew. Travis felt like the brother she'd never had, and they teased each other unmercifully. But Mac, a few years older, was the guy she'd bonded with on a deeper level.

Those kind brown eyes invited her to say things to him she wouldn't dream of saying to anyone else. She'd discovered how to make him laugh, and so she'd often bring up outrageous topics on purpose to crack him up. Yet even when he was joking around, she sensed something more going on with him. Maybe it was melodramatic and silly to imagine he had a secret sorrow, but . . . she thought he did.

"So," Travis said. "Are these matters weighing on your mind to the point that you're not up for another best two out of three?"

"Absolutely not." She wasn't a very good darts player, but she was usually an enthusiastic one. She hadn't been today, though. "Game on."

"Ha!" Travis walked to the board and pulled out all the darts. "Anastasia Bickford is in the house!"

"I was just getting warmed up." She accepted her share of darts from Travis. "Stand back, boys. Let me show you how it's done."

Two hours later, Travis was the undisputed champion, as he usually turned out to be. There was a reason he insisted on playing darts every afternoon. Mac was competitive, but he didn't want the victory with the same intensity Travis did.

Tonight Mac had played well, but she'd caught him glancing at her with a worried expression. He'd been reluctant to agree to the riding lessons, and she wasn't sure why. Now wasn't the time to ask him, though, with so many people around.

She should have taken care of this pesky phobia years ago. She was amazed that her fear hadn't come through in her art. Or maybe it had, because her renderings of the Ghost always had a sense of power and . . . danger. People expected wild animals to be dangerous, so adding that subtle element might have given the drawings extra appeal.

After Travis was declared the darts champion of the universe, he offered to buy a round of drinks, but she'd hit her limit of social interaction for the day. She could do it for a few hours at a time and then she had to retreat. Her art came from a place of solitude, not a place of bustling activity.

She turned to address the people who'd gathered to watch the competition. "Thanks so much, everyone. But I'm heading home." That was another dilemma. She used to share the stately Victorian at the far end of Main Street with her mother and stepsister, but after Georgie and Vince had become engaged, they'd rented a little house.

That had left Anastasia alone with her mother. She loved her, but they had almost nothing in common. Still, it was her home, and since she'd just announced she was going there, she might as well do so.

After retrieving her messenger bag, she headed out the door of Sadie's. The best part of the sunset had faded, but she savored the afterglow. Sunset colors were tricky and she had more luck capturing them with watercolors than acrylics. She didn't realize Mac had followed her out until he caught up with her on the sidewalk.

She glanced at him in surprise.

"We didn't exactly make a plan for the riding lessons."

"Oh. You're right. What's good for you?"

"Early morning. Around six."

"You're kidding. The sun's not even up then."

"Almost, though." He matched his stride to hers. "The horses are fresh and you can get it out of the way first thing so you don't spend the whole day worrying about it. Then we can each get on with our day."

She looked over at him. "The horses may be fresh, but I'll be virtually unconscious. I'm not an early riser."

"What time do you usually get up?"

"Eleven."

"Eleven?"

His shock made her grin. "I've been known to get up at ten thirty, but that's rare."

"So what time do you go to bed?"

"Usually around two, unless I'm stoked about a project. Then it could be four or five. I've discovered I'm very productive after midnight."

"Hmm." He walked beside her without speaking for a little while. "So let's say you had to get up earlier to catch a plane or something. What then?"

"I never book flights that leave in the morning. If I'm forced to, it's ugly."

"But you spent four years in art school. You must have had *some* morning classes."

The memory made her groan. "Yes, and it was *horrible.* I ditched so many times it's a wonder I passed any of them. Eventually I worked my schedule around so none of my classes started before eleven. If I could get an evening class, I jumped on it."

"So you're a night owl."

"Yep, that's me." She shrugged. "That's the way I'm built." They'd reached the slate blue Victorian with the white gingerbread trim. A light was on in the parlor where her mother had installed a large flat-screen. She'd be watching it and having a pitcher of martinis by now.

Anastasia was home, or what served as home. She paused by the gate. "When I first came up with this idea, I was thinking we could do it around five thirty, after I've finished my stint at Sadie's. Around now—twilight."

He stuck his thumbs in his belt loops and gazed at her. "That's awkward timing for the horses because Ed feeds them then. And I could be wrong, but aren't you extending your time at Sadie's into happy hour beginning next week? I could have sworn I saw some signage to that effect in the window."

"You're right, darn it. I'd completely forgotten about that bright idea." She itched to pull out her sketch pad and draw him as he stood in that typical cowboy pose. She always wondered if guys realized they were framing their crotch when they did it or if the gesture was unconsciously provocative.

In Mac's case it had to be unconscious. He never tried to be sexy. He just was. If she asked him about the pose, she was fairly sure he'd blush. Then he'd make an effort never to put his thumbs through his belt loops again. Her world would become less visually interesting and she'd have only herself to blame.

A sketch of him standing like that would sell instantly, too. A woman might not understand the subliminal message, but she'd buy the sketch and it would give her a little buzz to look at it. Anastasia would get a little buzz drawing it, too. Good thing she had a photographic memory so she could get the creases in the denim just right and replicate the stitching on his fly.

Then he lifted one hand to wave it in front of her face. "Hey, cut it out."

She blinked and glanced up. Now *she* was blushing. "Um, I was . . . You probably got the wrong idea just now."

"I sure as hell hope so." His expression was forbiddingly stern.

"My interest in . . . in . . ."

"My package?" His tone was mild but he was no longer relaxed. He'd squared up his stance and now stood with feet apart and arms crossed.

"Not just that! You in general! It's purely artistic, I promise!"

"Are you sure?" His brown gaze issued a challenge. "Because after Ida's comment, I—"

"What comment?"

"She thinks you like me."

"Of course I do. I always have. You're a great guy."

"She wasn't talking about liking as in friendship. She meant liking as in wanting to be more than friends."

The conversation was affecting her heart rate for some stupid reason. But she didn't want him to know that, so she sighed and rolled her eyes. "You know not to listen to Ida. She loves to stir things up."

"That's what I told myself, and then I caught you staring at my package."

"I can explain that." She just needed to do it without making him self-conscious about sticking his thumbs in his belt loops.

He continued to stand there with his arms crossed in a defensive posture. "Go ahead."

"Now that I'm excited about drawing again, I'm constantly seeing things I want to draw."

"Like my crotch?" He looked horrified.

"No! All of you! While we stood there talking, I noticed your relaxed stance and thought it would make a nice sketch, but I couldn't very well whip out some paper and start drawing you on the spot. You'd think I'm crazy."

His mouth turned up at the corners.

"You already think I'm crazy, don't you?"

"Kind of. But in a good way." His shoulders lost their rigidity.

"Okay, I'll own that. I can get a little manic sometimes, especially about my art. In this case, I wanted to memorize every detail of how you were standing there so I could get the lines right when I went up to my room and started drawing. And the way the denim fits . . . in that area . . . is . . . complicated."

His eyes sparkled with repressed laughter. "Sometimes more than others."

"I suppose." Her cheeks felt so hot. They must be stop-sign red about now. "The point is, I'm viewing you through the eyes of an artist and that requires concentration."

"You were definitely concentrating." His mouth twitched.

"I do that all the time. Like if I decided to draw a—oh, I don't know—an earthworm, for example, I'd study it just as closely as I was studying—"

He lost it. "An *earthworm*?" His laughter boomed out. "I think I've been insulted!"

"Bad example." She'd made him laugh without trying to, but it still worked to ease the tension. She seriously doubted he had the equivalent of an earthworm tucked into his jeans or that he was the least bit insecure about what lay behind that zippered fly. She also wasn't convinced he believed her elaborate explanation as to why she was staring at it.

He finally composed himself enough to be able to talk. "Listen, do you have anything you have to do right now?"

"Other than going upstairs to draw a picture of your crotch?"

"Stop. Just stop. So, nothing you have to do?"

"Not really. Why?"

"After all this talk about you drawing things constantly, I have an idea. We're only a little ways from Ed's stable. Let's wander over there."

Her chest tightened. "For a lesson? Now?"

"No. You have your sketch pad with you. How about if you draw a horse?"

She stared at him as the idea registered. "That's brilliant."

"Have you ever drawn one from real life?"

"Like I said, they scare me. So I've avoided them. But if I start the process by drawing one, or several, that could be very calming." Or terrifying. She wouldn't know which until she tried it. "But I'm staying outside the fence."

"They're all in the barn now, anyway. It's feeding time."

"Then I'm staying outside the stall."

"That's fine. I was picturing you concentrating on their heads, anyway. And their eyes. Look into their eyes long enough and I'll bet you'll feel better about climbing on board one of them."

"You'll stick around while I do this?"

"Why not? All I had on my schedule was ripping out some old carpet. That can wait."

"Then let's go." The stables were only a short way from her house, but she'd never spent any time there, just like she'd never gone out to the little barn behind her house after that awful night. Georgie used to keep her horse, Prince, there, but the property she and Vince had rented included a barn, so Prince had moved out, too.

"How are the renovations coming along?" she asked as they approached the stable. She wanted to know, but talking about it would serve the dual purpose of distracting her. She did *not* like barns.

"Slow, but that's because I'm a perfectionist. At this rate I'll be finished in about ten years."

"You should get Georgie to help you. She's extremely handy with tools."

"She's offered, but I'm having fun doing it by myself. I've never owned a house before, so this is a brand-new experience for me." He pushed open the main gate to Ed and Vivian's property. It included the stable, a couple of corrals, and their house, which doubled as an office.

Ed and Vivian sat on the front porch and they both called out a greeting.

Mac waved at them. "Okay if I give Anastasia a tour of the stable?"

"Sure thing." Ed smiled at her. "Don't think I've ever seen you down here, young lady."

"Nope!" She smiled back, although it felt more like a grimace. "First time."

"But not her last!" Mac sounded quite happy about that.

She wasn't. She looked at him so she wouldn't have to look at where they were going. "I'm glad you bought a house here. It shows that you have confidence in Bickford's future."

"I do, and I've always liked the town."

They were mere steps from the barn's double doors, which stood open and ready to swallow her up. She kept the conversation going. "Vince would love to buy Mom's place because he knows how much Georgie wants it, but Mom won't sell while the market's going up."

"And if she sold it, where would you live?"

She shrugged. "I'd figure something out. I wish Georgie could get that house. Her ancestors built it and she maintains it even though she's not living there anymore. She should have it. I've tried talking to Mom but she's stubborn."

"So I hear. Hey, are you okay?" He peered at her. "You look pale."

"I'm scared of horses, but I'm also scared of barns."

"I'm sorry. I didn't know that. I thought a barn would make it easier because the horses are all confined in their stalls. Do you want to forget going in?"

She stood there breathing hard and feeling like an idiot. Learning to ride had been her idea, not Mac's, but he had agreed to help her and his suggestion that she draw the horses was a good one.

Her ultimate goal was to ride a horse out to the canyon where the Ghost kept his band, and draw him from life. If she couldn't even enter this barn, then none of that would take place. People entered barns all the time. No big deal.

She swallowed. "I want to go in. This is important."

"Then take my hand." He laced his strong fingers through hers.

"Thank you." The warmth of their entwined fingers spread through her and chased away the chill of dread. She would have done this without his welcome support, but his presence, and now his touch, made it so much easier.

He squeezed her hand. "Let's go."

Eyes open, heart pounding, she walked into a barn for the first time since she'd been a fanciful little girl of six. The scent of hay and the sound of horses moving in their stalls brought it all back. Her throat closed and she felt dizzy.

"You can do it." Releasing her hand, he put an arm around her shoulders and urged her forward.

His solid bulk beside her was the only thing that kept her from turning around and running outside. His grip was firm and his pace steady.

"You're fine," he murmured. "I'm here. I promise nothing will happen to you. Just keep walking."

He had far more confidence in her than she had in herself, and for that reason she kept going. She couldn't let him down. She couldn't let herself down, either.

A large horse with a reddish coat poked its head out of the stall to gaze at them.

Mac paused. "Hey, Jasper. I've brought somebody to meet you. This is Anastasia. She wants to do your portrait. You up for that?"

The horse blew out through his nose, and Anastasia hung back.

Mac's grip on her shoulder tightened. "They do that kind of thing sometimes when they meet people. Nothing worrisome about it. Jasper and me, we're buddies. Technically, he's not my horse, but I've had the use of him for trail rides and we have an understanding. Don't we, Jasper?"

The horse gazed at them with eyes so big they reflected an image of Mac. The artist in her was fascinated by those eyes fringed with dark lashes. Mac had been right that she needed to concentrate on those, which seemed filled with understanding. She might be imagining that quality, but if imagining it helped, she'd go with it.

"Feel like sketching this guy?" Mac gave her shoulder another squeeze. "He's my favorite, so I'd be much obliged if you would."

"Of course." It was the least she could do.

"Let me get you a place to sit." He let go of her.

She held back a cry of dismay. The support of his arm had meant more than she'd realized.

"You can use this." He brought over a canvas camp stool.

Without his support she felt a little wobbly, so she sat on the stool.

"I'll wager Jasper's never had his portrait done." Mac rubbed the horse's nose. "He'll love it."

The affection Mac obviously felt for the horse inspired her to pull out her sketch pad. If she could capture that emotion, she'd have something new for her portfolio.

She sketched the man first, but then she turned her attention to the horse. Such a sleek coat, such an interesting play of muscles in Jasper's neck. His ears fascinated her, too. Little hairs gave them an almost fuzzy appearance.

And the eyes. She'd have to use all her skill to capture the expression in those liquid brown eyes. Her heart rate slowed and her breathing evened out as she became completely absorbed in the task. She hummed softly under her breath.

Mac's voice roused her from her intense concentration. "You said you could chat while you draw."

"Do you want to chat?"

"Not exactly. I want to know what happened."

She didn't have to ask what he was talking about. "Nobody knows about this besides Georgie."

"You can trust me."

"I know." She kept working on the portrait of Jasper. "That's why I asked for your help."

"If I'm going to help you, I need to know the story."

She'd realized that, too. "Then maybe this is as good a time as any to tell you about it."

CHAPTER 3

When Anastasia had said that horses scared her, Mac had thought she had the usual garden-variety fear based on a horse's size and her lack of familiarity with their behavior. Oh, no. He'd signed on to help her with something much bigger. By rights she should see a therapist.

But therapists weren't thick on the ground in Bickford. Besides that, she didn't have a lot of time to mess around with driving up to Amarillo or down to Lubbock for sessions. Filming, and the publicity that would go with it, began in three weeks.

He hoped his help would be enough. All he could do was his best. So far, this drawing exercise seemed to be working okay. She'd finished one sketch of Jasper and had begun a second.

"When I was six," she began, "I'd seen several movies where the girl in the story rode bareback . . . somewhere. Either she was racing over the plains or galloping on the moors or leaping stone walls in Virginia. It looked so easy."

He wished he could have known that six-year-old. He would have been a worldly kid of thirteen, though, and might have thought she was a nuisance. Adolescent boys just discovering their sexuality tended to focus on cheerleaders and seminude movie stars.

She leaned closer to her drawing and added some detail he couldn't see from here. He wondered if she'd forgotten about telling him her story. Just as he was about to prompt her, she started up again.

"Georgie and my stepdad each had a horse but my mother wouldn't let me ride." She glanced up from her work, her expression puzzled. "I never thought of this before, but do you suppose *she's* scared of horses?"

"Maybe. You could ask her."

Anastasia shook her head, which made her glossy ponytail swing gently. "She'd never admit it to me."

"I'll bet it wasn't easy for you to admit it to me, either."

"No, but I had to if I wanted to fix the problem, and better you than anyone else I could think of." She met his gaze. "Horses are beautiful, you know."

"I do know." *And so are you.* Her shirt had a lot of green in it, which made her eyes seem more green than brown. She had really long lashes, too. At times they added to her sex appeal, but today, maybe because they were talking about her childhood, they made her appear young and vulnerable.

"I had a professor who told us we could never let fear stand in the way of our art. I've been doing that."

"But your pictures of the Ghost are great. I don't see how they could get any better."

She smiled. "Oh, they will. Even watching the video you took that one time can't replace firsthand experience. Just looking at Jasper tells me that. My drawings of the Ghost might be technically good, but once I see him, they'll be so much better. I'll be able to capture his spirit."

He gazed at her in admiration. "I can't wait to see the picture you draw after you've seen him."

"I can't wait, either." She smiled. "But don't worry. I won't steal a horse and ride off into the night by myself. I learned my lesson on that score."

"That's what you did?"

"Of course! I'd seen those movies."

"Six years old, never been on a horse, and you thought you could ride bareback all by yourself." But around the same age he'd jumped off the roof wearing a cape, so who was he to talk?

"I was barefoot and only had on a nightgown. I was going to race on Prince, Georgie's horse, through a moonlit meadow. For all I knew, fairies and elves would show up."

His heart ached for that little girl's brave fantasy.

"I got on him and he started off at a walk."

He waited, knowing the story had to get worse.

Her hand moved quickly over the paper as if keeping up with her racing thoughts. "But walking lacked drama, so I yelled at him and kicked him again. He broke into a trot, although I didn't understand what that was then. I screamed, and he panicked, I guess. He was a lot younger then." The pace of her breathing picked up. "I'm not sure what happened after that, but I think he might have started to gallop. We were going pretty fast."

Mac closed his eyes in dismay. "You could have been killed."

"On some level I knew that. This huge animal was out of control and I was about to die. I was hysterical, which only made him go faster. Then I yelled as loud as I could, and he stopped abruptly. I went right over his head."

He sucked in a breath. Even though she was sitting in front of him and obviously fine, the scene was horrific to contemplate. Maybe elves and fairies had been in the meadow watching out for her, after all.

"I could have been seriously hurt, but by some miracle I was only dazed and banged up a little. Prince hung around at first, but in my mind he'd turned into a demon horse and I screamed at him to get away. Eventually he headed for home."

"And you were alone out there."

"Not for long. It was summer so Georgie had her window open. Later she told me that she'd heard somebody out in the barn. She knows me pretty well, so she must have guessed I'd do something like that. She checked my room, threw on some clothes, and came after me."

"And you were completely traumatized."

"Not only by that, but I'd defied my mother. I was terrified of what she'd do if she found out. She doesn't like being disobeyed."

"So I gather."

"Georgie smuggled me back into the house, cleaned me up, and promised never to tell anyone." She glanced up from her sketch pad. "Although it probably doesn't matter anymore, you're one of three people in the world who know about my stupidity."

"It wasn't stupid. It was creative. Little kids think they're invincible. Even some big kids." He wanted to gather her close and comfort her, but that wasn't a good idea. Besides, she was still working on her second sketch of Jasper. He would never dream of interrupting her while she was working.

"This was a fabulous idea, Mac. Drawing Jasper and trying to get the right expression in his eyes makes me see him as an individual, a creature with needs and fears just like mine."

"As a prey animal, he has more reason to fear you than you have to fear him."

She looked up in surprise. "But he's *huge*. Why would he be afraid of little old me?"

"Ever heard that phrase *Eyes in front, born to hunt. Eyes on the side, run and hide*?"

"I have." She glanced at Jasper. "But I always thought of rabbits and deer versus coyotes and bobcats. Jasper seems much more capable of defending himself."

"Not necessarily any more than a deer. And we're definitely in the predator category, yet we expect him to carry us on his back, which puts him at potential risk if we should want to hurt him."

Her expression grew thoughtful. "I never considered that."

"If you put yourself in his place, and I know you can do that or you wouldn't be able to draw Ida with that rebellious gleam in her eye, it might change everything."

She laughed. "Ida is my second favorite subject."

He decided not to ask who her favorite subject was. He had a feeling he already knew. She claimed that her interest was purely artistic. He hoped that was true and Ida was on the wrong track.

If Anastasia didn't cross the line, he certainly wouldn't. He had so many reasons not to make a move. Being alone with her in the barn had demonstrated what he'd been trying to deny. He wanted Anastasia Bickford.

But he was no longer driven by his hormones, thank God. At one time in his life he wouldn't have been able to teach her how to ride without giving in to temptation. But he had to have faith in himself and believe those days were behind him.

When she'd first asked, he'd shied away. But now that he'd heard her story, he was glad he'd eventually said he'd do it. He wanted to help remove this block to her creativity. He believed in her future as an artist, and if he could contribute to that, great.

"I could work on this drawing forever, but I think I've kept you long enough." She carefully started tearing the pages from her sketch pad.

"That's okay. As I said, the carpet can wait." And he didn't want this moment to end. He'd have to watch himself. He might be able to keep from reaching for her, but if he started craving her company that would be almost as bad.

"I'm sure you'll feel better if you get a start on it tonight." She stood and handed him the drawings. "These are for you."

"Oh, I couldn't take those."

"You don't want them?"

"Of course I *want* them. But your stuff is worth a fair amount of money these days. You can't go giving away a—"

"Your time is also valuable, so consider this the beginning of our barter agreement. You'll need some art for the walls of your house, anyway. You can get Georgie to mat and frame them for you. She's really into that these days."

"She's good at it, too."

"Thank God for that. You can't imagine the damage I can do with a sharp blade."

Mac nodded. "Yes, I can."

"Hey, you're not supposed to *agree* with me." She tucked her sketch pad in her messenger bag and slung it over her shoulder. "You're supposed to say I just need a little more practice, or I'm probably not as bad as I think I am. Something along those lines."

"Sorry." He grinned at her. "I've been hearing stories ever since I moved here. According to those stories, you're a brilliant artist but you're also a klutz. I'm glad Georgie's convinced you to let her mat and frame for you."

"She didn't exactly convince me as much as order me away from the matting knife on pain of death. That was after I nearly sliced open an artery." She held out her arm to show him the cut. It had healed, but an angry red slash remained on her delicate skin.

He winced and resisted the urge to lean down and kiss the spot. "Does Georgie know you were planning to ask me for riding lessons?"

"Not yet, but I'm going to tell her unless you don't want me to."

"Even if I didn't want you to, we couldn't keep it secret. We'll be using Jasper and probably Cinder, so Ed and Vivian will know. Eventually the rest of the town will figure it out, too, but they don't have to hear the whole complicated story."

"I'd appreciate that. Like I said, I'm no longer terrified of repercussions from my mother, but I see no reason to stir up old issues. Those horses were a source of friction between her and my stepdad."

"Then we'll just say you need to learn so you can sketch the Ghost in his natural habitat." He gazed at her. "It's hard to believe you've never seen the meadow or Sing-Song Creek."

"Only in pictures."

"Why not hike out there? I know it's a substantial distance, but—"

"It is, and I've never been much of a hiker. I keep stopping to draw something and before you know it, the day's gone and I'm too far out to make it back before dark. I don't know much about camping, either. On horseback is the way to go, especially if someone is with me who will keep me moving."

"I can do that, although I enjoy it when you start sketching something. It makes me take a closer look. I'm guilty of seeing things in a superficial way."

She shrugged. "We all do that sometimes."

"I'll bet you don't do it much. These are great." He studied the two sketches she'd given him. The first one of him stroking Jasper's nose made him smile, but the second one of Jasper by himself peering over the stall door tugged at his heart.

She'd captured Jasper's eager interest in whatever the humans were doing. Not every horse cared, but Jasper watched the people in his life as if they were a constant source of entertainment for him. Anastasia had seen that and put it on paper. What a gift she had.

But looking at the sketches made him think of one more step she should probably take while she was here and feeling reasonably mellow. "Before you leave, why not pet him a little bit?"

"Pet him?" The anxiety in her voice was obvious as she gave the horse a nervous glance. "Do I have to?"

"No, but he'd like it if you did. Think about this from his perspective. He loves being rubbed and scratched, so you'd be doing him a big favor."

She gazed at the horse. "Is that right, Jasper? Are you looking for a little scratch?"

Jasper bobbed his head, which was probably only a reflex that had nothing to do with nodding. But his timing was perfect.

Anastasia turned to Mac with a wide smile. "Did you see that? He does!"

"Then go right ahead." He wasn't about to disabuse her of the notion. She was once a girl who'd believed in fairies and elves. She still might have some of those fantasies, and if he could add a magical horse, why not? Besides, Jasper was a really smart animal. Somebody might have taught him to nod when asked a question.

"Would you please hold my bag?" She held it toward him.

"You bet." The canvas bag was old and almost color-less from age and much use. She'd probably had it for years, maybe since high school. Whenever he pictured Anastasia, and he did quite often, she was carrying this bag over her shoulder or resting it beside her chair while she worked. He handled it with care.

Moving slowly and cautiously, she approached the stall. "I've never done this before, Jasper," she mur-mured. "I don't know much about horses in general and you in particular, but if you want a little scratch, then you deserve one for being such a good boy and a cooperative subject."

Mac swallowed a chuckle. Jasper hadn't been given much choice. He was stuck in that stall. But he was a friendly horse, which was why Mac had chosen him for the portrait session.

She lifted a hand toward the horse and then hesitated. "Mac, where do I start?"

"You could stroke his nose, first. He likes that, too."

"Promise he won't bite me."

"He won't bite you. But if you're worried about it, keep your fingers together so they don't look like car-rots."

"Carrots?" She pulled her hand away. "He could mis-take my fingers for carrots? I'm not doing this. I need my fingers. My fingers are my life."

"Here." He stepped forward and took her hand. "We'll do it together."

"We could put this off, you know." But she allowed him to guide her to Jasper's forehead while his hand pro-tectively covered her precious fingers.

Good old Jasper stood quietly as Mac moved her hand slowly down his nose. Then he repeated the mo-tion.

"He's very soft," she murmured.

"Yeah." But she was even softer and she smelled great, like ... cookies baking. "Now we'll scratch his neck." He moved her hand under Jasper's mane.

"Okay, I think I have this." Her voice quavered a little.

"You sure?"

"Yep. He'd have to be some kind of contortionist to bite my fingers while they're up under his mane. Thanks for getting me over the hump."

"No problem." He stepped away with regret, another warning sign. He was enjoying this teaching business way too much. On top of that, watching her scratch Jasper's neck made him want things he shouldn't, like her delicate fingers lightly scratching his chest, or his back, or his thighs, or ....

He stared up into the rafters of the barn while he disengaged from that line of thought. What had he decided only moments ago? That he was capable of giving her riding lessons without letting the experience become sexual?

Well, he was capable of that, damn it. Now this project had become a matter of pride, a test to see whether he'd evolved. She'd trusted him with a secret that only her beloved stepsister, Georgie, knew. She needed his help to take her Ghost-inspired art to the next level.

Using that situation to introduce sex into their relationship wasn't playing fair. He was better than that. He'd prove that to himself if nothing else.

"You were right," she said. "He really likes this."

Taking a deep breath, Mac brought his attention back to Anastasia and the horse she was caressing. Jasper, the lucky nag, was blissed out. His head hung low and his eyes had drifted half-closed as Anastasia ran her fingernails over his silky neck in a rhythmic pattern.

Mac couldn't keep watching that. Certain things were likely to happen if he did. If she thought his crotch had been interesting while they'd stood outside her gate, she'd find a whole other artistic challenge there if he didn't get out of this barn ASAP.

He grabbed the first excuse that came to mind, the one she'd given him earlier. "I've been thinking about that carpet." His nose would grow for sure with that whopper. "I would feel better if I get some of it pulled up tonight." And the physical labor would help him deal with some very inappropriate thoughts about her.

"Told you so." She gave Jasper one final scratch. "See you later, handsome." Then she turned toward Mac. "Thank you. Petting him was exactly what I needed to do. The idea of riding him or any horse still scares the snot out of me, but I've made progress."

"Yes, you have." Her open expression filled him with joy and another less noble emotion. But he'd conquer this attack of lust or know the reason why. He handed back her messenger bag. "Then I'll see you here at six in the morning?"

She groaned. "I *knew* you were going to say that. All right, but I'm warning you that I'll be a zombie."

"That'll actually be better than if you're totally awake."

"I don't see how. My coordination isn't great under the best of circumstances. If I'm half-asleep, I could slip right out of the saddle."

"In the first place, I wasn't planning to have you get up on Jasper tomorrow."

"Jasper? Isn't that your horse?"

"Not exactly, and for the next two weeks, he'll be your horse. I trust him to take good care of you."

She smiled. "That's incredibly sweet."

He fought off the wave of tenderness that made him want to pull her close and kiss those smiling lips. "It's incredibly practical. We can't risk another bad experience, considering what's at stake."

"Yeah, I guess not."

"So tomorrow you'll brush Jasper before putting on his bridle and saddling him up. Then you'll take it all off again and brush him some more. That's plenty for the first day."

She gazed at him as she hoisted the messenger bag more securely onto her shoulder. "I knew I'd made the right choice."

"We'll see. No promises."

"I don't need promises. Just knowing you're on the job is enough for me. See you at six." She rolled her eyes. "I can't believe I just said that. See ya. I have to go home, drink warm milk, and read a boring book."

"Good luck with that." She made him laugh, which might be more arousing than anything else about her.

"It'll never happen. I'll be up until two like always and shuffle in here like the living dead."

"I look forward to it." She had no idea how much.

CHAPTER 4

Whew. That had been exciting in more ways than one. Anastasia left the stables on an adrenaline high that was partly due to the interaction with the horse and mostly due to the interaction with the man. She wanted to sketch the picture of Mac she still carried in her head, but she didn't feel like going home.

Instead she walked along a back road that meandered through the sparsely populated area west of Main Street. Her mother wouldn't be expecting her for dinner. After her mom's nightly happy hour, she usually nuked a single serving of something prepackaged and let Anastasia fend for herself.

That was perfectly fine. Evelyn's life seemed to revolve around reality TV and e-mailing with friends from Abilene, where she used to live before marrying Georgie's dad. That left Anastasia free to make her own plans.

Mac had asked her what she'd do if her mother sold the house. Of course she'd miss it. The Victorian had been home for more than twenty years. But she'd never felt she quite belonged there. Georgie did, though. The Bickfords had settled the town and built that house.

Thinking of that, she realized why she'd unconsciously

walked in this direction. She wanted a sisterly chat. Vince was in Houston, so this could be the perfect time. She pulled out her phone and dialed Georgie's number. "Hey, can I invite myself over for dinner?"

"Sure, if you're okay with pasta and a salad. When Vince isn't here I eat light."

"Do you have enough for both of us?"

"I do."

"I'm on my way." She needed to tell Georgie about the riding lessons, but that wasn't the only item on her agenda. Her reaction to Mac was more potent than she'd counted on. When he'd stepped in to show her how to touch Jasper, she'd desperately wanted to touch him instead. She could use some advice from her big sister.

As she cut across a field to get there, she almost stopped to quickly sketch a gnarled mesquite. Nope, the twenty minutes it would take her would be twenty minutes Georgie would have to wait and worry. Not a nice payback after getting herself invited to dinner.

But she made a mental note of the mesquite's location so she could come back another time. The rebirth of her creative drive had been life-changing. She'd come home from art school burned out from too much structure and disappointed in love.

Not only that—the sheer number of aspiring artists had intimidated her into thinking she'd never make it. They all seemed so much better and more confident than she was. But in the past six months that depressing attitude had been banished to the far corners of her psyche.

Mac, and to a lesser extent Travis and Vince, was the reason. She'd always be grateful for that. When she'd first seen Mac, she'd had an uncontrollable urge to get that handsome face down on paper.

At the time she hadn't come in contact with a guy that gorgeous in a while, so her response had been understandable. She and Georgie lived in a town essentially without single men, let alone good-looking ones. Once the town had started going downhill, the unattached men in their twenties had all moved elsewhere to find work.

The arrival of Mac, Travis, and Vince had been the catalyst for change, both in the town and in her. She'd ended up sketching all three of them, and their awed response had poured water on the parched earth of her creativity. Now she couldn't seem to stop drawing things.

Even better, she had buyers for her art. Knowing someone would pay for one of her pictures had rebuilt her confidence and her savings account. If she decided to move or was forced to, she could handle that.

She came in sight of Georgie and Vince's rental, a cute one-bedroom bungalow on three acres. It belonged to a couple who'd also moved to find jobs when the town could no longer provide any. Like many people in that situation, they hadn't found a buyer so they'd been thrilled at the idea of renting the house.

Georgie seemed to like the place okay, but obviously the barn was the most important feature. She'd wanted Prince nearby, and Vince had recently bought a gorgeous black horse named Storm Cloud. They rode together every chance they got, and Anastasia envied them that. Even though she was afraid, the little girl she used to be still dreamed of riding bareback across a meadow.

She wasn't as keen on the moonlit part of the fantasy, though. After listening to Georgie, she understood that racing across a field at night could end up crippling the horse and maiming the rider if a gopher hole happened to be in the wrong place. But riding along a trail in the moonlight with a handsome cowboy who looked a lot like Mac Foster . . . Oh, yeah, she could picture that.

The rental house had a patio wall in back and a low

decorative wall in front with a wrought-iron gate. The barn to the right of the house sat back about twenty yards. Anastasia had ignored the barn in the past, just as she'd learned to ignore the one out behind the Victorian after that fateful night.

Today, though, she looked at the barn with interest. She could draw Prince and Storm Cloud and give the sketches to Georgie and Vince. They'd probably like that.

They already had a lot of her work on their walls, including an early sketch of the Ghost and the one she'd done of Vince soon after the guys had arrived in town. But a sketch of the two of them on their beloved horses would make an awesome wedding present.

As she approached the bungalow, Georgie must have been watching for her because she came out the front door and down the flagstone walk. The flagstone was a nice touch, and the house had some charm. The owners had offered a rent-to-own deal, but Georgie and Vince weren't doing that. Anastasia knew her sister was biding her time, waiting to reclaim her ancestral home.

"Hey." Georgie's welcome was reflected in her brown eyes as she came toward the gate. She'd piled her honey blond hair on top of her head and she wore her favorite at-home outfit—an old shirt and faded jeans. Her relaxed expression had become the norm ever since she and Vince had figured out they were madly in love. "I'm so glad you called. But you'll need a jacket for the walk home unless I drive you."

She laughed. That was so Georgie. "You can loan me a hoodie if it would make you feel better. But I'm not letting you use your gas to take me that short distance. Have you started cooking yet?"

"Not yet. Why?"

"Let's take a walk down to the barn, first."

Georgie came to an abrupt halt and stared at her. "The barn? Who are you and what have you done with my sister?"

"I've taken a major step toward overcoming my fear of horses. Now I want to go pet yours."

"This I gotta see." She came through the gate and gave Anastasia a hug. "What major step?"

"I asked Mac to give me riding lessons."

Her mouth dropped open. "You did not."

"I did." Laughing, she crossed her heart. "I promise I'm not making this up."

"You're taking riding lessons? That's fabulous!" Georgie hugged her again, tighter this time. "Congratulations, sis."

Anastasia got a little choked up at that. "Thanks. You're the only person who understands what . . . what a challenge this will be."

"I know." Georgie's eyes were moist, too. "But why ask Mac? I would teach you. Gladly."

"I know you would, and I considered asking you." Anastasia met her gaze. "But face it, Georgie. You wouldn't be tough enough on me."

"I would so!"

"You would not. You won't even let me walk home without loaning me a jacket. You're incredibly protective, and I love that you're such a softie where I'm concerned, but I need someone who'll push me to do things even when I don't want to. He's expecting me at Ed's by six."

"In the *morning*?"

"Yep, and I'll be there. I tried to weasel out of going so early, but it's the best time for him and for the horses. He stuck to his guns and I gave in."

Georgie laughed. "Well, I see your point. I would have worked around your normal sleep schedule. I've been doing that for years. Who knew you'd get up for a six a.m. riding lesson?"

Anastasia grinned. "I didn't—that's for sure. But I really want to conquer my fear so I can eventually ride out and see the Ghost with my own two eyes."

"So that's what this is all about."

"I've felt like a fraud for months, knowing that I've never seen him in person, and now with the film crew arriving in three weeks . . . that fact will come out, I'll bet. Even if I was lucky and it didn't become an issue, I still want to fix this. So will you take me out to the barn?"

"Absolutely, if you're sure you can handle it."

"I'm sure."

Georgie started across the yard. "Is this like a desensitizing exercise before the big day tomorrow?"

"More like a continuation of what I just did with Mac over at the stable." She walked beside Georgie. "He suggested I go into the barn and sketch one of the horses."

"Now *that* is a great idea. Good for Mac. So how did it go?"

"That's the other thing I need to talk to you about."

Georgie glanced at her. "If you're going to tell me you have a crush on Mac, I already know that. You've had a crush from the first day you met him."

"It's not a crush, damn it. Well, maybe it was at first, but now he's just a friend. A friend with a really nice body and a face I enjoy drawing. And good hair. I like his hair. But that doesn't mean I have to go to bed with him."

"Of course you don't *have* to." Laughter simmered in Georgie's voice. "But I have a feeling you want to."

"No, I don't, and I can't allow myself to, either. That would interfere with everything—my concentration on my work, the easy friendship we have, and the riding lessons. He point-blank asked me about the crush because Ida—bless her heart—told him I was crushing on him. I told him I was interested in him for artistic reasons. He's fun to draw."

Georgie's laughter spilled out. "And what did he say to that?"

"I think he bought it."

"If he did, I have a bridge I want to sell him."

Anastasia groaned. "You think he was humoring me?"

"No, I didn't mean it like that. He probably believes your explanation, but it's only part of the story. You're an artist, after all, and I'm sure he is fun to do—I mean, *draw*." She started laughing again.

"Oh, for God's sake. You and Ida make a good pair."

Georgie wrapped an arm around her and gave her a quick squeeze. "Okay, I'll stop teasing you."

"That's good, because I seriously do need some advice on how to handle the situation. I don't want it to get out of hand. But let's table it until after I say hello to your horses, especially Prince. I have a long overdue apology to deliver."

"He doesn't hold grudges." Georgie slid the bar aside that held the barn doors closed.

Easy for an adult, Anastasia thought. Not for a six-year-old. "I wasn't very nice to him." She expected to feel at least some anxiety as she walked into the small barn with her sister, but instead the scent of hay and horses made her think of Mac. He'd been so patient with her. And so damn sexy. That was the thought that made her shiver.

Georgie noticed. "You okay?"

"Yes." She took a deep breath and looked around. The barn was much narrower than Ed's. His had stalls on both sides of a wooden aisle, but in this setup all four stalls were in a row down the right side.

Both horses stuck their heads out to see who'd come

in for a visit. Prince was in the first stall and Storm Cloud was in the last one. Georgie went over to Prince and stroked his nose the way Mac had stroked Jasper's. "No treats, but I brought you a friend," she murmured.

Anastasia studied the horse that had carried her into the night in a terrifying race across the field. In her imagination he'd been gigantic and he'd breathed fire. She'd seen him since then, of course, but only from a distance.

Slowly she walked toward him. "I remember him as being bigger."

"Probably because you were smaller." Georgie turned to her. "Do you want me to bring him out?"

"No, no, that's okay. Maybe the next time I come over." Once she was close enough, she reached out the way Mac had taught her and scratched Prince's neck.

"You're not hyperventilating. That's good." Georgie moved away to give her plenty of room to maneuver.

"I did at first with Jasper, but then I got over it." Mac's soft breathing and his masculine scent had made her forget to be afraid. But she'd been so distracted that she hadn't spent much time observing the horse she'd been touching.

This time she could. She'd heard Georgie describe Prince as a bay, which meant he was brown with a black mane and tail. But Prince wasn't just brown. If she decided to paint him someday, she'd have to mix in red to enrich the color, and maybe a smidgen of yellow. His coat reminded her of polished cherrywood, except wood was static and his coat was not.

As he shifted his weight, the ripple of muscles underneath his coat gave it subtle shading. Getting that down, either using watercolors or acrylics, would be tricky, but she could do it. She'd studied the skeletal and muscular structure of several animals, including horses, in one of her classes.

When drawing the horses in class she'd made it a purely intellectual exercise to keep her emotions in check. She'd done the same thing when drawing the Ghost. But sketching Jasper today, she'd let herself engage. She did that now with Prince even though she wasn't drawing him.

Her face, reflected in his large brown eyes, was distorted as though seen through a peephole in a door. She edged to the left so she could really look into Prince's warm gaze. And it was friendly, too. She saw nothing but goodwill there.

Getting braver, she stroked his nose the way Georgie had. "Do you think he remembers me?"

"He might have a vague memory of your smell. If you screamed, he might remember."

"I think I'll skip that part." She combed his forelock with her fingers. "I'm sorry I screamed at you, Prince. That wasn't respectful and I promise not to do it again."

He responded with a gentle snort. Startled, she drew in a breath, but he continued to look at her calmly as if to say that she didn't have a single thing to be afraid of. She went back to stroking his nose.

"Do you think you'd ever want to ride him?" Georgie's question caught her by surprise.

"You'd let me?"

"Of course I would. You could ride Prince and I could ride Storm Cloud."

Anastasia smiled. "Did you hear that, Prince? My sis just invited me to go riding with her. That would be a first."

"I'd love it if you would, but I don't want to rush things. Let me know when you're ready."

"See what I mean?" She glanced over her shoulder at Georgie. "You're so careful with me. To most people, you're this powerhouse with high expectations, but you've always treated me as if I might break. Why is that?"

Georgie's expression softened. "The easy answer is

that I respect your talent, but the real truth is that from the start you liked me. So of course I wanted to take good care of you. I'd never had a sister before. Charmaine resented the hell out of me, but for some strange reason you didn't."

"Are you kidding? I thought you were cool beans, riding around on Prince and cracking that whip. I was jealous, but I also wanted to be you."

"You still want to learn how to use a whip?"

"Oh, God, yes. But I always figured I had to be able to ride first, like Zorro."

"Not necessarily."

"Still, it would make a good motivator. Once I've conquered the riding thing, we can move on to whip practice."

"It's a deal." Georgie smiled. "Listen, I'm getting hungry. I'm all for this new direction of yours, but could we skip petting Storm Cloud for now and go cook up some pasta?"

"We could do that." Anastasia gave Prince one last pat. "Catch you later, big guy."

As they walked back to the house, she sighed. "I've missed out on a lot, huh?"

"You mean because you didn't want to have anything to do with horses?"

"Yeah. This is a horse-oriented town, especially now that the wild horses are so much a part of our growth."

"You've sold a lot of pictures of the Ghost. That's not what I call missing out."

"I'm not talking about economically. I mean being in sync with everyone else around here. The only other person I know who doesn't like horses is my mother. She should like them because they're the force behind escalating property values and the flood of tourists who buy my art. But she doesn't."

"Her loss." Georgie walked through the gate she'd left open and continued on up the flagstone walk.

"I'm determined she'll sell you that house someday."

"You know, I think she will. She never liked Bickford. I think she hoped my father would expand his holdings and eventually outgrow the town. That was never going to happen, even if he'd lived."

"I really loved him."

Georgie's voice grew husky. "Me, too. Still miss him."

"He would have liked the idea of Wild Horse Canyon Adventures."

"I think he would have." She opened the front door and ushered Anastasia into the cozy home she'd created. "But he'd hate the fact that Vince and I are living together and haven't seen fit to stand before a preacher yet."

Anastasia followed her into the kitchen. "I hope you know the entire town is on pins and needles about the wedding date. Last I heard, somebody had started a pool for guessing the day, maybe even the time."

"Somebody?" Georgie put a large pan of water on to boil and took a box of pasta out of the cupboard. "Somebody by the name of Travis Langdon?"

"That would be the one." Anastasia rummaged in the refrigerator. "I'll put together the salad."

"That would be great." Georgie chopped veggies and dumped them into a frying pan. "This is something I assemble and then stick in the oven for a little while. We'll have time to talk about you and Mac."

"You know what? I've decided we don't need to. I'll be too zonked at six in the morning to worry about anything. My hormones will be AWOL at that ungodly hour." She began tearing lettuce into a bowl. "I'd rather talk about the holdup on setting the date for the ceremony. As your official maid of honor, I have as much right to ask as anybody. What's the problem?"

Georgie turned, knife in hand, and waved it in her direction. "You're in the pool, aren't you?"

"Who, me?" She tried to look innocent.

"Anastasia Bickford, did you come over here just so you could get the inside scoop and win the money?"

"Actually, no, but it's not a bad idea."

"Aha! You *are* in the pool."

She shrugged. "It's the most interesting thing happening at Sadie's and I'm there a lot. I figured my guess is as good as anybody's, maybe better. But I'm as baffled as they are. You're a perfect match and you both know it. Why not get on with the knot-tying part?"

Georgie stirred the veggies without looking at her. "We've been arguing about the venue."

"Really? You both like things casual. What's to discuss?"

"He wants to get married in that little box canyon we discovered that's the overnight stop for the trail rides. But I think Sadie's would work better."

"Because of Mom?"

"To be honest, if that was the only sticking point, I'd go along with Vince's idea and let her figure out what she wanted to do. It would be beautiful out there. Much more significant than getting married in Sadie's."

Anastasia's chest tightened with love for her sister. "But you knew I couldn't get to that canyon."

Georgie nodded. "Vince keeps saying we can just throw you on a gentle horse and you'll be fine, but I know different."

"And you didn't say why that wouldn't work, not even to your dearly beloved." She hadn't expected that kind of loyalty, considering how close Georgie and Vince were, but it sure felt good.

"It's not mine to tell."

"Oh, Georgie." She walked over to hug her sister. "You really are too easy on me."

"I was there that night. I know how it affected you. I couldn't ask you to climb on a horse just so I could get married in the spot of Vince's choosing. The place isn't important, but the people who will be there are extremely important."

Anastasia took a deep breath. "Set the date, sis. I'll be there."

CHAPTER 5

Mac was awake at five, a full two hours before sunrise. By five thirty he was drinking coffee and eating peanut butter toast he could barely taste. He hadn't been this much on edge since the day he'd faced a justice of the peace with Sophie.

He'd known deep down that decision hadn't been a good one. Although he had similar jitters this morning, he couldn't get a fix on whether he was doing the right thing or something totally insane. But he'd agreed to it, and once he said he'd do something, he by God did it.

He didn't have many rules to live by, but that was one of them. Normally he didn't give his word without a lot of thought, but this time he'd allowed himself to make a snap decision. He hoped it wouldn't come back to bite him.

After Anastasia had left the stable yesterday he'd had a talk with Ed about what was going to take place. Some kind of payment schedule had seemed appropriate, but Ed wouldn't hear of it. Georgie was one of his favorite people in the world, and if her little sister wanted to learn how to ride, Ed was glad to help. When he'd discovered Mac wasn't taking any money, either, that had settled the matter.

Since Mac was up early, he threw on his denim jacket and headed on over to the stable to help Ed feed. His house was only a quarter of a mile away. While most residents had built west of town, a few maverick types had bought land to the east. Mac had liked the idea of being in a slightly wilder, less developed area.

That meant he was making the trip to the stable in the pale predawn light, but he'd walked over there so many times in the past few months he didn't need to see very well. The stars were just starting to fade and the crisp, cool air felt good. The weather had stayed nice, but sooner or later they'd see some snow. His house had a wood-burning fireplace and he wanted to test it out.

The reality of owning a house hadn't quite set in yet. He'd told himself it was an investment, not a lifestyle decision, and the way Bickford was recovering he'd make money if he sold tomorrow. But with every improvement he made, he became more attached to the place.

And why not? He liked the town, his job, and the people. The population was heavily weighted toward senior citizens, but they knew how to have a good time. He could find a friendly poker game most nights at Sadie's.

Years ago the saloon had featured live music and dancing, too. Steve and Myra Jenson were determined to get a good country band booked now that they could afford to hire one. The first group had been loud and profane. The second one had played well and hadn't cussed, but they hadn't managed to show up on time. Steve and Myra were holding another round of auditions.

Ed called out a greeting when Mac walked into the barn. "Sorta thought you might show up."

"Getting up early is in my blood, I guess."

"Good timing. I was just about to start."

"I figured." Mac pulled on his leather gloves and grabbed a flake of hay while Ed did the same. They usually shared this chore before a trail ride, so they had their routine down. Mac took one row of stalls and Ed took the other.

Jasper was first to get fed, which worked out well. He'd easily be finished eating by the time Anastasia got here. Mac could halter him, too. No sense in waiting until she showed up to do that.

Delivering flakes of hay to each stall calmed the horses, but it calmed Mac, too. A daily routine was about the only thing he missed about ranch work. In this job, he and Travis were on duty for two days straight every weekend, but their weekday schedules varied.

Sometimes they repaired sections of the trail that had washed out. Other days they fetched supplies from Amarillo. If Vince and Georgie brought in a new horse, Mac and Travis were usually in charge of working the kinks out.

Some weeks were crazy and some were quiet. This one should be quiet, so Anastasia had picked a good time to ask for lessons. There would be one more overnight trail ride this weekend, and then everybody would begin focusing on the film crew's arrival. Georgie hadn't booked a trail ride for the weekend prior to their coming to town so the path could be groomed and the campsite put in tip-top condition.

Anastasia wouldn't be finished with her lessons by next week, but if they kept up with the six a.m. program, they should be able to get an hour in every weekday morning. Maybe by then she'd have adjusted to waking up before dawn. He didn't know very many night owls. Ranch people had responsibilities first thing in the morning. Most of the seniors in Bickford got up early, too. He thought Anastasia would get used to it.

But when she arrived precisely at six looking as if someone had pulled her through a knothole backward, he wasn't so sure. She must have put her hair in a ponytail the night before, because it was half in and half out of it. He'd expected she'd show up without makeup, which she didn't need to be pretty, but she must have slept in her clothes.

She hadn't bothered to zip her quilted vest, and underneath it her shirt was a wrinkled mess that was no longer tucked into her jeans if it ever had been. The jeans didn't show wrinkles, but the cuffs were bunched around her boot tops. Most people either pulled them over the boots or tucked them in, but she hadn't taken the time to do either.

They weren't the same clothes she'd had on yesterday, though. She'd obviously changed outfits. At first glance he wouldn't have recognized her except for the canvas messenger bag slung over her shoulder.

He got no cheery smile from her, either. She gazed at him in silence, her usually bright eyes dull and unfocused.

"Good morning, Anastasia."

"Morning." Her voice was hoarse.

"Ready to work with Jasper?"

She nodded.

Ed walked up to stand beside Mac. He surveyed Anastasia for a moment. "Young lady, how about if I fetch you a cup of coffee from the house?"

She nodded again.

"I'll be right back." Ed hurried out of the barn.

She stayed put, as if somebody had nailed her boots to the floor.

Mac nudged his hat back with his thumb. "Guess you weren't kidding about that zombie thing."

Once again her reply sounded like a rusty hinge. "No."

"But you made it on time. Congratulations."

"Thanks."

He resisted the urge to fix her hair, or straighten the cuffs of her jeans, or tuck in her shirt. She needed tending to, but he wasn't the person who should do the tending. He was touched, though, that she'd done what she had to in order to make it here by six. Obviously it hadn't been easy for her.

"Is it okay if we hang your messenger bag on one of those wall hooks?" He gestured toward a section that Ed had constructed specifically for ladies' purses.

A friend of Ed's had welded horseshoes together to make eight hooks that Ed had nailed to the wall. Women who arrived for short rides armed with purses could leave them here. Only one lady had ever questioned the security of this arrangement, and the insulted expression on Ed's weathered face had convinced her that she didn't have to worry.

"You'll need to have both hands free," Mac added.

She looked at the messenger bag hanging from her shoulder as if surprised to see it there. If she'd been operating on automatic this morning, she might have scooped it up out of habit. Or maybe she intended to stick around and draw horses after the lesson.

She swallowed and handed it over. "That's fine."

As Mac looped the strap over the first hook, Ed came back with a steaming mug in one hand and an energy bar in the other.

"It's hot." He handed her the mug carefully. "Don't burn your tongue."

"Thank you." Her voice sounded slightly more normal.

"Just in case you didn't have time for breakfast, Vivian told me to bring this." He opened the top of the energy bar and peeled down the wrapper before handing her that, too. "It's strawberry. Most people like strawberry."

"Thanks." She took a cautious sip of the coffee and closed her eyes. "Ah."

"Apparently you had the right idea, Ed. Thank you." Mac wished he'd thought of it. He could have brought a thermos of coffee. He didn't have energy bars, but he could have made her a P B and J.

Ed chuckled. "I recognize the look. My daughter's a night owl. She moved to California and took a job writing computer code for a company that doesn't care if she works nights or days so long as she finishes her projects. She told me once that she wouldn't be able to keep my hours if I put a gun to her head."

Mac glanced at Anastasia. "Then I guess I should be even more flattered than I was that you got out of bed to be here."

"You should." She took another swallow of the coffee and bit into the energy bar. Her eyes were growing brighter in tandem with the rising sun.

It was compelling, watching her wake up with the sun, but he couldn't let himself continue to do it. Staring at her for any length of time was a bad idea. His thoughts were either tender or lustful, and neither of those emotions had any place in the proceedings.

He cleared his throat. "Tell you what. While you drink your coffee and eat your energy bar, I'll take Jasper out of his stall and tie him to the hitching post outside. That way he'll be ready for you to brush him."

"Okay." She remained standing in the exact middle of the aisle.

"You might want to move over to the side while I do that."

"Oh!" Showing quite a bit more animation, she backed toward the wall where her messenger bag hung.

Ed glanced at Mac. "Guess I'll let you get on with it

while I go have my breakfast. Let me know if you need anything."

"Thanks, Ed. I will." As Ed left the barn, Mac looked at Anastasia with what he hoped was an encouraging smile. "This'll be so easy. Like falling off a log."

"Right." She shoved the unfinished energy bar into her vest pocket.

"You have time to finish that while I take him out."

"Not hungry."

Apparently she was awake enough to be scared. He felt her attention on him as he grabbed a lead rope and unlatched Jasper's stall. Up to this point she'd seemed to have forgotten why she was here.

Maybe the caffeine had kicked in, because the prospect of a horse walking right past her obviously had penetrated her sleep-fogged brain. After clipping the rope in place, Mac started to lead Jasper out of the stall.

Anastasia had backed closer to the wall and stood clutching her coffee mug in both hands as if it could serve as a shield. With her straggling hair, untucked shirt, and hastily pulled on boots, she looked like a waif lost in the storm. His heart lurched.

This must be the vulnerability that Georgie saw in her little sister and now he saw it, too. But Anastasia had asked him to be tough on her, to push her out of her comfort zone so that she could overcome her fear. He hadn't realized how difficult that might turn out to be.

Instead he wanted to hold her, comfort her, and protect her from anything scary. That attitude wouldn't help her at all. Taking a deep breath, he vowed to be the kind of teacher she needed.

He paused. "On second thought, why don't you put that mug down and come on over here on his right side? We'll lead him out together."

Her eyes widened and she swallowed. She also didn't move. She remained frozen to the spot.

"He likes you. You're the person who scratched his neck for so long that you nearly put him in a trance. He knows you're back and he's hoping for more of the same. You don't want to disappoint this poor horse, do you?"

"No." She crouched down without losing eye contact and put the mug on the floor. Then she straightened. Holding his gaze, she walked slowly toward him.

In any other context, it would have been an extremely sexy thing to do. But he was fairly sure she didn't have sex on her mind. She was fixated on him so she wouldn't have to look at the big scary horse standing *right there.*

"Great. When you get over here, take hold of his rope and we'll go out the door. It's not far. Remember, he thinks you're great."

She nodded. Once she had a grip on the rope, she faced forward immediately. "It's a lot different when he's out of the stall." Her voice was tight with strain.

"I know. That's why I wanted you to get used to him while he was contained. Your sketches are of a kind horse, a cooperative horse, one who likes people, especially pretty ladies who scratch his neck." He glanced past Jasper's nose so he could look at her and he was gratified to see a tiny smile blooming. "Ready?"

"Ready."

"Then here we go." He started forward.

"In case you wondered, I slept in my clothes."

"Never would have guessed."

Her smile widened. "You're either a liar or incredibly unobservant."

"Okay, I guessed. And for the record, I had no idea what I was asking of you."

"I don't function well at this hour, so I showered and

dressed before I went to bed. Otherwise I might have shown up with no clothes at all."

And he pictured that because he couldn't help himself. He'd never seen her naked, but he had a good imagination, and the view was breathtaking. He took a mental cold shower and focused on the task at hand. "And look at that. You made it on time."

"My body was here. My brain was not."

"How about now?"

"The coffee helped, but that energy bar was nasty. Ed was so sweet to bring it, though. I had to eat some. Tonight I'll make a P B and J and set the timer on the coffeemaker. There's no way I can get up in time to make breakfast, but I can do that before I go to bed."

He'd been about to offer the same thing, but he held back. Having her supply her own coffee and snack was more empowering. Somehow he had to stifle his natural impulse to take care of her. It would be an ongoing project.

As they walked through the double doors and into the yard, she sucked in a breath.

He went on alert. "What's wrong?"

"Mac, look at the *sky*."

He'd been too engrossed in thinking about the next step to notice the sky. A few scattered clouds were tinged with pink and orange. He always enjoyed looking, but it wasn't the most spectacular sunrise ever. "Very nice."

"Nice? It's gorgeous!"

That's when he realized that although he'd seen hundreds of sunrises, she had not. Sure, she'd been forced to wake up for a few. She couldn't have reached this age without witnessing some along the way. But depending on the circumstances, she might not have been in a mood to enjoy them.

"You're right," he said. "It's gorgeous." But he wasn't looking at the sunrise. He was looking at the glow reflected on her upturned face. With her hair coming undone, he didn't have to stretch very far to picture waking up with her after a night of making love. Then they'd step outside to greet the dawn, just as they were doing now. Dangerous thoughts.

"If I got up at sunrise more often, I'd see a sky like this. I could do some sunrise watercolors."

"You could."

She blew out a breath. "Forget it. Making it over here nearly killed me. Sunsets are beautiful, too."

"Yep."

"But totally different." She continued to gaze at the sky. "These colors are more subtle and they change much faster. A sunrise would be harder to capture than a sunset."

He didn't respond. He loved them equally for different reasons, and because he wasn't an artist, he'd never thought in terms of capturing anything. He counted on people like Anastasia to give him a permanent record of those things.

But he'd just thought of another way to push her out of her comfort zone. Because she was so involved in the sunrise, he decided to try it. "Hold on to Jasper for a minute. I need to get the tote with the brushes and currycombs."

"You're leaving?"

"For just a minute. Stand right here and hold on to his halter and the rope. It'll be fine."

"Easy for you to say."

It wasn't at all easy for him to say. He wanted to coddle her exactly as Georgie had been doing for twenty years. But Anastasia wanted out of her cocoon, and he'd help her make the break.

By the time he returned with the plastic tote, she'd turned away from the sunrise and was scratching Jasper's neck and murmuring things to him that Mac couldn't hear. His plan had worked. Left alone with the horse, she'd established a connection.

The woman stroking the brawny roan bore no resemblance to the one who'd stood petrified in the barn as she'd waited for Jasper to emerge from his stall. Apparently the dynamic could change that fast, especially if he took himself out of the equation. Lesson learned. Sometimes he just had to get out of the way and let things happen.

The obvious progress she'd made in less than an hour caused him to rethink his approach. She could spend a little time grooming Jasper, and she needed to learn the basics of saddling and bridling a horse. But before they left the stable this morning, he wanted to see her up on Jasper, despite what he'd said yesterday. She wanted him to push her, and that's what he intended to do.

CHAPTER 6

Anastasia was finally awake enough to realize she was a hot mess. While Mac tied Jasper to the hitching post, she pulled the elastic from her hair and redid her ponytail. Then she tucked in her shirt and pulled her jeans down over the tops of her boots.

She wouldn't win any style contests, but at least she wouldn't look as if she'd been on a three-day binge.

He turned as she was straightening her vest and smiled. "Feeling a little better?"

"Getting there. Probably couldn't do any algebra problems yet."

"Well, it's pretty hard to screw this up, although it's not quite like brushing a dog." He took a mitt out of the tote and put it on his right hand. "I'll show you this first part and then you can take over."

"I've never brushed a dog, so I don't have to unlearn anything."

"Really?" He paused to gaze at her. "No dogs in your life at all?"

"Georgie and my stepdad had one when we first moved to Bickford, but he got sick and died soon after we got here. My mother put her foot down about getting another one." She paused. "Now I wonder if she's afraid of dogs, too."

"Are you?"

"No, not at all. I like them. Cats, too. They're like living sculpture. But Mom doesn't want animals so I'd have to move to have any, and I haven't decided where I want to be, yet."

"I picture you with a cat. Maybe it should have a black, orange, and white coat in interesting patterns so you'd have fun painting it."

"I picture you with a dog. A big old, fluffy one that likes to chase balls and fetch sticks."

He grinned at that. "And then curl up on a rug by the fire on winter nights. Oh, and I'd need a cat sleeping in the rocking chair by the fire, too."

She savored his vision of cozy domesticity. "Are you planning to get a dog and a cat, then?"

"Been thinking about it, now that I have a house. Only problem is, I'm gone every weekend."

"I could look in on them for you." She said it without thinking. She'd never set foot in his house, and here she was offering to take care of his animals when he was gone, assuming he adopted some. But he'd agreed to teach her to ride, so maybe taking care of his animals would repay that debt.

"Thanks for the offer." He smiled. "But dogs usually expect to eat first thing in the morning. Automatic feeders are a possibility, but dogs need the human touch. I think they'd rather see a real person."

"Oh."

"So unless this early-rising thing becomes a habit . . ."

"I'd be amazed if it does. Considering that, I probably shouldn't have said anything. Sorry." The stupid part of this conversation was that she wanted him to have a dog and a cat. Now that he'd described his ideal image, she could see it so clearly she could've made a sketch of it.

"No problem. I don't even have any pets, so feeding them on the weekend isn't an issue."

"Listen, you need that dog on the rug by the hearth and the cat in the rocking chair. If you get those animals in your house, I'll set my alarm on the weekends and take care of them."

He laughed. "Anastasia, that's—"

"Only fair after you're doing this riding thing for me. I saw your expression when you described that scene and it's so you, Mac."

"I can't imagine why you'd say that. I've been on the move most of my adult life. Anybody who knows me would tell you that if I bought property it was with the hope of selling it at a profit."

"But you plan to keep that property, don't you?"

"I'm thinking about it."

His willingness to settle somewhere, to fix up a house and live in it, appealed to her. Compared to Mac, the guys she'd known in art school seemed immature and irresponsible. She thought Mac might be a little older than she was, but she'd never asked. "How old are you?"

"Thirty-two. Six years older than you."

It thrilled her that he had that information about her age on the tip of his tongue. He'd been paying attention. "How do you know how old I am?"

"When I first started working at the guest ranch you were sixteen. I was there for six years. Four years later I came back and by some miracle we're both ten years older. Amazing how that happens."

"Amazing." He really did have beautiful brown eyes. When she looked into his eyes, she could tell something was always going on in his mind.

Like now, for instance. His gaze was warm and friendly, but she could tell he was thinking beyond the moment, maybe imagining a time when he had his house the way he wanted it along with a dog, a cat, and ... someone special, too? That would be one lucky lady who shared his home.

Awareness flickered briefly in his eyes. Of her? He glanced away and cleared his throat. "We're not making much progress on this grooming business."

"Guess not." She was probably dead wrong, but she couldn't help wondering if he'd mentally placed her in the picture he was creating.

If so, he wasn't thinking that anymore. When he looked at her again, he was all business. "When you're grooming a gentle horse like Jasper, you don't have to worry because he's not jumpy. Some people use a curry-comb, but I like this mitt. Start at his shoulders and rub his coat in circles, like you're polishing a car. It coaxes the dirt out so later you can brush it away."

As Mac worked, Jasper shivered in delight.

She could understand the reaction. Those strong hands must feel really good, and he was so efficient and assured. She didn't want to risk having an affair with him and getting sidetracked from her work, but she couldn't deny he was sexy as all get-out. For the first time in her life she was attracted to a man, not a boy. It was a delicious feeling, one she'd enjoy privately and then let it go.

"Be gentle with his belly, but make sure you get the area where the cinch goes, which is right here." He rubbed that section. "Don't worry about his legs. When you're done with this side, go around and start at his shoulder on the right side. Think you have the idea?" He turned back to her.

"Yes." She took the mitt and their hands touched. It wasn't the first time that had happened. He'd held her hand when they'd walked together into the barn and again when he'd showed her how to pet Jasper.

Maybe those instances had generated a cumulative effect, because this brief touch created a buzz that traveled up her arm before fanning out to all points beyond. She tingled all over. If he could accomplish that with the merest contact, what would happen if . . . But she'd already decided against going there so it was pointless to speculate.

He stepped back and gestured toward Jasper. "Have at it."

All right. She wasn't here to indulge in fantasies of Mac. She was here to conquer her fear of horses. Maybe she was focusing on her attraction to him because that diluted her emotional reaction to being around horses. She couldn't be sexually excited and afraid at the same time.

Taking a deep breath, she approached Jasper. Earlier, while Mac had gone to fetch the tote with the grooming supplies, she'd interacted with the horse by imagining he was still enclosed in a stall and she was petting him the way she had the previous afternoon. She'd concentrated on his head and neck.

Now she was confronted with the entire horse. Looking into his eyes helped, but it was physically impossible to use the mitt effectively while looking into his eyes. She rubbed his coat in circles the way Mac had.

As she did, her artist's eye took note of the powerful muscles. The little girl who'd been traumatized by the size of an animal like this quailed at the thought of his brute strength. Her imagination pictured him rearing like the Ghost did in her well-known drawing.

Anyone caught under his hooves could be seriously hurt, even killed. But Jasper wore a halter and was tied to a hitching post with a rope. He couldn't rear.

Besides, he had no reason to. She told herself that

over and over as she worked the brush over his back, his rib cage and his haunches. She'd nearly convinced herself he was perfectly harmless as she began to walk around to his other side.

"Watch his back hooves."

She froze in place. "What do you mean?" The terror returned.

"Sorry, sorry. I shouldn't have said it like that." He nudged his hat back as he came over to her. "My mistake. I should have explained that when you cross behind a horse, they can't see what you're doing and it can make them nervous. Remember the predator/prey thing we talked about?"

"Uh-huh." Although she wasn't feeling it, now. She was back to being intimidated.

"We don't want to give them any reason to be nervous. Jasper's so calm he'd probably be fine, but it's good to get in the habit of either walking right behind them, so they can't kick you, or making a wide circle, so their hooves can't reach you."

"He might deliberately *kick* me?"

"Not likely, since he's calm and well-trained, but some horses might, more as a reflex than an aggressive act. I want you to be safe."

She swallowed. "Me, too."

"For the most part, horses have no intention of hurting you." He met her gaze. "I don't want you to be afraid, but I want you to be alert. Think of a piece of heavy farm equipment. The tractor isn't out to get you, but if you walk in front of it without setting the brake, it might roll over you. Nothing intentional about it."

"Mac, I get spacey sometimes. I daydream. I've tried to correct that tendency, but it seems to be a permanent part of my makeup. I can see myself forgetting to set the brake on that tractor."

"Not if someone teaches you to make it a habit."

"I'm not so sure about that." She wanted to bag the whole program. Horses were as scary as she'd first thought, and that wasn't going to change just because she wanted to be a more authentic artist. Mac himself had said that nobody would guess she'd never seen the Ghost in person. Why was she torturing herself?

He put his hands on her shoulders and looked into her eyes. "I'm sure. I'm going to work with you so that you'll be able to ride into the canyon and be safe doing it. Don't give up."

Wow, that was effective. The warmth of his hands flooded her body with sensual images and the determination in his brown eyes melted her fear like sun on snow. "Okay."

"Excellent." Giving her shoulders a squeeze, he stepped back. "Just make your decision about whether to walk close behind or far away and then do it that way every time. I recommend the close-behind maneuver because sometimes you don't have the extra room to walk way around. But it's up to you."

Keeping far from those hooves sounded great to her, but she was willing to bet most experienced riders stayed close. It was more efficient. "How close?"

"Close enough to rest your hand on his rump as you circle behind him. In fact, it's a good idea to do that. Make it part of the habit. Then he knows exactly what's going on."

She'd better do it now, before she lost her nerve. Resting her left hand on his rear end, she made the journey around to his other side.

"Good job."

"Thanks." She hadn't thought much about his voice before. His charm had been more visual than auditory. Maybe because she was too busy with the horse to look at him, his voice had more impact than usual. Whatever the reason, hearing it made her feel as if all was right in her world.

She decided to keep him talking and find out if the effect lasted. "How did you happen to become a wrangler?"

"Grew up with it. My dad and mom met on the job. He was a wrangler for a big outfit and she was a cook."

Sure enough, his rich baritone was wonderful for calming her nerves. "And now?"

"They're back doing the same thing. They tried ranching on their own when I was a kid, but it was a struggle. Besides, I think they like working alongside other folks. They're social people."

"Is that the same ranch where you and Travis were working before you took the job here?"

"Nope. It's outside of Dallas. I was there for a little while, but I was at that age when you want to strike out on your own, so I did."

"Do you have any . . . No, never mind. This is starting to sound like a game of twenty questions. Sorry about that."

He laughed. "No worries. I get it. Talking can relax a person if you're on edge. How're you doing?"

"I'm just about finished."

"I mean mentally."

She paused to evaluate. "Better."

"Then come back around. The brush is next."

"Be right there." On an impulse, she took off the glove and scratched under Jasper's mane the way she had the day before. "You've been a patient boy, Jasper. I appreciate it."

He turned his head and bumped his nose gently against her chest.

"Oh!" Startled, she jumped back.

"He did that because he likes you. It's a gesture of affection."

She took a deep breath as her heartbeat returned to normal. "All righty, then. I like you, too, Jasper." Giving him one last scratch, she walked around his hindquarters exactly the way she'd done it before.

"You're doing great, you know."

She smiled at him. "Thanks. Good teacher."

"A better one would have told you how to circle the back of the horse in advance." The sun warmed the area in front of the barn and Mac had taken off his jacket.

"Actually, the way it happened was better." She didn't need her vest anymore, either, so she took it off. Her phone was in there, so she transferred it to her jeans pocket.

"I don't see how it was better. I scared you enough that you were ready to quit on me."

"Yeah, but if you'd started out by telling me I could get kicked if I wasn't careful, I would have been freaked from the get-go." She laid her vest over the end of the hitching post next to his jacket. "At that point, I'm not sure you could have talked me into staying."

"I'm glad you did."

"Me, too." It was another of those moments when his gaze locked with hers, a moment that could turn into something if either of them made a move.

Instead they broke eye contact at about the same time and he began demonstrating how to use long, sweeping strokes of the brush to flick away the dirt she'd stirred up with the mitt. That left her free to watch him and she took that artistic opportunity. She'd never sketched him from the back, now that she thought about it.

The view was excellent from this angle, too. She couldn't pull out her sketch pad but she could take out her phone.

At the click of the phone's camera, he turned. "Did you just take a picture?"

"For reference."

"What kind of reference?"

"In case I ever want to do a sketch of you brushing Jasper."

"But my back's turned." He seemed sincerely confused by the concept.

Bless his heart, maybe he didn't realize he had great-looking buns. "I know. That's what makes it . . . different." And sexy as hell. She tucked her phone away, glad she had the shot for later.

He shrugged. "If you say so. I'll take your word for it. I'm no artist—that's for sure." He walked over and handed her the brush. "Same as before. Start with his left shoulder, work toward the back, then walk around to his right and start at the other shoulder."

"Got it." She began brushing and sure enough, dirt flew. His coat had looked glossy before they'd started this, but it would probably shine like wet paint when they finished.

"What were you going to ask last time, when you interrupted yourself?"

Aw, he wanted to put her at ease. How sweet. She thought back. "Whether you had any brothers or sisters."

"Just me. Mom said they were lucky to have even one. Some medical issue, I guess."

"Isn't Vince an only child, too?"

"He is. I think that's one reason we bonded like we did when we met at the guest ranch. He really is like the brother I never had."

"Travis, too?"

He laughed. "Yeah, like the pain-in-the-ass little brother I never had. He has a couple of sisters. I've seen pictures but I've never met them, and I think that's on purpose."

"I see."

"He has no reason to be so protective. I've told him a dozen times that I wouldn't date either of his sisters."

"Why not?"

"Because if things didn't go well, and with my record that's entirely possible, it could ruin the friendship. I wouldn't take that risk."

"You have a bad record with women?" In all their discussions, this subject had never come up.

"You could say that."

"In what way?"

He sighed. "In every way. And I deeply regret I mentioned it. How about if we talk about something else?"

"We can do that." But she was intrigued. How could a gorgeous, caring man like Mac have a bad record with women? Maybe over the next couple of weeks he'd let down his guard enough to tell her.

CHAPTER 7

Mac could have kicked himself. In his eagerness to provide conversation so Anastasia would relax, he'd accidentally broached his least favorite topic in the world. Or rather, he'd tossed off a remark that would lead to it if he answered her question.

Marrying Sophie had been the biggest mistake of his life, and he wished to hell he could erase that part of his memory so he'd never have to think about it again. As it was, he thought about it way more than he wanted to. Every damn time he did, guilt turned his stomach into a cement mixer.

Anastasia had graciously come up with a new topic. She'd asked him how he planned to finish the floors in his house once he'd pulled up all the old carpet. Flooring was the kind of neutral subject that wouldn't get him into trouble and he was grateful.

But he'd been around her enough to know that she wouldn't forget the issue he'd refused to talk about. She still wanted to know the answer to her question. He'd take bets on it.

He should probably tell her all about Sophie. If she had a crush, and he was beginning to think she might, that would take care of it. But he didn't want to tell her. First of all, he didn't enjoy talking about that chapter in his life, but that was secondary.

Mostly, he didn't want to say anything because he'd get knocked off his pedestal. Her attention, whether for artistic reasons or something more personal, stroked his ego. He hated to admit that, but it was true. Even though he'd promised himself nothing would ever happen between them, he basked in the glow of her not-so-subtle interest.

Not every guy had a woman drawing sketches of him all the time or taking pictures of him on her phone for reference, whatever that meant. It was going to his head and he shouldn't let that happen. But it felt so good. Once he told her about Sophie, she wouldn't view him in the same way. He wanted to postpone that moment indefinitely.

"I think that's it for the brushing." She peered at him over Jasper's broad back. "What's next?"

"We saddle him. You can hang out with him while I fetch the saddle and blanket." So far, so good, he thought as he hauled both items out of the tack room and propped them on the hitching post. Picking up the brush, he flicked it over Jasper's back a few more times. "You want to get all the dirt off. If you put a saddle on a horse with grit on his back, it'll irritate him and give him saddle sores."

Her eyes widened. "Are they that delicate?"

"You'd be amazed how delicate they are. Anyway, here's how we'll do this. I'll lift the saddle so you can pull out the blanket and put it on him."

"Sounds like a plan." She seemed almost nonchalant.

He coached her on the positioning of the blanket. Then he showed her how to pile the stirrups and cinch on top of the saddle before she carried it over to Jasper.

She picked it up. "Kind of heavy."

"You can do it." He had to suppress his natural urge to help her with that burden. She was strong enough to carry the saddle and lift it onto Jasper's back.

And when she'd done that, she turned to him with a smile of triumph that made everything worth it. "That wasn't so bad."

"I never doubted you'd get it up there. Now you need to fasten the cinch."

She was a little more hesitant about that because it involved ducking under Jasper's belly. But she soldiered on and eventually the cinch was tight and the stirrups were down. She dusted off her hands. "What next?"

"The bridle, which is slightly more complicated. The first time I'll do it, and then we'll switch sides and you can try."

"Sounds good."

As he carried the tote into the barn and took the bridle out of the tack room, he thought of how far she'd come since yesterday, when she'd been afraid to walk into the barn. He couldn't take all the credit, either. She was a brave woman.

Jasper had done his part, too. The horse belonged to Frank Bryson, a retired lawyer in his eighties who didn't ride anymore but seemed to enjoy the idea of owning a horse. Mac would love to buy him, but Frank might not sell. Even if he did, Mac doubted he could afford Jasper after sinking so much money into his house. Knowing Frank, he'd paid top dollar for the big roan.

Anastasia was stroking his nose and talking to him when Mac came out of the barn. He wondered if she'd ever get to the point where she'd want a horse of her own. That would be a real triumph.

She might set her sights on Jasper because he was the first horse she'd worked with. He wouldn't mind losing out to her if it meant she had come far enough to think of buying a horse. Frank might be more likely to sell to her, too, because he'd watched her grow up here.

Sometimes Mac envied the people who'd lived in Bickford for years. They shared a special connection with one another that he couldn't expect yet. Vince had more of an inside track, even though he hadn't bought property and Mac had, because Vince was engaged to Georgie. That had given him an instant seal of approval.

Jasper turned to look at him as he walked up with the bridle. Fortunately Jasper was pretty good about taking the bit, although Mac anticipated Anastasia wouldn't be crazy about that part.

"First thing," he said, "is to make sure the horse can't walk away from you while you're putting on the bridle."

"They'll do that?"

"Sometimes, so I'll start by slipping off his halter and fastening it around his neck. That way he's still attached to the hitching post. Then I'll put the bit in position and ease it into his mouth. Can you see what I'm doing?"

She crouched down and gazed up. "Now I can. He has gigantic teeth."

"Which he uses on hay and grass. He's a little resistant this morning, so I'll stick my thumb in his mouth so he'll accept the bit."

"Yikes. Good-bye, thumb."

"Not if I do it right. There's a gap between his front teeth and his back ones. That's right where my thumb goes."

"And if you do it wrong?"

"I won't do it wrong and neither will you when it's your turn."

"I definitely won't do it wrong because I'm not doing it at all, Charlie."

"The name's Mac."

"I don't care if your name is God. My thumb is not going in that horse's mouth."

He held back a smile. He also chose not to argue the point. Technically he could skip all of this and teach her to ride well enough to go out to the canyon with him. On the surface he would have satisfied her request. He or someone else could groom, bridle, and saddle her horse for her.

But he didn't go along with that for anyone who wanted to learn to ride, and especially for someone who was afraid. Having someone else do those things would distance her from the animal. She might be able to minimize her fear that way, but she'd never completely erase it.

He wanted her to stop thinking of a horse as somehow *other*. The more intimate her interaction, the less she'd believe that, or at least that was his theory. He was operating largely on instinct, though. He'd never met someone as terrified of horses as she'd appeared to be.

"Now that he's taken the bit, this part goes over his ears. Ease them forward because they're cartilage and sensitive."

"I love Jasper's ears. The sun's shining through the little hairs right now. So sweet."

"All of him is sweet, even his mouth." But he took the time to glance at Jasper's ears and see what she meant about the sun shining through the tiny hairs lining the edges. It was kind of cool.

"His teeth aren't sweet. They're enormous and could end my career in seconds."

"That won't happen. Are you watching how I'm finishing this up? This is important." Maybe it was time to be more assertive. She was right that she could get a little spacey. He could see the danger if she allowed herself to be distracted by something visually interesting and forgot what she was doing.

"I'm watching."

"All right. Now I'll reverse the process so you can do it. You'll need to come around to this side. He's used to being bridled from the left. Most horses are."

"Okay, but I'm only doing it if he takes that bit." She rounded the horse's hindquarters and came up beside him. "I'm not sticking my—"

He glanced over at her. "I never realized how stubborn you are."

"Only about certain things, my thumbs being two of them."

"Then let's hope Jasper cooperates. Hold the bridle like this."

She was awkward at it and he had to move in and help her. Damn, she smelled good. He forced himself to ignore that. Jasper took the bit easily this time. Mac had been prepared to coax her to use her thumb if necessary, but it wasn't. Crisis averted. Maybe by the time she needed to do that, she'd be so mellow about Jasper's teeth she wouldn't think anything about it.

"That's it. He's bridled." The lesson was taking longer than he'd figured on, but it didn't matter. It wasn't like she was paying him by the hour.

"I need a picture of this!" She pulled out her phone and took several shots of Jasper all tacked up.

"Ready to climb aboard?"

She whipped around so fast she almost dropped her phone. "C-climb aboard? I thought you said—"

"I know, but you've been making such great progress. You don't have to go anywhere, just sit there for a little while and get used to the view." He paused. "I'll take your picture so you can show Georgie."

She studied Jasper for quite a while. Finally she took a deep breath and let it out before handing him her phone. "Okay."

It wasn't an enthusiastic statement, but he'd take it. Shoving her phone in his pocket, he walked over to Jasper. "Let me adjust the stirrups for you." He'd been the last person to use the saddle and the stirrups were way too long for her.

"Shouldn't I do that?"

"Next time." He didn't want a delay to make her nervous and potentially cause her to change her mind. After years of adjusting stirrups for greenhorns, he had a pretty good idea where they should be for someone of Anastasia's height and build. They'd be good enough for now.

She came closer. "Now they're so high I don't know if I can get my foot up there."

"I could go search out a mounting block, but we can do it the old-fashioned way." He linked his hands together and held them below the stirrup. "Grab the saddle horn and put your left foot here. I'll boost you up."

"Mac, I'm scared."

He looked into her eyes and her pupils were dilated. She was also breathing faster than normal. "You'll be fine. I'll be right here."

She glanced up at the saddle. "I'll be clumsy. What if he doesn't like that and starts moving around and stuff?"

"This is your friend Jasper. You've spent time grooming him and petting him. He's not going to be annoyed because you're new at this."

"How do you know?"

"I've spent six months getting acquainted with him. It's not his personality to be nervous and jumpy with greenhorns. He's patient."

She gazed at the horse. "Is that right, Jasper? Are you going to stand there like a good boy when I climb on you?"

He bobbed his head like a trick pony.

"Mac, did you make him do that? Have you trained him to respond to some subtle hand signal?"

"No, I have not. Somebody might have taught him to bob his head when he hears a rising note in a person's voice. I haven't paid attention to whether he does it on cue or not."

"Maybe later on we can test it. For now I'm going to take it as a sign that I should get on this horse." She took hold of the saddle horn and placed her booted foot in his supporting hands. "Here goes nothing."

"Correction. Here goes everything."

"Right." She put her weight on his linked fingers and, despite her concern about being clumsy, she swung up into the saddle as if she'd been doing it forever.

The sound of her cute little tush dropping into the saddle was music to his ears. He glanced up and she was looking down at him from her new perch. Her color was high and her eyes were bright. She was so beautiful he forgot to breathe.

"I'm on," she murmured, as if talking too loud would disturb the perfection of the moment.

He kept his voice down, too. Hushed tones seemed to fit the mood. "How's it feel?"

"Scary. But exhilarating, too." She adjusted her feet in the stirrups. "I'm not as far away from the ground as I remembered."

"You were very small." Anxiety curled in his gut whenever he thought of her riding out into the night all by herself.

"The saddle and the stirrups help. Sliding around on Prince's back was terrifying. I only had his mane to hold on to and I . . . I probably jerked some of the hair out." She winced. "I know I did. I had a handful of horse hair when I landed. I remember that now."

"I could lead you around if you want to—"

"Not today. Today I'll just sit here and get used to it."

"And have your picture taken."

"Oh, yeah. I forgot."

"Still want me to do that?"

"Yes. I have to show Georgie."

He moved back a few feet and pulled out her phone. Usually when he worked with first-time riders he had to remind them to sit up straight. Apparently he wouldn't have to remind Anastasia. Pride, and maybe a lingering touch of fear, kept her back straight as a lodge pole pine.

Her wide smile of accomplishment tinged with panic tugged at his heart. He'd never helped someone overcome a handicap, and that's what her fear had become. Being a part of her struggle was an honor.

He snapped several pictures from different angles. You could never have enough of a good thing.

"Done?"

"Let me check them out." He scrolled through the pictures, knowing they were fine but also wanting a chance to send one to his cell. He didn't ask her if he could have one. He just did it without worrying about why.

After he'd sent it over, he glanced up. "Want to take a look?"

"No, I want to get down. Adrenaline rush. Feeling a little wobbly."

He could hear it in her voice. The party was over for today. "Stay right there. I'll help you." He tucked her phone away and walked over. The last thing she needed was to take a tumble climbing off the horse because she wasn't steady on her pins.

"I feel silly. I was fine a minute ago, and now I'm shaking all over."

"Probably a combination of adrenaline and lack of food."

She chuckled softly. "And lack of sleep."

"That, too. Grab onto the horn and slide your right foot out of the stirrup."

"Okay." She white-knuckled the saddle horn. "What next?"

He assessed the situation. She wasn't kidding about being shaky. He could see her trembling and he didn't want to take any chances. Tomorrow she could dismount on her own.

"Slide your left foot out, too. I'm going to lift you down." Reaching up, he grasped her around the waist.

"Mac, I can—"

"Tomorrow you can. Now let go of the horn."

"I feel like such a baby." But she put both hands on his shoulders.

"You're not a baby." She sure as hell was a woman, though. The second he'd touched her, he'd been forcefully reminded of that. She was so warm.

The dismount wasn't smooth, but it would have been a lot worse without him holding on to her. She hadn't taken her right foot completely out of the stirrup, so she got hung up as she tried to lift her leg over the saddle. While she worked her way out of that tangle, his hat fell off and her breasts quivered within inches of his face.

Finally she got loose and made it to the ground, although she was off balance. He continued to steady her as she searched for her footing.

"Sorry." With a breathless little laugh, she glanced up once she had both feet planted. "That was awkward."

"Not too bad." Now was the time he should let go of her and she should let go of him. It didn't seem to be happening. "At least you didn't fall."

"Thanks to you."

"You okay?" He was stalling. If she lifted her hands from his shoulders, he'd release her and step back. If she didn't, then he was going to kiss her.

She knew it. Her eyes had a gleam that told him she was thinking about what that would be like. She was cu-

WILD ABOUT THE WRANGLER   89

rious about so many things. She was probably curious about that, too.

"I'm fine." She said it softly, as if she didn't want to break the mood. Her fingers tightened against the fabric of his shirt. Instead of letting go, she was hanging on.

His heart beat faster. She wanted him to kiss her. In that case, he was about to satisfy the lady's curiosity.

Then Jasper bumped his nose against her shoulder. She squealed in surprise and whirled around. And that was the end of that.

"Jasper, goodness! You scared me!" She dragged in a breath.

"He just likes you." And so did he. Way too much.

CHAPTER 8

Not only had Jasper startled her; he'd saved her from a very dumb move. She'd been about to let Mac kiss her. Apparently lack of sleep and lack of food had made her both shaky and stupid.

She considered acknowledging what had almost happened and letting him know it wouldn't happen again. No, that would just embarrass both of them. Instead she'd pretend that they hadn't been a split second away from a lip lock.

To that end, she adopted a jolly tone. "Guess I'm up for unsaddling this big guy, huh?"

"That's okay." He retrieved his hat, put it on and tugged down the brim so it almost hid his eyes. "I've put you through enough for one morning. I'll handle it. In fact, I might take a little ride, give him some exercise."

"Then I guess unsaddling him makes no sense."

"Nope. We can cover that tomorrow. Oh, here's your phone."

She took it back and there was that slight brush of fingers again, one she shouldn't even notice. Except from now on she would always notice. "Thank you. And thank you for the lesson. It was awesome." She picked up her vest from the end of the hitching post. "Big day today."

"Yep. We made lots of progress."

"We sure did!" She almost added *by golly* to the end of that statement. If she had, it would qualify as the most sickeningly cheerful thing she'd ever said. "I'll just grab my messenger bag and be on my way. See you in the morning!" She started into the barn.

"Are you taking the rest of the day off?"

She turned back to him. "No. I'll be at Sadie's doing portraits as usual. Why?"

"I was planning on going in for a beer later on."

"Oh, right. Of course. Then I'll see you there, won't I?" She followed that with a big grin. She was so rattled it wasn't funny. It might be funny to Georgie, though. Georgie was definitely going to get an earful today.

He regarded her with a bemused expression. "Seems like it."

"Bye for now!" She waved and walked into the barn, but it was a wonder she hadn't walked into a wall, instead. By the time Mac showed up at Sadie's, she would have her act together. If the possibility of a kiss had scrambled her brain to this extent, she'd hate to think what an actual kiss would do.

The barn was a cool refuge, and she paused to drag in a breath. He'd said he might take Jasper out for a ride. If he really meant that, maybe she could stay in here until he was gone. That would save her from making any more idiotic comments.

Come to think of it, she wouldn't mind sitting down for a moment. She'd had quite a morning, and it wasn't even nine yet. Normally she'd still be zonked out in her bed at home. Instead she was in a barn, of all places, trying to recover what was left of her wits.

A straw bale sat near the wall where her messenger

bag hung waiting for her. She decided to rest on it for a while and give Mr. Hot Cowboy plenty of time to lengthen the stirrups for his long legs and ride off into the sunrise.

His tight buns would rest in the same saddle she'd recently vacated. She might not want to think about that. But she did anyway. She wondered if the leather was still warm and if he'd notice that.

In some ways she regretted not kissing him just now. She'd sketched his mouth so many times she knew it by heart, but she didn't know what it felt like, only what it looked like. And it looked like a mouth made for kissing.

It was wide and bracketed with smile lines, which gave it character. He had a full lower lip and an upper lip the exact shape of a bow. Not every man had such a classical mouth. She wondered if kissing him would have affected how she drew that mouth. It would be an interesting experiment, but—

"Anastasia?"

She leaped up as Mac walked into the barn. "What are you doing here?"

"Checking on you."

"I thought you were going riding."

"I was." He crossed to her. "But when you didn't come out, I thought something might be wrong. I didn't want you to be in here crying, or—"

"Crying? Why would I be crying?"

"I don't know. I sometimes get confused about why ladies cry." He stepped closer. "What *were* you doing in here all this time?"

She gazed up at him. She was hungry, overtired, and dazed by the new awareness between them. She'd always told him the truth before, so she did it now. "I was thinking about your mouth."

He sucked in a breath.

Now that she'd said that, she felt the need to explain.

"You have an almost perfect mouth, and I can't help wondering what it feels like. But I don't think we should start anything."

"I don't think we should, either." His voice was husky.

In the cool privacy of the barn, she felt herself slide across some invisible line of propriety. "Could I just touch it?"

"I guess." His eyes darkened.

"I draw things better after I know what they feel like."

"Makes sense." His expression became unreadable, almost as if he'd gone deep within himself.

She really did want to do this, even though she dimly realized it might be a bad idea. But when would she ever get another chance? Reaching up, she started at the center of the bow and stroked to the corner.

He closed his eyes.

"You have nice lashes." She'd noticed that before, but she'd never been this close. They were thick and dark as they lay against his cheeks.

"You should see them when the sun shines through."

"Okay, that was funny. Now hold still and let me finish." She ran her finger slowly over his lower lip. The texture reminded her of a rose petal, but the color was harder to describe. Maybe she'd seen it in the dawn sky this morning. She'd check again tomorrow.

She came back to the midpoint of his upper lip and drew her hand away. "Done. Thank you."

His eyelids drifted open and he let out a slow breath. "All right, then."

Looking into those dark eyes was a mistake. Her heart was already beating pretty fast after touching his mouth, and what she saw in his gaze made her want things she shouldn't.

Taking another deep breath, he turned and started to leave the barn.

She didn't want him to go. She wanted . . . A soft whimper escaped before she could swallow it.

He turned back. "Anastasia?"

"I don't know what's wrong with me, Mac. I don't want you to go away. I want . . . I know this is a mistake, but I want you to . . . kiss me. Please. If you would be so kind."

He cleared his throat. "You're probably just having an emotional reaction to the lesson."

"Probably. But I . . . One kiss. That's it."

He took off his hat and laid it on the straw bale. "We're both liable to regret this."

"I'll never ask you again."

Slowly he cupped her face in both hands and looked into her eyes. "One kiss and that's it."

"Yes." Her heart beat like a wild thing. "I just need this. You can make it quick, but please make it good."

He searched her expression for a moment longer, and then his mouth came down on hers.

Oh. Ohhhh. She sagged against him as he thrust his tongue deep and kissed away every inhibition she'd ever counted on to shield herself from this kind of raw passion. He wasn't tentative and he wasn't gentle.

With the firm pressure of his mouth and each stroke of his tongue he told her exactly what he wanted and how much he wanted it. He left no doubt in her mind as to the level of intensity he'd bring to a sexual encounter. Caging her face with his strong fingers, he coaxed her to open wider so that he could ravish her even more thoroughly.

When he lifted his head, she was dizzy with cravings that dwarfed any she'd ever felt before. Yet he'd only kissed her. If he'd suggested they head off to his house to spend the day in his bed, she would have gone.

His voice was hoarse as he rubbed his thumbs over

her cheekbones and gazed into her eyes. "Did that do the trick?"

She swallowed. He'd done what she'd asked, and if she asked for more, well, that would lead to the very thing she'd decided to avoid, to both safeguard her creativity and preserve their special friendship. "Yes."

"I meant every bit of that kiss, so we should make sure it doesn't happen again, okay?"

"Okay." Apparently that's the way he wanted it, too. That settled the matter.

Slowly he released her.

She uncurled her fingers from his shirt and stepped back. "I've wrinkled you."

"Doesn't matter."

She couldn't help noticing that his jeans fly didn't look like it had before, either.

He saw the direction of her gaze and smiled. "I'd appreciate it if you wouldn't sketch that."

"I won't." As the effect of the kiss began to wear off, embarrassment made her cheeks hot. She'd begged him to kiss her. How humiliating. "I shouldn't have asked you to kiss me. Sorry about that. I don't know what came over me."

"Emotional overload, anxiety, lack of sleep." He gave her a soft smile. "Don't worry about it. As you could no doubt tell, I enjoyed myself."

"Me, too. It was a great kiss. I just can't believe I came right out and asked you to do it."

"No worries." He took a deep breath and ran his fingers through his hair. "So I guess I'll see you back here tomorrow."

"Yes." She picked up his hat and gave it to him. "I'll be here at six. And I won't . . . This won't . . ." She gestured vaguely. "It won't happen again."

"That's for the best." He glanced at the messenger bag hanging on the wall. "Ready to take off, now?"

"Yes." She unhooked the bag, slung it over her shoulder, and walked outside with him. The sunlight made her blink. "Are you going to ride Jasper?"

"Yep. He could use the workout and so could I."

"How soon do you think I can go out on the trail?"

"That's up to you. You'll tell me when you're ready."

That might be very soon. Right after kissing him she hadn't been able to think of anything but sex. Then she'd moved from that to embarrassment for her behavior, and now she was full of restless energy. All that energy had to go somewhere. Might as well channel it into this project. "What happens tomorrow?"

"Same grooming routine. Then saddling, bridling, and some actual riding in the corral."

"I'll be more awake, I promise."

He chuckled. "Don't make promises you can't keep."

"I'll keep it. As long as I don't nap, I'll be so exhausted I'll fall asleep early. And tonight I'm not sleeping in my clothes, either. That sucks."

"I know. I've had to do it a few times and it's not my favorite, either." He paused next to Jasper. "Well, my ride's here."

"So I see." She stepped around him and stroked Jasper's neck. "Thanks, big guy. See you tomorrow." Then she moved back and gestured toward the horse. "Go ahead and mount up. Show me how the pros do it."

"Now I feel as if I should take a running jump from behind and vault into the saddle."

"That doesn't sound like fun for the horse."

He smiled. "Congratulations. You just visualized the scene from Jasper's perspective. See how far you've come?"

"I know. We'll be on that trail in no time."

His eyebrows lifted. "You sound motivated."

"Energized." She met his gaze. "That really was a great kiss."

"Yeah." For a moment she thought he might reach for her again, but then he turned away with a soft oath.

"Go on, Mac. Get the heck out of here."

"Sounds like an excellent idea." After quickly retrieving the reins, he shoved a boot in the stirrup and swung into the saddle with the grace of a natural athlete.

She hadn't thought about the fact that he was coordinated, probably a lot more so than she was. Coordination was a good trait in a riding teacher and an even better trait in a lover. Oh, well.

He looked mighty good on that horse, though. He sat up there as if he'd been doing it forever, which he practically had. Touching the brim of his hat, he glanced down at her. "See you at Sadie's."

"See you then."

He trotted the horse out through the open gate of the stable property. She now understood what a trot was and how difficult it could be for a beginner. But Mac sat that trot without bouncing at all.

Once he cleared the gate he nudged the horse into the next gear, which she was fairly sure was a canter. The fluid motion of horse and man was beautiful to see. She watched him until he was out of sight and then started home.

He stirred her blood, no question about that, but now wasn't the time for a love affair, and she must have been out of her mind to ask for that kiss. That would teach her not to attempt one of the biggest challenges of her life on no sleep.

Before that explosive kiss, she'd planned to unburden herself to Georgie about her situation with Mac. But she wasn't about to tell Georgie or anyone that she'd literally begged him to kiss her or that the requested kiss had been mind-blowingly good. That was between her and Mac.

But she had pictures on her phone she wanted to show off. Her mother would still be asleep and wouldn't want to hear about horseback riding lessons even when she woke up. Georgie would be dying to hear about them. So after a little food and more caffeine, she'd walk down to the Bickford General Store that Georgie ran and show her the pictures.

Out of necessity she'd become a halfway decent cook, although she almost never made breakfast. Messing around in the kitchen at this hour felt very weird, but she decided to whip up an omelet and to toast some English muffins. She was starving.

When the food was ready, she sat at the kitchen table with a fork in her left hand and the sketch pad to her right. She proceeded to draw — who else? — Mac. Except this wasn't Mac as seen from a distance. It wasn't a portrait, either.

Instead it was Mac as he'd looked after that never-to-be-forgotten kiss. She worked to capture the desire mixed with regret that she'd seen in his eyes. He'd called a halt, not her.

As she looked at the picture emerging, she wondered if he had reasons other than the obvious ones for not getting involved. There was her career, which might or might not be affected, and there was Georgie, who might or might not disapprove. But those issues could be dealt with if the attraction turned out to be strong enough. Judging from the way he'd kissed her, it was plenty strong enough.

He'd alluded to his bad record with relationships and then had asked to change the subject. She'd been curious at the time, and now she was even more so. Maybe something in his background kept him from acting on his feelings for her. If he considered himself no good with relationships, then she'd be off-limits in his mind.

The smartest thing would be to let it go. She didn't want to get involved any more than he did. Well, she *did*, but that wasn't the wisest course. Obviously Mac recognized that as well as she did. Still, she was virtually incapable of ignoring a puzzle.

The puzzle of Mac Foster gave her even more reason to move quickly from the basics of the riding lessons to getting out on the trail. She'd never been on a trail ride, but she had a vivid imagination. With eight people, the usual component for Wild Horse Canyon Adventures, it would be casual conversation, jokes, camaraderie. But with only two people, they could talk about things.

She had a hunch something lurked in Mac's past. Vince might know, which meant Georgie might know, but Anastasia wasn't going that route. Mac would tell her eventually. Maybe. She'd just be patient and see how it all worked out.

As she washed up the dishes she'd used, she was surprised by her mother walking into the kitchen in her black silk robe. At fifty-five, she was quite youthful looking, thanks to expensive creams and potions.

She seemed startled to find Anastasia at the sink washing dishes. "Why on earth are you up so early?"

"I had something to do."

Her mother came closer and sniffed. "You smell of horse. But that's impossible. You hate horses."

"I used to, or rather I was scared to death of them. I'm hoping I can get over that." She decided not to be specific about the riding lessons.

"I can't imagine why you'd want to." She wandered over to the coffeepot. "Oh, good. You made coffee." She took a mug out of the cupboard and poured the last of the pot into it.

Anastasia thought of her earlier suspicion that her mother was afraid of horses and maybe animals in general. "Did your family have horses when you were growing up?"

"Goodness, no. Nasty things. My mother wouldn't have stood for it."

"Dogs?"

"Oh, no. They shed and they're unpredictable. You never know when they could turn on you." She took a sip of coffee.

"Did that happen to you?"

Her mother glanced up in alarm. "Why would you ask a thing like that?"

"Mom, were you attacked by a dog?"

Her expression closed down. "That's not a fit subject for the breakfast table."

"We're not at the breakfast table. I'm finished and you're standing there with a mug of coffee."

Her mother's eyes widened. "You're certainly feeling your oats this morning, young lady."

Looking into her mother's eyes was like looking in a mirror. They had the same coloring, too. Anastasia could remember a time when her mother's hair had been the same shade of brown as hers. Now that it was turning gray, she experimented with various highlights. At her last salon visit, she'd gone almost completely blonde.

"Stop staring at me like that, Anastasia."

"Like what?"

"Like you're memorizing every line in my face so you can sketch it later. I've told you before that I don't like it when you sketch me. You make me look old."

"I think you're beautiful." And she'd tried to convey that in charcoal soon after returning from art school. Her mother had torn it up, so she'd never tried *that* again.

"Beautiful, huh?" She set down her mug and combed back her hair from her forehead. She'd always worn it with a wave dipping over that section. "See that scar?"

Anastasia had to move in close and search hard, but at last she found a long, thin scar near the hairline. It was white and looked as if it had been there awhile. "I never noticed that before."

"Because I keep it hidden, that's why! It's ugly. I hate it."

Anastasia thought it was barely noticeable, but she didn't want to argue. "What happened?"

"My best friend talked me into riding her horse and I stupidly went along. Then this vicious dog came out of nowhere, barking and snapping at the horse. It reared and I fell off on my head. They had to shave it and stitch me up. No senior prom for me!" She folded her arms. "Happy, Dr. Freud?"

"Oh, Mom." She started to put her arms around her.

"Nope, nope." Her mother raised both hands and backed away. "Don't go feeling sorry for me. It was my own dumb fault. I don't like animals and they don't like me. Now we stay away from each other and everybody's better off."

Anastasia sighed. After twenty-six years of being Evelyn's daughter, she knew that tone very well. Once her mother shut the door on a matter, it stayed closed. But at least one mystery had been solved.

She doubted her mother would be going out to Wild Horse Canyon to see her stepdaughter get married, either. Come to think of it, that would give her mother the perfect excuse not to go. She and Georgie had never been close.

Anastasia was going, though, no matter what. Thank goodness she'd made the decision to take riding lessons so Georgie and Vince could have the wedding they both wanted. And she'd get to be a part of the ceremony, the first time she'd ever been in a wedding party.

She'd been looking forward to it ever since Georgie had asked. As the maid of honor, she'd be expected to spend time with the best man, aka Mac Foster. The thought of hanging out with Mac always made her smile.

CHAPTER 9

Mac had discovered a dry wash not far from the stable with a stretch of nearly flat sand that continued for about half a mile. Whenever he wanted a good hard gallop, he took Jasper over there and opened up the throttle. He thought the big roan loved it as much as he did.

This morning he had a particular need for speed and Jasper seemed to know it. Sand flew from the horse's pounding hooves and Mac grabbed his hat right before it was ready to fly off. Hunched over the gelding's powerful neck, he let the thrill of the ride satisfy the craving for a different kind of thrill.

Too soon they reached a section where a scattering of boulders changed the character of the wash. Mac pulled up and turned Jasper around. He'd walk the big roan back so they could both cool down.

Riding full tilt down a sandy wash couldn't really substitute for hot sex, but for now it would have to do. He'd kissed Anastasia because she'd asked him to and he couldn't seem to refuse her anything, no matter how much trouble it might cause. He'd nearly wrecked himself in the process. Ending that kiss instead of moving ahead to the next stage had been torture.

No doubt he was in for more torture every time he came in contact with her, but at least she'd agreed that was the end of the kissing. He'd tried to believe that her interest in him was purely artistic as she claimed. After the energetic way she'd responded when he'd thrust his tongue in her mouth, he no longer believed it.

He'd better stop thinking about that before he ruined his efforts, and riding Jasper became painful. Anastasia was a challenge, but he'd known she would be when he'd agreed to be her riding instructor. Deciding to overcome her fear of horses told him she was in a transitional stage.

She probably didn't know quite what she wanted. Right now he was looking at four more lessons before he left for the weekend trail ride. The break would be good for both of them, give them some breathing room.

By Tuesday or Wednesday of next week, she should be ready to tackle the long trail out to Wild Horse Canyon. If they went early enough, she'd stand an excellent chance of seeing the Ghost. Mission accomplished with time to spare.

Everything should be fine if he avoided situations such as they'd just found themselves in. He shouldn't have to help her on or off her horse anymore. If necessary he'd bring out the mounting block until she was better at it.

And no more time alone in the barn. He really had been worried about her when she hadn't come right back out. Stress plus a lack of food and sleep could make someone faint. He'd had visions of her lying unconscious in there.

Discovering she was fine had been such a relief that he'd felt a little light-headed, himself. Then she'd started talking about his mouth. In some ways that was so her. Jasper's ears, his mouth—they were all items she wanted to study and then draw.

But she'd needed more, an outlet for all the anxiety

she'd felt after surviving a fairly intimate encounter with an animal she'd learned to fear. He'd been handy. Only problem with that—he'd confirmed that they had chemistry to burn. Ignoring that inconvenient fact wasn't going to be easy, but he'd do his best. Lots of hard rides down the wash should help.

By the time he rode back into the stable yard, he was a hundred percent calmer than he had been when he'd left. Ed had turned the rest of the horses into the fenced pasture behind the stable. Mac unsaddled Jasper and gave him a good rubdown before sending him out to join the others.

Then he leaned on the gate and watched the horses as he thought about whether to go home and fix himself some lunch or walk down to Sadie's. Anastasia would be at her table sketching portraits of the tourists by now. That was a good reason to head home. He wasn't giving up his habit of having a beer at the end of the day and playing some darts, but he didn't have to add lunch to the program. Not today, anyway.

"Will you look at that guy working his fingers to the bone?"

"I know. It's pitiful. Somebody should give him the weekend off."

Mac turned with a grin as Vince and Travis walked toward him. "At least I've been on the premises instead of a certain jet-setter I know. Aren't you home early, Vincent?"

"Only my mother gets away with calling me that." Vince clasped Mac's outstretched hand.

Travis chuckled. "I think Mac just did get away with it unless you're fixing to clean his clock."

"Nah, too much trouble. I'm wearing my good shirt today."

"What's *your* full name, Mac?" Travis thumbed back

his hat. "I never thought to ask that most important question. MacDougal? MacKensie? Mackintosh?"

"Never mind." Mac gave Vince a warning look. Vince knew, but years ago he'd sworn not to give out that information. So far he hadn't, but Mac had called him Vincent, so all bets might be off.

Travis turned to Vince. "Do you know?"

"Yes."

"You gonna tell me?"

"No."

"Oh, yeah, you will. One of these nights, when you've had a few beers at Sadie's, some moment when you least expect it, I'll ask and you'll blurt it out. Guaranteed. Or maybe I'll create a contest called 'Guess Mac's Full Name.' That would be popular. I could—"

"Oh, for God's sake." Mac rolled his eyes. "Don't hurt yourself. It's Macario."

Travis shook his head. "No, it isn't. You're making that up to throw me off. Nobody's named that."

"I am. My mother found it in an old baby book. It means *blessed*. She wanted something different, and she calls me that, but my dad and everyone else who knows me calls me Mac. Happy, now?"

"Macario? For real?"

"Yep."

"I can see why you wouldn't want that widely known. It's a little . . . strange."

"I think it's Greek." Mac had been embarrassed about that name for as long as he could remember. It didn't sound manly to him. But he'd bet good money Anastasia would like it. She'd think it was unusual and interesting, like his mother had when she'd chosen it.

"Well, your secret is safe with me." Travis clapped him on the shoulder.

"Thanks." He wasn't sure that was true. Travis could

easily leak the information, and he hadn't figured out yet that if one person in Bickford knew something, eventually everyone in town would be in on it.

Maybe it didn't matter so much anymore. Years ago he'd been touchier about his image. The older he got, the less he cared what other people thought.

He glanced over at Vince. "What are you doing back here so soon? I thought your plane didn't get in until tonight."

"I was finished in Houston and I took a chance on an early-morning standby. Way early. I got on, and Georgie drove up to Amarillo to get me. I was back before she had to open the general store."

Mac smiled. "So did you two have a reunion in the back room?"

"None of your business." But the gleam in Vince's eye said it all. He was crazy about Georgie. Hanging out at the airport in hopes of getting on an earlier flight was the kind of thing he'd do so he could get home quicker.

Mac envied the hell out of him. He had a great woman and knew the right things to do and say to keep the home fires burning.

"But speaking of Georgie—I already told Travis about this—Georgie and I want to take over trail ride duties this weekend."

"No kidding?" Mac was surprised. "Don't you want to cuddle at home instead of wrangling eight greenhorns?"

"Believe it or not, we can find time to cuddle on weeknights. And Georgie misses seeing the Ghost and his herd. We haven't led a ride in a while and we both enjoy it. Now that she has good part-time help, she can leave the store more easily."

"In other words," Travis said, "me and Mac have us a vacation coming up."

"Huh." Immediately Mac thought of Anastasia. That

would give him two more days for lessons, but they
wouldn't have the little break from each other he'd
counted on so they could turn down the heat some.

"You look as if you don't know quite what to do with
the time off, buddy," Vince said.

"I sure know what I'm doing with it." Travis danced a
little jig. "I'm off to Clovis, New Mexico, to spend the
weekend with dear old mom and dad and my two sisters.
Want to come with me, Macario?"

"Watch it."

"Just funning with ya. Want to come?"

"I thought you didn't approve of me meeting your
sisters."

"Turns out they're both engaged now, so I figure it's
safe. So do you want to? Mom's a great cook."

"Thanks for the offer, but I think I'll stay here and
work on my house." He probably should have accepted
the invitation and removed himself from temptation for
those two days. Instead he was thinking about how the
extra lessons would benefit Anastasia. He also had no
inclination to leave her if he didn't have to. He should
probably be worried about that.

"We won't take Jasper on the trail ride, then," Vince
said, "so you can use him while we're gone."

"Okay." That worked out nicely.

"I'll be taking Storm Cloud and Georgie will be on
Prince, so that leaves two extra horses. I haven't decided
who else should stay home."

"How about Cinder? He's still a little feisty for beginning riders."

"Yeah, that makes sense."

Travis shook his head. "You're making a mistake not
spending the weekend with my folks, Mac. Hot apple pie
à la mode. That's all I'm sayin'."

"Yeah, but I could start sanding the floors."

"Or you could be eating pot roast and watching football on a ginormous flat-screen."

Mac laughed. "Someday you'll have a place of your own and then you'll understand why I want to sand those floors."

"I doubt it. I'm living large at the Bickford Hotel, where the floors have already been sanded and I have daily maid service. Sadie's is down the stairs and to the left. Can you say that?"

"Nope."

"There you go. When I come back stuffed with pot roast and apple pie, I'll mosey over and admire your sanded floors. Then I'll head to Sadie's for a beer. And speaking of Sadie's, I'm hungry. Either of you interested in going down there for lunch?"

Vince shook his head. "I'm making sandwiches at home and taking them to the store so I can have lunch with Georgie."

"I'm eating at home." Mac was glad he'd made that decision earlier so he didn't have to think about it.

"You're both getting really boring—you know that?" Travis touched the brim of his hat and grinned. "See ya later, losers."

After he left, Vince turned to Mac. "I owe you, buddy."

"What for?"

"Georgie told me you're teaching Anastasia to ride."

"I am, but what does that have to do with you?"

"You have no idea." Vince blew out a breath. "It means I can finally get married to the most wonderful, stubborn woman in the world."

"I don't get it."

"We don't argue about much, but we've argued about this one thing. I think we should get married in Wild Horse Canyon, but we'd all have to ride out there."

Now Mac understood. "Including Anastasia. Does she know about this?"

"She didn't, but she does as of last night. Georgie kept insisting that she wouldn't force Anastasia to ride a horse just so we could have the wedding out there. She wouldn't even ask if she'd consider it. Instead she pushed for having it at Sadie's."

"The canyon's better, especially if you do it where we've set up camp in that box canyon with the waterfall."

"Way better. Sadie's is great and I love it, but I want something significant and, well, romantic."

"Besides, Sadie's is where you and Georgie had all your confrontations."

"That, too. And the box canyon is where we ... came to an understanding, more or less."

Mac knew that was doublespeak for their first sexual encounter, but he didn't say so.

"So when Anastasia told Georgie you were giving her riding lessons, Georgie finally broke down and confessed we'd been delaying the wedding because we couldn't agree on the venue. She called me last night with the news, which is one of the reasons I wanted to get the hell home, both to set a date and thank you in person."

"So have you decided on a date? Travis set up a pool at Sadie's."

"I heard about that, too. Welcome to small-town, USA."

Mac chuckled. "No kidding."

"Are you in the pool?"

"Yep. I think the whole town's in it. When's your date?"

"Before I tell you, what's your evaluation of Anastasia's riding skill? She doesn't have to be an expert or anything. How's she doing?"

"Well. It was only the first lesson with Jasper."

"Yeah, but can she walk him around? That's really all she needs to be able to do. Charmaine did it with no prior experience and she was fine."

"I'll be able to tell you more after tomorrow's lesson." Gradually it dawned on Mac that Vince didn't know anything about Anastasia's fear of horses. Vince had assumed, like everyone else, that she just wasn't interested. And Georgie, loyal sister that she was, hadn't told him any different.

"All right. I'll check with you again tomorrow."

"She's making good progress."

"I'm sure she is. She can be determined when she sets her mind to something. Look, I want you to consider this weekend as a vacation, but as a big favor to me, could you work in a couple of lessons for Anastasia?"

Mac nodded. "I was planning on it."

"Good. That was one of my motivations for suggesting Georgie and I take over the trail ride this weekend, so I could free you up. It never occurred to me Travis would invite you to his folks' place."

"I probably wouldn't have gone, anyway." He grinned. "God knows I wouldn't want to be responsible for one of those sisters breaking her engagement."

Vince laughed, but then he stopped laughing and gazed at Mac. "There's a rumor Anastasia has a crush on you. I think Ida's behind it, and I've been on the receiving end of her manipulations, but . . . Georgie's noticed a lot of pictures of you showing up in Anastasia's sketchbook."

"That's all under control." At least he hoped to hell it was.

Vince hesitated. "I'm not going to tell you what to do or not do, but she . . . she believes in the fantasy—a hero on a white horse and happily ever after, all that stuff."

"I figured as much. As we both know, I'm not that hero."

"Your opinion, not mine. Your marriage didn't work out, but why is that all your fault?"

"Because *she* left *me*. I didn't even realize she was

unhappy until she walked out the door. We'd been having regular sex, and I thought that meant things were fine."

Vince smiled. "Usually it does mean that. Has it ever crossed your mind that Sophie was the one with the problem?"

"No, because when she left, she told me I didn't understand her at all. Which I guess I didn't since she was heading out the door and I had no idea why."

"But what if she—"

"Vince, I appreciate you sticking up for me, but you're my friend. Of course you'll think it was her fault and not mine. I also got a call after the fact from her mother, who said the same thing. I didn't understand her daughter and it was my fault the marriage was ending."

"You were young. She was even younger. Nobody knows what they're doing at that age."

"Yeah, but the thing is, I still don't." He rubbed the back of his neck. "Anyway, you need to go make lunch for Georgie. Don't worry about Anastasia. I know I'm not the right guy for her."

"I wasn't *worried* exactly."

Mac laughed. "Yeah, you were, and I understand. You're about to be married to the woman's protective big sister and you want peace in the family. Don't blame you."

"Which reminds me, we sort of got off the subject of when Anastasia could handle that trail."

"When do you want her to be able to handle it?"

"A week from Saturday."

Mac stared at him in shock. "You plan to squeeze your wedding in before the film crew gets here?"

"We've had the license for months. Georgie has the dress. So we're only missing dresses for Anastasia and Charmaine."

"Dresses?" He wondered how Anastasia would do riding in a dress.

"Yeah, they'll have split skirts. You've probably seen pictures of weddings on horseback. We're going for an old-fashioned look."

"Okay."

"Renting everything for the guys will be easy. If we get married in the box canyon there won't be decorating involved. The reception will be at Sadie's and Henry Blaylock is a genius of a chef. He'll be able to whip up a reception menu in no time. I don't mind having the reception there. I just want the ceremony in the canyon."

"Wow. You're far more organized than I thought. What's the rush?"

"Other than the fact that I'm madly in love with my fiancée, only one thing has added a note of urgency. Georgie found out last week that she's pregnant."

"For the love of God, Vince. Didn't anybody ever explain to you about condoms?"

"Sure." Vince smiled. "But it's a lot more fun without them."

"I'm sure it is, although I've never had the pleasure. And I guess I can understand. You were expecting to get married any minute."

"I thought it would be long before this, but Georgie wouldn't talk to her sister about the horse thing. Surprised me, but I couldn't budge her."

Mac would bet not, knowing the whole story. "Is anybody else aware of this situation besides you, me, and Georgie?"

"The doctor in Amarillo."

"Naturally, but besides that. Anastasia, for instance?"

"Georgie would rather not tell her and put more pressure on her about the riding thing. I honestly don't get it.

Riding at a walk or maybe an easy trot out to Wild Horse Canyon should be no big deal."

Mac kind of liked that he knew something about Anastasia that Vince didn't. "I won't say a word, either. And I think she'll be ready to go out there a week from Saturday, especially with the two extra days. But that's totally up to her, and she needs to know this new plan ASAP."

"She will. Once I tell Georgie you think it's doable, she'll call Anastasia and see what she thinks. We won't finalize anything until Anastasia agrees to it."

"If you made it the following weekend, you'd give Anastasia more time and your wedding would be on national TV."

"Exactly what I'm trying to avoid. I'm happy to be the spokesperson for Wild Horse Canyon Adventures. But this is a private celebration."

"Gotcha. And congratulations, stud." He clapped Vince on the shoulder.

Vince's grin was a mile wide. "Hard to believe, huh? I'm gonna be a daddy."

"You'll be a great one." And there was that prick of envy, again. His decision not to remarry meant he'd never feel the joy that Vince was experiencing right now. He'd just have to accept that, but right now he was jealous as hell.

CHAPTER 10

Like a starstruck teenager, Anastasia had been waiting for Mac to walk in the door of Sadie's ever since Travis had arrived for lunch around one. When Mac didn't join him, she wondered if he'd stayed away on purpose. That would be a shame. She knew he liked coming in here for the food, the beer, and the camaraderie.

She'd been busy with portraits ever since coming in at twelve, but eventually she had a break. Travis was still sitting at the bar eating his lunch and talking to Ike. So she walked over to say hello.

He turned to her with his usual cheerful smile. "Hey, beautiful. Looks like business is booming in your corner of the world."

"Fortunately, yes. How are you?"

"Most excellent, pretty lady. Vince and Georgie just gave Mac and me the next weekend off."

"Is that right? What about the trail rides?" And would Mac stick around to give her extra lessons?

"Vince and Georgie want to take a turn at the helm. You know how Georgie loves going out to see those wild horses."

"She does. It's her passion. Well, other than Vince."

"That's a fact." Travis polished off the last of his sand-wich.

"What are you going to do with all that free time?"

"Drive to Clovis."

"Ah. Good choice. I'm sure your family will be happy to see you."

"I know. Who wouldn't be?" He winked at her. "Tried to get ol' Mac to go along on that trip, but apparently he'd rather sand floors. If he's any example of how home-ownership turns a person into a drudge, count me out."

"To each his own, I guess." Then Mac wasn't going anywhere this weekend. But he was officially on vaca-tion. That might mean he wouldn't want to give her les-sons. "Where is he, by the way? I was surprised he didn't come in with you."

"You and me, both. He said he'd eat at home. Now if Mac happened to be a gourmet cook, I could under-stand that. But he's not." Travis gestured to his plate. "He'd never come up with a meal like that, not even on his best day. Henry's cooking is not to be missed. Am I right?"

"You're right. Nobody cooks like Henry."

"Agreed." He leaned closer. "On another food-related subject, my sources tell me that you had dinner with Georgie last night. Any word on the wedding date?"

"Nope." She gazed at Travis. "You missed your calling. You should have been a bookie. Or a PI. Or a standup comic."

"With all my many talents, why is it that you haven't tried to seduce me?"

She patted his arm. "Pretty as you are, it would be like having sex with my kid brother."

"First of all, I'm older than you, and second of all, you don't have a kid brother. I keep track. I know these things."

"No, I don't have a kid brother, but if I did, he would be exactly like you, only younger." She glanced over at her table and noticed a man lingering there. "Excuse me, but I think I have a live one."

"That's okay. I need to finish my beer and get back to the stable. I'm trying to talk Ed into putting in an automatic watering system for the barn. The money's there and I could install it for him, but he's resistant. He's still using a hose and a bucket."

"Ed's old school."

"Tell me about it. See you later for darts?"

"I'll be here." She returned to her table.

A man who looked to be in his early fifties stood leafing through the portfolio she kept there for just that purpose. He glanced up and smiled.

He had very white teeth, made even more startling by his deep tan. She suspected he was proud of those teeth. And maybe a little vain about the gray at his temples, judging from the way he smoothed his hair back.

"Can I help you?"

"I'd like a charcoal portrait." He held out his hand. "The name's Ryan Nesbitt." He said it as if she should recognize it. He had a sure grip and the air of someone used to wielding power.

"I'd be glad to." She gestured to the chair she used for her subjects. "Have a seat."

As he sat down, he glanced around the room as if searching for something. "I wish I had a cowboy hat."

"You'd like your portrait with one?"

"Yeah, I would. It seems appropriate if I'm getting it done in Sadie's, the watering hole for Wild Horse Canyon Adventures. But this was a last-minute decision and I don't have a hat."

"I may know someone who'd loan you his."

"That cowboy you were talking to? He has a great

hat. And it's seen enough wear to give it character. Think he'd let me borrow it for a little while?"

"I'll go ask." She walked back over to the bar and noticed Travis still had some beer left. "My client wants to know if he can borrow your hat for his sitting. I can be done before you finish your beer."

Travis grinned at her. "What's it worth to you?"

"Not much. If you won't do it, I'll go find Steve and see if he has one I can use. This place is lousy with cowboy hats. I'm offering to immortalize yours." She lowered her voice. "And from the looks of this guy, his portrait will hang in a place of honor. With your hat on his head."

With a dramatic sigh, he picked up his beer, drained it, and slid off the stool. "In that case, allow me to deliver this important hat in person."

She laughed. "Okay. You can stick around and chat with him while I draw."

"Might as well. I already know he has good taste in art and hats." Travis snagged a vacant chair as they walked over to Anastasia's corner. "I'm Travis Langdon." He held out his hand as he set the chair down. "I understand you could use a temporary hat."

"That I could." Ryan stood and shook hands with Travis while he introduced himself with the same flourish as he had with Anastasia. Either he was a mover and shaker or he was good at imitating the type.

Travis sat down before taking off his brown Stetson and handing it to Ryan. "There you go. I hope it fits."

"Looks like it will." He glanced at the label inside. "Nice."

"I'm particular about my hats. Where're you from?"

"L.A." He settled the hat on his head and instantly transformed himself into a cattle baron. He had that kind of charisma.

"That was my guess," Travis said. "What brings you to Bickford?"

"Actually I was in Amarillo visiting a friend and stopped by an art gallery there. Saw some of Ms. Bickford's work. Bought the one of the cowboy sitting on the barstool."

Anastasia stopped in midstroke. "You did?"

"That would be my friend Mac," Travis said. "She has a bunch of drawings of Mac on a barstool."

"Well, I really liked it. So naturally I asked about the artist and the gallery owner directed me to Bickford and Sadie's."

She stared at him, still not quite believing what he'd said. "This is the first time anyone's ever bought something and then come down here to meet me."

"I'm surprised. You're very talented. I'd think people would be beating a path to your door."

"I tell her that all the time," Travis said. "She's great."

She shook herself out of her daze long enough to smile at Ryan. "Thank you. But that's the only gallery where I have my work for sale, so my exposure is limited."

"The *only* gallery? Nothing in Dallas or Santa Fe?"

"Nope."

He looked puzzled. "Why is that?"

"Just haven't gotten around to contacting anyone else." She didn't want to admit to this worldly man that she was shy about asking a gallery owner to display her art. Georgie had talked her into doing it once, and they'd discussed contacting other galleries elsewhere, but she couldn't see the point when she had so much business right here.

"I see. Well, I predict your anonymity won't last."

"That's what I think, too," Travis said. "She did a sketch of me a while back. Awesome. And I was wearing that same hat."

Ryan chuckled. "You could sit here and charge guys for the use of your hat as a prop."

"That's not a bad idea. Except I won't charge you. It's on the house."

"I appreciate that."

"No problem. But you talking about the hat as a prop tells me you might be connected with Hollywood somehow. Am I right?"

"Very observant."

"Actor?"

"No. No talent for acting. I'm just one of the guys who helps make films happen."

"Cool." Travis nodded.

Anastasia expected him to keep digging until he'd identified exactly what Ryan Nesbitt did in Hollywood. She was curious, and Travis must be, too.

To her surprise, he veered onto a different topic. "We're hoping the old movie theater down the street opens soon. It's one of those single-screen beauties that they don't build anymore."

"I saw that as I was walking down here. I love those historic movie houses. There's one in my hometown I'm itching to restore."

"Velvet upholstery and velvet curtain over the screen?"

"Oh, yeah, and gilt trim everywhere."

"And wall sconces from the forties."

"Exactly!"

Anastasia listened in astonishment as Travis kept up with the guy as they compared notes on the wonders of old theaters. She'd had no idea Travis knew that much about them. Their animated conversation left her free to fully concentrate on the sketch, which was a luxury she didn't often have. She drew Ryan with the image of a cattle baron in her mind, because she thought he'd like seeing himself that way.

As she worked, she considered the incredible fact that

he'd driven down from Amarillo specifically to meet her. No one had ever done that before.

Georgie and others kept saying that she had what it took to make it big, but they were her friends and family. They were supposed to believe in her talent. This man was a stranger. No one had twisted his arm to get him down here. He'd come because he'd liked her pictures in the gallery. He'd even bought one.

Therefore she was a little more nervous than usual when she finished the sketch and turned it around for him to see. After all this buildup, a negative reaction would be difficult to take.

His eyes widened, and she wasn't sure if that was a good thing or a bad thing. Then he broke into a wide smile. "Amazing! You made me look like I belong in that hat!"

Giddy with relief, she almost leaned over and kissed him for giving her the perfect compliment. "That's what I was going for."

"Well, you nailed it. That'll look great in my office. I'll have it framed in old barn wood." He glanced over at Travis. "I don't suppose you'll sell me this hat."

"Sorry. It's broken in."

"That's why I want it. But I respect the fact that you won't sell it to me." He handed it back with obvious reluctance. "If I owned that hat, I wouldn't sell it, either." He stood. "Guess I'd better get going. My friend's expecting me back for dinner."

Anastasia and Travis stood, too. She took the money he handed her and thanked him.

"No, no, thank *you*. You really should raise your prices." He held up the folder with his portrait in it. "This will be worth significant money someday. So will the one I bought this morning."

"Now you're making me blush."

"Get used to blushing, young lady. You have a bright future." He shook hands with Travis and gave Anastasia a quick hug. Then he was gone.

Travis stared after him. "Who *was* that guy?"

"I don't know, but I thought for sure you were going to dig until you found out. Then you stopped digging. How come?"

"I got a clear message that he didn't want to tell us exactly what he did. If we didn't recognize his name, and he knew right away we didn't have a clue, then he'd enjoy being anonymous for a little while. People probably hit him up for favors if he tells them his title. But I guarantee he doesn't mop floors over there."

"I don't think so, either. Whew. It's been quite a day. I need coffee and lots of it." She walked over to the bar and ordered a cup.

"You haven't had lunch, either."

"Oh. I forgot about that."

"Hey, Ike," Travis called out. "Better bring our famous artist a sandwich to go with the coffee. She looks a little peaked." He guided her onto a barstool. "Scoot on up there before you fall over."

"Good idea." Ike delivered her coffee and she thanked him before cradling the mug and taking a sip. Ah. Then Travis took the barstool next to her and she glanced over at him. "Aren't you supposed to be somewhere?"

"I'm going, right after I find out why you're so desperate for coffee today. Long night of sketching?"

"Long night, early morning."

"Yeah, right." He chuckled. "What'd you do, get up at ten forty-five instead of eleven?"

That's when she realized she hadn't meant to say anything about her early morning to Travis. He was fun to have around, but he couldn't always remember when to keep his mouth shut. He might be getting better, though.

Just now he'd pulled back from questioning her client about his job in Hollywood. And he'd been very sweet about loaning his hat. He'd be insulted if he found out long after the fact that she'd been taking riding lessons from Mac.

She took another sip of coffee before looking over at him. "You have to keep this under your hat."

"You mean this hat?" He pointed to it. "The one that some rich Hollywood dude was ready to pay a small fortune for? Is that the hat to which we're referring?"

She sighed. "Yes. I can see that's a story that's never going to die."

"Not if I can help it. So why are you so tired?"

"I was over at Ed's by six this morning."

"I'm sorry. What?"

"You heard me. I was at the stable by six because Mac is teaching me to ride."

His mouth dropped open. Then he took off his hat and peered inside. "That information is never going to fit under this hat. Just sayin'."

"Please don't spread it around."

"I can understand why you'd say that. If people hear that Anastasia Bickford is up by six, they'll think that life as we know it is about to end. I'm a little concerned about it myself."

"I just don't want to make a big deal about this riding thing."

"Then you should have scheduled your lessons for eleven. Nobody would notice that."

"Believe me, I tried. Mac insisted they had to be early so we could each get on with our day."

"I can see how well that's working out for you. You're mainlining coffee and about to fall off your barstool."

"Tomorrow will be better. I'll go to bed early."

"You look like you should go to bed now."

She shook her head. "Then I'll really be messed up. I'm determined to stay awake until ten, go to bed, and sleep until six."

"Good luck with that. Ah, here's your food." He gestured to the plate Ike had put in front of her. "Try not to do a face-plant into it."

"Thanks." She smiled at him. "Seriously, don't say anything about this, okay?"

"Okay. But I'm assuming Ed knows."

"He does."

"Who else?"

"Georgie, and probably Vince by now."

"Probably, although he didn't say anything to me. But now I understand why Mac isn't going to Clovis with me. He's too busy sadistically torturing you at six in the morning."

"He's got the right idea. That way we don't interfere with any of the regular work around here. And *now* are you going down to talk to Ed about automatic watering systems?"

"I am. See you for darts later." He paused. "Or maybe that's a bad idea, all things considered. You could put somebody's eye out."

"I'll be *fine*. Now get out of here."

"I'm gone. Try to stay vertical." He gave her shoulder a squeeze and left.

The coffee helped but the food made her sleepy again so she had more coffee. And more coffee. By the time happy hour rolled around and Mac walked in with Travis, she was totally wired.

"Hi!" She hopped up from her table and knocked over her chair. "Whoops."

Travis swept his arm in her direction. "Behold your overcaffeinated pupil."

"I see that." Mac approached her with a smile and picked up the chair she'd knocked over. "But I understand congratulations are in order. Travis said some high roller from L.A. is very impressed with your work."

"Apparently." Her accelerated heartbeat could be from all the caffeine in her system, but she thought it was probably because Mac was standing right in front of her with a proud expression on his face.

"I hope you don't care that I told him," Travis said. "After I did, I thought maybe you'd want to break the news, but it was too late."

"That's fine. You probably told it better than I could, anyway."

"That's true. You suck at bragging on yourself unless we're talking darts."

"That reminds me. See the sign on my table?"

Mac glanced over at it. "Taking a dart break?"

"Yep, that's my plan. Are you two ready to lose?"

Mac's brow furrowed. "What if you get another great customer like you had earlier? I don't want to screw that up. If they see the sign, they might leave."

"So let 'em. I've been looking forward to this dart game all day." Mostly because it was her only excuse for spending time with him until they met again tomorrow morning, which seemed like ages from now.

"Okay, but I'm going to keep an eye on that table for you."

"Thank you, Mac." She drank in the sight of him. He'd changed his shirt since this morning, and if she wasn't mistaken, he'd shaved before coming here. She caught a whiff of shaving lotion, and normally when he showed up at this hour he had a five o'clock shadow going on.

She had to believe that had something to do with her and the kiss they'd shared, even if he'd never admit it.

For her part, she'd ducked into the women's bathroom about fifteen minutes ago to freshen up before he got here. She'd felt a little silly doing it, but knowing he'd changed his shirt and shaved made her feel a lot less silly.

He made no move to walk over to the dart board. "Travis said the guy bought a picture of me when he went to the gallery in Amarillo."

"That's right. Sketches of you sell." That wasn't the biggest reason why she did them, but it sure was a bonus. "I should probably pay you a modeling fee."

"Don't even think about it." His warm brown gaze searched hers. "How are you? According to Travis, I'm putting you through hell with this early-morning routine."

"I'm fine." Especially now that he was here. She drew strength from his solid presence.

"Would seven o'clock be any better? We could probably get away with seven."

"And miss the sunrise? Not on your life. I'm sure the first morning was the hardest." She hesitated. "So you have the weekend off, I hear."

"I do. That means we can schedule lessons Saturday and Sunday morning if you're up to it."

"Absolutely." She couldn't seem to stop looking into his eyes.

"I'm waiting," Travis called out in a singsong voice. "I see a sign that says 'Taking a dart break' but I don't see any dart playing going on."

"Hang on, hotshot," Mac called back. "We have a few things to discuss over here." He kept his attention on Anastasia. "Vince is leaving Jasper at the stable this weekend so we can use him for your lessons. Vince is pretty excited about the lessons. Did Georgie call you?"

"I don't think so." Then she remembered and clapped her hand to her forehead. "I turned off my phone when I got busy. I never turned it on again." She pulled it out of her pocket and switched it on. "What did she want? I hope it wasn't critical."

"Uh, in a way."

Sure enough, she had three calls from Georgie but no message. She glanced up at Mac. "Is something wrong?"

"Call her."

She did, and a few moments later she disconnected and gazed at Mac. "They want to get married a week from Saturday."

"I know. Vince told me. Do you think you can do it?"

"I guess I have to."

"No, you don't. If that's too much pressure, then they can get married here in Sadie's."

"Vince would never understand."

"Too bad. I do."

She was impressed that he was more concerned for her struggle than for his best friend's wedding plans. "Do you think I can be ready by then?"

"Yes, if we work hard, but this is your decision."

"I can't let them down. Or myself. In order to stand a chance of seeing the Ghost before the film crew arrives, I'd have to be out in the canyon by then, anyway."

"Yes, but he won't be around during a wedding. You can't combine the two events. He'll take his herd and disappear that day."

"Then I'll have to ride out there with you before then. After the wedding is cutting it too close."

"Maybe."

"I'm going to do it, Mac. I want you to push me as hard as you need to in order to make that happen. First the canyon ride. Then the wedding." She smiled. "It'll be fine. I'm the maid of honor and you're the best man, so you'll have to keep track of me out there."

"I would in any case."

As she met his gaze and battled the urge to melt into his strong arms, she began to understand the problem she'd created for herself with one amazing kiss.

CHAPTER 11

Mac spent an hour of sweet frustration playing darts with Anastasia and Travis. Somehow he managed it without touching her, or at least not much. She was adorable with that caffeine buzz in progress. He finally talked her into drinking a beer because he was afraid with all the coffee she'd consumed she'd never sleep.

Then Georgie and Vince showed up and they all had dinner together. Travis repeated the Ryan Nesbitt story and made sure his hat was featured prominently in the telling. Mac hadn't laughed so much in a long time. That helped relieve the tension that gripped him whenever he looked at Anastasia. She was too beautiful. That was the main problem.

He was grateful to Georgie and Vince for showing up, because they decided to walk Anastasia home so they could talk about wedding stuff. He didn't dare offer, and he was a little sick of how chummy she was getting with Travis.

There wasn't anything sexual between them. Anybody could see that. But they were so easy with each other. Ever since this morning, he and Anastasia seemed to have lost that ability and he missed it.

After dinner he went home and ripped up some more carpet until he was tired enough to sleep. Honestly, he was like a kid on Christmas Eve knowing that he'd be spending the early-morning hours with Anastasia. She wasn't used to sharing those hours with anybody, which made his time with her even more special.

The next morning he resisted the impulse to make her a P B and J, but he brewed extra coffee and put it in a thermos. If she didn't need it, he could always drink it later. Ed greeted him with a twinkle in his eye.

That made him a little nervous. He'd assumed Ed hadn't observed anything out of the ordinary the previous morning. But then again, it was Ed's stable and he could have come upon them kissing and quietly left again.

There would be no kissing this morning. They had a deadline to meet, a couple of them, and he would do everything in his power to help her do what she wanted to do.

When she walked into the barn at exactly six, she was in far better shape than she'd been the morning before. Her cuffs were down, her shirt was tucked in, and her hair was tidy. She held a Spider-Man lunchbox in one hand and a thermos in the other.

He bit the inside of his cheek so he wouldn't laugh, but she looked like a third-grader headed off to school. Yet he knew she had to be extremely proud of herself for arriving more pulled together and carrying breakfast.

He cleared the amusement from his throat. "Good morning."

"Good morning." Her voice was a little thick with sleep but at least she was forming words and speaking distinctly. "I brought this." She held up the Spider-Man lunchbox.

The image of a third-grader arriving for the first day

of school was reinforced. "I see you did. That's good. Um, nice container."

"I've had this since third grade."

Bingo.

"It's more environmentally friendly than a paper sack."

"Can't argue with you, there." From the corner of his eye he could see Ed leaning on a shovel and trying to hide a smile. "How about taking a seat on the hay bale and eating your breakfast? Jasper's just finishing his. We can give him a little while to digest."

"Works for me." She plopped down with a little sigh.

Ed put his shovel away. "Everything seems to be under control, so I'll head up to the house."

"Thanks, Ed." But as the stable owner left, Mac realized that they were barely five minutes into the session and he'd already broken one of his newly minted rules. He was alone in the barn with Anastasia. Again.

Fortunately she wasn't awake enough to notice. She was concentrating on unscrewing the stainless steel cup from the top of her thermos. "Coffee." She said it like some people would say *gold bullion*.

Then she surprised the hell out of him. After pouring herself a cup, she glanced up. "Want some? I have an extra mug in the lunchbox."

"Um, sure." He was flabbergasted and touched, too. She'd not only brought a sandwich and coffee for herself; she'd thought of him and was willing to share her precious coffee. He wasn't about to tell her he had brought an entire thermos of it in case she'd forgotten.

Setting her cup on the floor, she snapped open the lunchbox and took out a mug. She stared at it for a second, shrugged, and poured his coffee. "Here you go. You like it black like me, right?"

"Right." He couldn't remember the last time he'd

been so moved by a simple gesture. "Thank you." The coffee was strong, just the way he liked it. "Great coffee."

"I make good coffee."

He took another sip. "Yes, you do." The lavender mug had writing on one side and a picture on the other. He'd been so intent on her thoughtfulness that he hadn't paid much attention to either the words or the picture. As she started in on her sandwich, he took the time to look at the mug.

First he read the slogan written in bright orange. SAVE A SHIRT. PAINT NAKED. He turned the mug around, and sure enough, there was a naked woman standing in front of an easel.

He chuckled, but that wasn't his only reaction since the woman on the mug had brown hair and a ponytail. Whether it was supposed to be her or not, the image had captured his imagination and a response was rapidly traveling south.

"Sorry about that. I swear it was an accident." Her cheeks were tinged with pink. "I just grabbed one that would fit in the lunchbox. I'm so used to that one I don't really see it, if you know what I mean."

"I guess." He'd be seeing it in his dreams tonight, probably in an animated version. He took another sip and tried to forget the picture on the mug. Nope, couldn't do it. "So you've had it awhile."

"Since first year of art school. I took a ceramics class."

"And made this?" Then it had to be a self-portrait.

"Yep." She swallowed more coffee. "I was trying so hard to be outrageous and artistic. Full of myself, in other words." She looked at the mug and frowned. "I should probably get rid of it."

"But it's who you were then." She might have reined in that outrageous streak but it wasn't gone. He'd seen flashes of it during some of their conversations. "I'd keep it."

"It's sort of embarrassing, though."

"I won't describe this mug to Travis, if that's what you're worried about."

She smiled at him for the first time this morning. "Good idea."

He had to ask. If he didn't, the question would drive him crazy. "Do you?"

"Do I what?"

"Paint naked."

"Sometimes."

Wham. Lust was on the loose in his eager body.

"I have this man's shirt I use as a smock. If it's in the wash, I'd rather paint naked than not paint at all."

He swallowed. "You could get another shirt." He imagined her wearing one of his shirts and nothing else while she stood in front of her easel. Then he'd have to keep his hands off her while she worked. He would, too.

"Nope. That's my lucky paint shirt. I paint good pictures when I wear it."

"What about when you don't wear it?"

Her gaze locked with his and heat simmered there. "We shouldn't be having this conversation."

"I know. Blame it on the mug. What happens when you paint naked?"

She opened her mouth as if she meant to tell him. Then she glanced away. "Let's drop it."

"You're right. Sorry. I'm going to take a walk while you finish your breakfast." He stepped into the cool morning and stopped to draw a deep breath.

So he was out here but he was still holding the mug and he really wasn't sure where to walk that wouldn't draw attention. He finished off the coffee while he thought about it. The only real option was to head out the gate and onto the road, and Ed might notice him doing that and wonder what the hell he was up to.

Good question. What had he been thinking, pursuing the question of her painting naked? He didn't need to know whether she did or not, and he certainly didn't need to know if the pictures were any different. In no time at all he'd crossed whatever lines he'd supposedly drawn yesterday.

"It's my fault."

He turned to find her standing in the doorway of the barn, her hands shoved in the pockets of her quilted vest. "No, it's not," he said. "I could have kept my big mouth shut."

"I'm the one who brought the stupid mug."

"It's not a stupid mug. It's funny and sexy. If yesterday hadn't happened, then we'd both be laughing about this mug."

"See, it *is* my fault. I asked you to kiss me and now we have this . . . problem."

"You were stressed. I could have refused to kiss you, but I didn't, so I share the blame."

She blew out a breath. "But I should have seen which mug I was grabbing and picked another one. I know we have to be careful."

"You were half asleep, damn it! The most important part of this episode is that you made coffee and thought to bring along a mug to share it with me. That blows me away."

She gave him a tiny smile. "It does?"

"Yeah. Your impulse was pure even if the mug isn't. So let's rewind this whole situation and start over. You brought coffee to share, which is not only a sweet gesture, but it shows you're more awake this morning. How did you sleep?"

"Like the dead until around three. So I got up and sketched for an hour and amazingly got back to sleep again. Getting up at six was a little rough, but nothing like yesterday." She gestured to her clothes. "As you can see."

"I noticed right away. And FYI, I love the Spider-Man lunchbox."

"I actually took it to art school and used it there. Getting it out again brought back memories."

"Good ones, I hope."

Hesitation flickered in her eyes. "Mostly." She glanced over his shoulder. "Oh, Mac, turn around and look."

The awe in her voice tugged at his heart as he turned to greet another sunrise with her. She responded to it with more enthusiasm than anyone he'd known, but she was the only artist he'd ever known, so that made sense. Sunrises would always remind him of Anastasia, which was ironic, considering how she'd avoided them all her life.

She walked up to stand beside him. "I already have so much to thank you for, but getting me up to see a sunrise twice in a row is high on the list."

He glanced over to see the pink light touching her skin with a rosy glow. "I'm glad the sacrifice has some rewards."

"Lots of rewards." She gazed at the changing colors. "I don't know if I could paint fast enough to capture it, and a picture won't do it. There's no point in taking out my phone."

"I know. I've tried with mine. You need a fancy camera, and even then . . . ."

"I have a fancy camera but I don't use it much. For reference my phone does a fine job." She watched in silence for a moment. "I think Georgie's pregnant."

"You do?" He stared at her.

She nodded. "And from the panicky way you responded, I think you knew that, but you aren't supposed to tell me."

He wasn't going to lie to her, so he decided not to confirm or deny that statement.

"It's the only explanation that makes sense. Otherwise they'd wait until after the film crew is gone."

"Maybe they're trying to avoid getting too close to Halloween, or Thanksgiving, or maybe they don't want to get snowed on. Once we hit November, anything's possible. The weather now is perfect."

"Totally plausible, but Georgie didn't say any of those things to me yesterday. Also, she didn't drink wine with dinner last night or the night before. She likes a glass of red wine with dinner."

Mac continued to keep quiet. Georgie should have realized she couldn't fool her little sister. Anastasia was too sharp.

"See, she doesn't want to tell me she's pregnant and put more pressure on me to learn to ride, but she doesn't want to give me a dishonest reason, either. She said it was because they were so eager to tie the knot, which is the truth as far as it goes."

"I don't think people in Bickford would care whether she's pregnant."

"Aha!" She whirled to face him. "So she is!"

He backed up, hands raised. "You didn't hear it from me."

"Oh, Mac." She laughed. "I won't give you away. I'll pretend I don't know a thing."

"But we'd better get to work. You'll be taking Jasper out of his stall this morning."

She blinked, and some of her self-assurance disappeared. "I will?"

"You told me to push you."

"I know. I'm thinking about the moment I got Prince out of his stall and what happened after that. I never really had control of him."

"You're bigger now. You'll have a rope and he's already wearing a halter. It'll be just like yesterday except I won't be the one taking him out."

She nodded, but she didn't look convinced she could do it.

"Just yesterday you stood in the yard with him while I fetched the tote and you seemed okay with that."

"But we were both standing still. When we were moving, you were in charge." She swallowed. "But I'll do it."

"You need to get used to handling him alone. When you're out there with the wedding party and everybody's on horseback, all kinds of unexpected things can happen. If you have even a trace of that old terror left, you could react in a way that puts you and others at risk."

"And my sister's pregnant."

"Just barely. Don't forget she's going on the trail ride this weekend, so it's not like she can't be married on horseback the weekend after that."

"Good point."

"She'll be fine. We'll all be fine, but I want you to be best buddies with Jasper before the big day." He gestured toward the barn. "After you."

"What do I do, first?" Tension laced her words.

"Breathe."

"Ha-ha."

"No, I mean it." He set the mug down next to her lunchbox on the hay bale. "Take a nice deep breath and blow it out slowly."

She stopped in the middle of the aisle and followed his instructions.

"Good. Any better?"

"Some."

"Then do it again." He took the lead rope out of the tack room while she pulled in another deep breath and let it out. Then he walked up next to her. "Okay, now?"

She glanced at him. "If I say *not quite* you'll know I'm stalling, so I won't say it. I'm fine. Or as fine as I'll be until I jump this next hurdle."

"Then take this lead rope, go into the stall, and clip it to his halter."

She took the rope. "You make it sound so easy."

"It is easy. He likes you. He'll be thrilled that you want to take him out of the stall and groom him."

"Thrilled, huh?" She paused in front of the stall and Jasper stuck his head over, as always. "Hey, Jasper." She stroked his nose. "Want to take a short walk with me?"

He bobbed his head.

Mac observed that with interest. "Funny I never noticed how consistently he does that. I must not ask him questions."

"Because you already know all the answers."

"Don't I wish. Need any help opening the door?"

"No. I watched you." But she hesitated. "What if he starts to come out before I have the lead rope clipped on?"

"He shouldn't, but just say *back*, and he'll back up."

She squared her shoulders and opened the door. Jasper, bless him, stayed right where he was. Her movements were tentative, but she stepped into the stall and hooked the lead rope to his halter. "Now what?"

"Just turn around and start out of the stall. He'll come right along with you."

When she faced him again, anxiety shone in her eyes. "Will he step on me?"

"No. But I'll walk along beside you so you can gauge the pace."

"Thanks." She was quivering a little, but she did exactly as he'd directed her and soon they were headed down the aisle. Jasper did what he'd been trained to do, walking steadily along beside her.

"You're doing great. When we get outside the barn, let's walk him around a little so you can get used to the feel. Turn left, turn right, maybe take him around in a circle."

"All right."

"I'll step over by the fence and give you room to maneuver."

She glanced at him in panic.

"You'll be fine. Jasper's crazy about you." He wondered if she'd ever catch on that he was projecting his feelings onto the horse. Jasper liked her, but he liked everybody unless they were mean to him. Mac's feelings, on the other hand, were quite specific to her and they were growing stronger with every minute.

He leaned against the fence and watched her with pride and an emotion he dared not identify. He'd always thought she was adorable and a very talented artist. But because of this project he was learning things about her he wouldn't have known otherwise, personality traits that made her more appealing than ever.

At the age of six she'd been intrepid. If her mother hadn't forbidden her to ride, she'd be an accomplished horsewoman like Georgie. She wouldn't have needed him to teach her anything. He shouldn't be glad that she'd suffered that trauma at a young age. But guilty though it made him feel, he was.

CHAPTER 12

The grooming went faster than the day before, but the saddling and bridling went slower because Mac made her do it pretty much by herself. Thank goodness she still hadn't been required to stick her thumb inside Jasper's mouth. The day would come, Mac assured her. She hoped by then Jasper would seem like a lap dog and she'd have the courage to do it.

Mac decided to use a mounting block for her to climb on Jasper. Then he had her climb back down again, to make sure she could do it by herself using the block. After the fiasco yesterday she was relieved that he'd chosen that method.

The less time they spent touching each other, the better. She avoided looking at his mouth just as she had all through dinner the night before. But she couldn't very well avoid looking at him. He was her teacher, after all, her broad-shouldered, narrow-hipped, bodacious teacher.

"Let's have you mount and dismount a few more times," Mac said. "Maybe if you practice that you'll feel like trying it without the mounting block, although I grant you Jasper is a tall horse."

"He is, but that's good. I need to conquer the fear of

being up high, and he's helping me do that." She climbed on again, using the block, sat in the saddle for a moment getting the feel of being up there, and dismounted again.

Mac propped his hip against the hitching post and folded his arms as he watched her. "I just thought of something we're missing. If we're going out into the corral this morning, you need a hat."

She laughed. "Where's Travis when you need him?"

For some odd reason Mac looked annoyed. "We don't need Travis. I can round you up a hat." He pulled out his phone. "Let me see if Ed has one we can borrow. I'll bet he does."

Interesting. If she didn't know better, she'd think Mac was jealous of the relationship she had with Travis. That was illogical on many levels. She and Mac had decided they wouldn't become involved, for one thing, so jealousy shouldn't even be on the table. Yet it seemed to be there.

Mac had to recognize that she wasn't attracted to Travis. Nothing about their interaction was sexually charged, whereas she was pretty sure people had guessed there was chemistry between her and Mac. Like Ida, they were waiting to see if anything would come of it.

She continued to practice her mounting and dismounting while he talked to Ed.

"Ed's bringing down a couple of hats Vivian doesn't wear much. She'll happily loan you one."

"That's nice of her." She mounted for at least the fifth time. She was losing count. She wondered if Jasper was as bored as she was. "I should probably buy one if I'm going to become a rider."

"Wouldn't hurt."

She sat there judging the distance to the ground. The more she'd fooled with the mounting block, the less she liked it. There wouldn't be one waiting for her in the canyon.

She might not have to get off and back on again during the wedding, but if she wasn't good at it she'd be trapped on Jasper the whole time. "Would you please move the block? I want to see if I can get down without it."

"Sure." He moved it well out of the way. "Have at it."

She'd mastered the trick of getting her right foot out and her leg over the cantle in one smooth motion. Putting her weight on her hands, she slipped the left foot free and began sliding down.

"You've almost got it."

"How far?"

"About six inches."

"That's far enough." She hopped down, spun around, and lifted her hands in the air. "Nailed the landing."

"Yeah, you did." His gaze had taken on that melted-chocolate look that turned her insides to mush.

He liked her a lot, and they were only two days into this. Over the weekend they'd have more hours together. They were probably fooling themselves that they could keep things strictly platonic.

Ed showed up with the hats, one brown and one black. In order to put them on, she had to take her hair out of its ponytail. She didn't have a mirror, either. Both hats fit, so she had to rely on Mac and Ed to tell her which one was better.

Ed refused to choose one over the other. "They both make you look prettier than a picture," he said. "You can't go wrong with either one."

"The brown," Mac said without hesitation.

"How come?"

"It goes the best with your eyes."

Oh, Mac. She wondered if he had any idea how Ed would interpret that statement.

Not surprisingly, Ed gave her a knowing smile. "There

you go. The brown it is. Vivian said to keep it as long as you need to. It was in the closet gathering dust. I can testify to that because I'm the one who brushed it off before I walked down here."

Anastasia settled the hat on her head. "Thank you, and please thank Vivian for me. I'll buy my own hat soon and then I'll return it."

"I probably shouldn't say until I check with her, but my guess is she'll give it to you if you want it. Our daughter doesn't wear such hats and Vivian really doesn't use either of these. I bought her one with a special hatband studded with turquoise, and she wears that one."

"I'm sure she does." She'd always thought Ed and Vivian made a sweet couple and the hat story only confirmed that they were still devoted after many years of marriage.

"Okay, then." Ed tucked the black hat under his arm. "I'll leave you two to carry on." He gave them one last glance before heading back to the house.

That last look convinced her that he knew something was going on between her and Mac. He might have even seen them kissing. But pointing that out to Mac wouldn't be particularly helpful.

"You look great in that hat." His admiration was obvious. Even if Ed hadn't witnessed the kiss, he would have noticed Mac's behavior this morning. "I don't think I've ever seen you wear one."

"I wasn't a cowgirl. I didn't ride. It seemed like an affectation to me, so I didn't consider it."

"Not even to keep the sun out of your eyes?"

"Nope. I've used shades."

"I guess that's right. You had a really wild pair you wore this summer. I'd forgotten about those." He gazed at her. "And you can't wear a pony tail with that hat."

"Nope." No doubt about it. The hair down and the hat on had put him in some kind of a trance. If she stepped into his arms right now he'd kiss her again.

And then he'd be upset, because he was attracted but reluctant. He could still be worried about Georgie's re-action, although Anastasia suspected it might be some-thing besides that. But now wasn't the time to quiz him, with Jasper saddled and ready to go. She had the hat and she'd learned to dismount by herself. Time to ride.

"Let's see if I can climb on without the mounting block."

That seemed to snap him out of it. "I'd like you to be able to do that."

"Then here goes." She grabbed the saddle horn with her left hand. Holding the stirrup with her right, she stood on tiptoe and managed to get her left foot securely in place. After that it was easy. She was on in nothing flat.

"Good." He put a hand on Jasper's shoulder and glanced up at her. "You look like a pro up there."

"It's the power of a hat. I saw what it did for Ryan Nesbitt yesterday. Apparently it's working the same magic for me."

"Could be." He looped the reins over Jasper's neck and handed them to her. "I'll lead you into the corral. How much do you know about neck reining?"

"Assume I know nothing."

"All right." But he kept looking at her with that light in his eyes. "I can't get over the difference the hat makes."

"It's an illusion, Mac. I'm no different." But he wasn't totally wrong. The hat did have a subtle psychological effect. With it on, she fit the profile of a competent rider.

The hat wasn't new, but it had been subtly shaped by a woman who could ride rings around Anastasia. Vivian had been a barrel racer when she was younger. She could probably do a credible job of running those barrels even now.

Compared to Vivian, the owner of the hat, Anastasia was a fraud. Now she had a third goal to add to her list. She'd started out wanting to see the Ghost in person. Yesterday she'd tacked on participating in her sister's horseback wedding. Her third goal had just been revealed. She wanted to become worthy of this hat.

The man who would help her achieve that had paused to open the gate to the corral, which was round instead of square. He had to let go of Jasper's bridle in order to pull the gate back so they could all enter. Yesterday she would have freaked out to be on a horse with nobody in charge but her.

Today, thanks to Mac's coaching, she didn't freak out. Well, maybe she was freaking out a little bit. Her heart was beating fast and her mouth felt dry. She was about to attempt something she'd been afraid to do for twenty years of her life.

Jasper stood quietly, ears swiveling back toward her. "I'm a little bit scared, Jasper," she murmured. "Will you take it easy for me?"

Jasper bobbed his head as he did every time she asked him a question. She realized now it was a trick someone had taught him, but it calmed her, all the same. Her hands had tightened on the reins, and she consciously loosened her grip. Easy does it.

Mac came back from closing the gate. First he gave her a quick lesson in neck reining, explaining that laying the reins on the horse's neck guided him away from that direction and moved him toward the opposite one. She tried to focus on what he was saying while her stomach churned.

"But you won't need to do much of that as you circle the corral," Mac said. "Once you start along the perimeter, Jasper will keep to the rail. He's done it a thousand times."

"Can we just walk around at first?"

"Absolutely. Walking is perfect."

Her throat felt as if she'd swallowed barbed wire. "What if he starts going faster?"

"He won't unless you ask him to. Let's stick with a walk for now."

"Which way am I going, clockwise or counterclockwise?" Her pulse raced.

"Either. He's used to both directions. You can go one direction and then reverse if you feel like it."

She wouldn't feel like it. Going round and round would be challenge enough. "I'll go clockwise, then."

"Okay. Reins in your left hand. That's it. Nudge him with your heels."

She gave Jasper a tentative tap with the heels of her boots.

"A little harder. And click your tongue."

When she did that, Jasper began to move. Her chest tightened and she grabbed for the saddle horn. But the pace was slow enough that she let go immediately, feeling a little silly for that instinctive reaction.

"Breathe," Mac called after her.

Oh. No wonder she was feeling a little dizzy. She was barely doing that, as if breathing would upset her balance. The saddle creaked as Jasper plodded along, his hoofs landing with rhythmic thuds on the soft ground of the corral.

If she fell off, it wouldn't be so bad this time. At this speed she wouldn't go sailing into the air, and no rocks or bushes were in her way. Gradually she realized that she'd have to work at falling off.

Her booted feet were tucked into the stirrups and getting them out wasn't all that easy. She'd struggled with that a couple of times while practicing her dismount. Instead of sliding around the horse's broad back the way she had as a kid, she was sitting on a saddle that cradled her backside. If things got really dicey, she could grab the saddle horn.

Slowly she began to relax. Jasper moved without any input from her. She was inside a corral, and Mac was in there with her, leaning against the fence, arms crossed. When he realized she was looking at him, he gave her a thumbs-up.

She circled the corral twice and nothing happened. "Is this what it's like out on the trail?" she called out to Mac.

"Pretty much. There are stretches where you can go faster, but trail riding is supposed to be leisurely, not a race to the finish line. I guarantee the wedding party won't be galloping out there with everybody all gussied up."

"Georgie said I'll be wearing a dress with a split skirt. That sounds complicated."

"You'll be ready when the time comes."

That was exactly what she needed to hear, and he had an uncanny ability to know that. "Will you be riding behind me?"

"I don't know, but you'll be with someone who's experienced, whether it's me or Georgie. Come to think of it, you may ride out with Georgie."

She decided she'd be okay with that. "Will I be on Jasper?"

"That's my plan and I can't imagine anybody objecting."

"Then I think I can do this, Mac. It's not so hard."

"Well, no, but there's a difference between riding in a circle in the corral and going along a trail with a horse in front and a horse behind."

"Of course there is. The second one sounds like a lot more fun."

He greeted that with a soft laugh. "Getting bored?"

His amusement sent a delicious shiver up her spine, and his words carried a subtle challenge. He wanted her to show some spunk. His reaction to the mug told her he liked that quality in her.

So did she, as a matter of fact. When her professor had told the class not to let fear get in the way of art, she'd known then that creativity and courage went together like peanut butter and jelly. Yet she'd allowed herself to be afraid of things. Horses, for one thing. Romantic entanglements, for another.

Some artists recommended good sex for inspiration. She'd never experienced inspiring sex, but she thought Mac would be capable of providing it. She'd have to give this some more thought, but for now, going round and round at a walk was getting old. "What's the next speed?"

"A trot. It's a little bouncy. Takes some getting used to."

"Is there a chance we'll do that one on the trail?"

"Definitely a chance, although probably not for long. We'll have mostly experienced riders, but as I understand it, Charmaine's only been on a horse once, for the inaugural trail ride."

"That's true, but she seemed to have a good time." Anastasia hadn't thought about this riding gig in connection with Charmaine. She liked her older sister a lot better now that they were adults and they weren't nearly as competitive.

But she'd enjoy the heck out of being a better rider than Charmaine when the wedding party rode out to the canyon. "What do I need to know about this trotting business?"

"First, let's see you reverse direction while you're just walking."

She thought back to what he'd said and laid the reins

against the left side of Jasper's neck. What a little miracle! He turned in that direction and started across the middle of the corral. "No, all the way around." She managed to get him going in the opposite direction. Apparently reining was like a steering wheel.

"Now, get your heels down and feel the connection with his body along your entire leg."

So much for relaxing in the saddle.

"When you nudge him into a trot, you'll bounce at first. Grip the saddle horn with your right hand so you can steady yourself and move with him instead of against him."

This was sounding way more difficult than she'd thought it would be, but she needed to be able to do it. Her list of reasons now included being able to ride better than Charmaine. She held on to the saddle horn, brought her legs in contact with Jasper's flanks, and looked over at Mac. "Ready."

He was no longer leaning against the fence, which should have told her something. "Nudge him and cluck your tongue."

She nudged and clucked, and all hell broke loose. Jasper launched into something that reminded her of the time she'd ridden her bike over a cattle guard. But that had been over in a couple of seconds.

This went on and on. She lost a stirrup and her hat fell into the dust. The fear she'd thought had been banished reared up like a fire-breathing dragon. Desperate and afraid, she called out to Mac. "Help!"

He was there in a heartbeat, taking hold of Jasper's bridle and bringing the horse to a stop.

"Oh, God." She gulped for air. "That was *horrible*."

"You did fine." He put a hand on her thigh. "Not bad at all, considering you're just starting out."

She gazed down at him. "I so wanted horseback riding to be magical."

"It can be."

"I don't think so."

"It can." He glanced down at the empty stirrup hanging there. "Let's try something."

Before she realized what he intended to do, he'd placed his foot in the stirrup and swung up behind the saddle.

"Can he carry us both?"

"He's a big, muscular horse. He can do it for a little while, and that's all we need. Put your foot back in the stirrup and relax against me."

If she'd been less rattled, that would have been a terrific idea. As it was, she was tight as a piece of canvas nailed to a frame.

"Come on, Anastasia. Loosen up." He wrapped one arm around her waist and coaxed her back against his solid chest as he took the reins. "This'll be fun."

"That's what they all say."

"You'll see." His breath was warm in her ear as he clicked his tongue. He must have done something with his heels, too, because Jasper began to move.

The walk felt familiar, but it was quickly followed by the bone-jarring trot. "Mac! Please don't—"

"Shh."

Then something happened and the bouncing was replaced by a smooth, easy movement that was *wonderful.* The scenery rushed by as Mac held her close and Jasper took them on a magic carpet ride. Round and round they went, and she never wanted it to end.

But it did eventually. The poor horse couldn't be expected to carry them both forever. Mac pulled back on the reins and subjected them to some jostling with a trot that quickly turned into a walk.

He stopped next to the spot where her hat had fallen.

He could have let go of her at that point, but he didn't. "What do you think?"

She sighed and rested her head against his shoulder. "That was magical." Having him there holding her had been a big part of the magic, but he was asking about the ride, not the bodily contact. "What was that gait?"

"A canter."

"Lovely. I don't suppose we'll be cantering on the trail ride."

"Probably not, but when you and I go out alone we can find places to canter the horses. Does that help?"

"Yes." She straightened. She shouldn't let herself lean against him with such abandon. "Thank you."

"You're welcome." He slipped down from the horse. "That's enough for today." His voice was suspiciously husky.

She was certainly stirred up, so she had to believe he was, too. "Should I—"

"I'll just lead you over to the hitching post. It'll be quicker that way." He scooped up her hat, dusted it off, and handed it to her. "Wouldn't want you to lose this great hat."

"Thanks." She still felt a little dazed as she put it on and allowed him to lead her out the gate and over to the hitching post. That moment on Jasper had been in broad daylight and she'd been riding in the arms of a man in a dusty corral instead of being off on her own in a fragrant meadow.

But the feeling had been exactly what she'd hoped for as a little girl of six when she'd taken Prince out of the barn. Mac had given her that. For that alone, he would always be her hero.

CHAPTER 13

Mac couldn't get rid of Anastasia fast enough. Once again he relieved her of taking off Jasper's tack and sent her packing. He hoped she understood that every second counted. He was so close to hauling her into his arms again it wasn't funny.

Correction—it was funny. Ridiculously funny. She hadn't merely wanted him to teach her to ride. Oh, no. She'd wanted him to make it magical. And here was the kicker—he got that.

He'd always thought riding was magical. His parents had taken him on moonlit rides and pointed out the constellations. His parents shared a love of riding. They'd passed that fascination on to him.

He thought about those things after he'd sent Anastasia home. Until she'd made that comment about wanting to feel the magic, he hadn't realized how much he wanted that for her. Not everyone had the capacity to appreciate magic. Sophie hadn't. But Anastasia . . .

As he rubbed the dirt and sweat off Jasper, he thought about the transformation when she'd put on that hat. Suddenly she wasn't a wannabe rider. He saw her as she hoped to become: a woman who was at ease with these animals. She'd hated trotting, which was no big surprise, and didn't mean she wouldn't one day be the rider she wanted to be.

But he hadn't been able to leave it at that. So he'd climbed on behind her, an ill-advised impulse, and he'd held her while demonstrating the joy of riding a canter. She'd responded as he'd known she would, with the same sense of wonder she brought to life itself.

And now he wanted her more than ever. What the hell was he doing to himself? And to her? These riding lessons were taking on all the trappings of an old-fashioned courtship.

That wasn't good. He thought of the guy from Hollywood who'd predicted that she'd soon be famous. Mac could see that happening. Considering her potential for greatness, she didn't need to get involved with some local yokel with a failed marriage on his résumé.

Vince rode into the stable yard on Storm Cloud soon after Mac had turned Jasper out with the other horses. He dismounted and thumbed back his hat. "What's on your agenda for today?"

"Ed has a farrier coming in from Lubbock."

"Oh, right. I forgot about that."

Mac chuckled. "You have other things on your mind. Anyway, I planned to help him. It's a big job, and Ed's not as limber as he used to be."

"Maybe Travis could handle it instead."

"I'm sure he could if he postpones his errands in Amarillo until tomorrow. What do you need me for?"

"I'd like you to ride out to the box canyon with me and help me figure out how to set up for the ceremony. Georgie's got some inventory issues at the store and can't go, but we have to start planning." He grinned. "She said I'm the one with the vision of how this will go, anyway."

"She has a point. Of the two of you, you're way more romantic. I'll call Travis and see if he's left yet."

He hadn't and agreed to come down and help the farrier.

Mac tucked his phone back in his pocket. "I'll go fetch Cinder. Do you think we'll be back in time for the farrier to take care of him, too?"

"Should be. I realize I'm pulling you off your regular job for this. But it's important."

"Definitely." Mac smiled to himself as he grabbed a lead rope out of the tack room and went out to the pasture. He'd known Vince a long time and he'd never seen him so happy and excited.

Six months ago Mac couldn't have pictured Vince planning his own wedding ceremony. He'd been the original rolling stone who never settled anywhere for very long. He used to claim that boredom caused him to move on. Obviously he wasn't bored now.

Mac saddled Cinder and mounted up. "We look like part of a drill team with these two black horses."

"We do." Vince laughed as they rode out the gate. "I told Georgie she should ride Cinder in the wedding so we could be on matching horses. She said I'd lost my mind. Prince has been with her through thick and thin, and one of the reasons she'd agreed to be married on horseback was that Prince could attend her wedding." They reached the trail head. "You want to lead?"

"You go ahead. This is your show."

Vince guided Storm Cloud down the narrow path. "Might as well check the trail while we're out here. Holler if you see anything that needs to be done."

"I will, although it was okay this past weekend." Mac followed Vince at a walk. He looked at the trail differently, though, now that he knew Anastasia would be riding down it soon. He had to duck to get under an overhanging mesquite branch. "On second thought, maybe I'll come out here with some loppers tomorrow."

"Good idea. How was the lesson today?"

Arousing beyond belief. "Fine. She stayed in the corral, walked a little at first, and then attempted a trot. We'll work on the trot tomorrow." He didn't plan to tell anyone about riding double while they cantered. She might, but he doubted it. That had been a special moment that wouldn't happen again.

"Trotting's hard in the beginning."

"Especially if you learn as an adult." Mac considered himself lucky that he'd been put on a horse at the age of two.

"And I did learn as an adult. Maybe if I'd grown up on the back of a horse like you, I'd wonder what all the fuss was about. You're the most relaxed rider I've ever known. You seem to become part of the horse."

"That's a really disturbing image, but thanks for the thought."

Vince laughed. "Now I'm picturing one of those mythical creatures, the half-man, half-horse deal. What are they called?"

"Centaurs. I swear I'm going to get you a reading list. You need to know these things if you expect to help your kid with homework."

"If I get stumped, I'll just call on Uncle Macario."

"Assuming I'm still in Bickford."

"You will be. You bought a house."

"Yeah, I probably will be." He glanced up at the rust-colored walls as they made their way deeper into the canyon. Being here felt right. "By the way, I appreciate you keeping the secret of my name all this time, but I've decided to start telling people before Travis does. Take the wind out of his sails."

"He might not tell."

"He might not mean to, but this is Travis we're talking about. I'm going to start mentioning it. It sounds a lot less awful to me now than it did when I was thirteen."

"Your mother would be proud."

"Hey, she's already proud. But that reminds me, can your folks make it for the wedding?"

"I talked to them about it right after I proposed to Georgie. Unfortunately my dad's health isn't great right now and my mom doesn't feel as if she can leave him. It was after I realized they couldn't be here that I started thinking seriously about having it in the canyon."

"Which probably leaves out your stepmother-in-law, too."

"Yeah, but Georgie told me she didn't want to base our wedding on what would suit Evelyn. I think that's a good call. Evelyn is one of the most self-centered women on the planet."

"I'm getting that. I've never met her, which is saying something in a town this size. Does she ever come out of that house?"

"Georgie and Anastasia take her on shopping trips to Amarillo every once in a while. She's flown over to stay with Charmaine in Dallas once that I know of. But she doesn't mingle with the residents of Bickford, if that's what you mean. I'm sure she thinks we're all beneath her." Vince's tone was bitter.

"You don't like her."

"Not much. She's been mean to the woman I love."

"Then I'm glad you decided to have the wedding on horseback. You and Georgie don't need her around to spoil the mood."

"Exactly." He nudged Storm Cloud into a trot.

Mac followed suit. Vince had picked up the pace without thinking, as a seasoned rider would do. Trotting was a natural gait if someone had been riding for years, but not if they'd been riding for days.

"Got a question for you," he called out to Vince.

"What's that?" He slowed Storm Cloud to a walk again.

"In a regular wedding, the guys get into position first and then the women follow. Does that mean we'll ride out ahead of Georgie and the others?"

"I guess it does. Why?"

"Maybe you could ask Georgie to keep the pace to a walk."

"Sure. She might be planning on that, anyway, but I'll talk to her about it."

"Good. I'll tell Anastasia in the morning. I think she'll be relieved."

"Or you could tell her tonight at Sadie's. Then she can be relieved that much sooner."

"I thought I'd stay home and rip up the last of the carpet."

"You can if you want, but Steve's got a country band he wants us to hear. He and Myra auditioned them over the weekend and since they'll be playing for the wedding reception, he wants us to give a listen tonight. See if we think the music's danceable."

"Oh." He gazed up into a slice of blue sky and spotted a hawk surfing the air currents. "So besides listening we're supposed to be dancing?"

"That's the idea. I'm looking forward to it. Like old times. What do you say?"

"Um, sure. I can do that." When Vince, Mac, and Travis had worked at the guest ranch near Bickford, they'd always gone dancing at Sadie's. Tonight, if he had any sense, he'd stay home and rip up carpet. But if he didn't go, dollars to doughnuts Travis would end up dancing with Anastasia a lot. They'd have a high old time together, and even though they were just friends, he still didn't like thinking about it.

And he would think about it constantly if he stayed home to pull up carpet, so he might as well go and dance with her. He'd never had the pleasure and they'd be expected to dance together at the wedding reception, so he could consider it practice.

Yeah, right. He was an excellent dancer and if she wasn't, so what? He could make her look like a better dancer than she was. He didn't need practice any more than he needed another reason to hold her. But if anyone was going to hold her on that dance floor tonight, it by God would be him.

"Good. It'll be fun." Vince nudged Storm Cloud into a trot again.

Mac was enjoying himself. Riding out here without worrying about greenhorns was a nice change. He could breathe in the crisp fall air and take time to notice the leaves changing. They didn't have spectacular fall foliage here, but splashes of orange and gold brightened the canyon.

When the path smoothed out, Vince urged his horse into a canter and Mac did the same. The rhythm was a bittersweet reminder of this morning—Anastasia's warmth, the gentle rise and fall of her breasts, the orange-peel scent of whatever shampoo she used.

Vince slowed again as they neared the meadow where the Ghost liked to hang out with his herd. The soft burble of Sing-Song Creek blended with the chirp of birds flitting through the bushes. The cottonwoods lining the bank of the creek had turned, and their yellow leaves glowed in the sun.

"I doubt the Ghost will be here in the middle of the day," Vince said. "But you never know."

"No, you don't. Just think, if you hadn't come up with that harebrained scheme to rope him last spring, none of this would have happened."

"That's true." Vince pulled Storm Cloud to a stop at the edge of the meadow and scanned the area. "I don't think he's around."

"Nope. But you'll probably see him this weekend on the trail ride. He's pretty regular in the evening and early morning."

"I hope we do. Georgie would like that. Me, too, actually."

"Then you can thank him personally for inspiring Anastasia to want to learn to ride. Now you can have the wedding ceremony of your dreams, assuming it doesn't rain."

"It won't."

"Should we haul a canopy out here just in case?"

"No." Vince guided Storm Cloud across the meadow toward the narrow trail leading to the box canyon. "The idea is to have the ceremony under the wide-open skies."

"I get that, but I guarantee the women who've spent hours on their hair and makeup will care a whole hell of a lot if they end up getting rained on."

"It won't rain." He clucked to Storm Cloud and started across the meadow toward the narrow trail into the box canyon.

And it probably wouldn't, Mac thought as he followed on Cinder. Luck seemed to be on Vince's side these days. Mac gave Cinder his head for the uphill climb on the far side of the meadow. What used to be a game trail obscured by thorny bushes had been widened last spring by Vince and his crew of volunteers.

As Mac drew closer to the box canyon, the sound of the waterfall became more distinct. Although he'd made this journey most weekends for close to six months, he still felt a thrill when he first saw it plunging straight down the side of the rust-colored canyon wall. The sun created rainbows in the mist surrounding it.

"I wanted to get out here and look at it now." Vince leaned on his saddle horn and gazed at the waterfall. "This is when I'd like to start the ceremony, although I know, considering the ride out, the timing might not be exact."

"Probably not. But the waterfall looks like this for a good hour every day."

"So it turns out our legal eagle Frank is also licensed to perform the ceremony."

"Yeah? That's great!" Or not. He had an unsettling thought. "I hope he's not planning to ride Jasper out here. I realize Jasper's his horse, but—"

"I've already talked to him and he's fine riding another horse so Anastasia can use Jasper."

Mac let out a breath. "Excellent."

"I'm picturing Frank with his back to the falls, and the rest of us facing them."

"How close do you want to get?"

"I don't know. Let's ride over there and decide."

Riding side by side, they skirted the campground area, a cleared space with a fire pit in the middle. At the edge of the campground stood a large chuck wagon that provided permanent storage for sleeping bags, tents for those who wanted them, and cookware.

Anastasia had never seen this, which seemed incomprehensible. Mac was determined to get her out here soon. He pictured her expression when she first saw the waterfall. She'd be entranced.

Imagining her reaction as he rode, he lost track of how close they were until he felt the mist on his skin. Pulling Cinder to a halt, he glanced over at Vince. "This is too close."

Vince grinned. "What? I can't hear you!"

"Exactly! You won't be able to hear Frank or Georgie, either, nimrod!"

Vince laughed. "Just wondered when you'd notice that!" Wheeling his horse around, he headed back the way they'd come. He stopped after about twenty yards and waited for Mac. "You were off in another world. I was beginning to think we'd end up standing under the falls before you came to."

"I was waiting for you to stop."

"The hell you were. What's got you so distracted, bro?"

Mac hedged. "There's a lot going on. The documentary, the wedding, the baby . . ."

"And the baby's auntie? Could she have something to do with your state of mind?"

"Look, nothing's going on."

"Oh, I think *something's* going on. I just can't figure out what. Georgie said Anastasia came to dinner Sunday night partly to discuss her interaction with you, but then she backed off and said it wouldn't be necessary."

"It's not necessary. Nothing's going to happen."

"Georgie thinks different. She's convinced that her sister wants you bad."

"We had a talk. We both agreed to keep things platonic."

"You'd better hope she doesn't change her mind. When she's focused, she is a force to be reckoned with."

Mac groaned. "I don't want to hear that."

"Maybe not, but I thought you should know. Are you planning to get her out here next week and test whether she can handle the trail?"

"Yeah."

"I thought she might be ready for that with the extra time you'll have this weekend. So when you do bring her out here, she'll love it."

Mac nodded. "She will."

"Georgie asked me to set a couple of ground rules, though, because this canyon can be very seductive."

"I don't need any damn ground rules. I won't be doing—"

"First ground rule: Don't break her heart."

"I can't break her heart if nothing happens, and it won't."

Vince continued as if he hadn't spoken. "And the second ground rule is: Carry condoms at all times."

CHAPTER 14

Mac hadn't come into Sadie's for lunch or happy hour, but Anastasia had hopes for later, when the band was scheduled to play. She remembered Charmaine telling her that Mac had loved to dance when he'd been a wrangler at the guest ranch. Anastasia had been too young to participate when Saturday night at Sadie's had been filled with live music and laughter.

The summer before her last year of art school she'd chosen to work for a gallery in San Antonio instead of coming home. And by the time she'd graduated, the live music had disappeared. But now it was back.

Tonight was to be a test of the band's popularity with anyone who loved to dance, because that would be important during the wedding reception scheduled in a week and a half. That meant Vince and Georgie would be there. So would Travis, who asked Anastasia to save him a dance.

She'd done that, but the man she was saving the rest of her dances for had yet to make an appearance. She'd run home to freshen up and change into a black knit long-sleeved shirt with a scooped neck and a new pair of jeans. She'd left her hair down.

Georgie had taken one look at her when she'd walked into Sadie's and then smiled knowingly. She understood the motivation for that trip home without Anastasia saying a single word.

As the band tuned up, Georgie drew Anastasia into a corner. "You're loaded for bear, I see."

"I've been doing some thinking."

"I can tell."

"I let fear keep me from riding horses, and that was extremely limiting. What else am I missing out on because I'm afraid?"

Georgie's reply was hesitant. "I understand what you're saying. You have a valid point. I just remember what happened your last year in art school."

"And whose fault was that?"

"*His.*" Georgie's brown eyes flashed fire. "I could have wrung his scrawny neck for treating you that way."

"No, Georgie, it was my fault that I allowed his behavior to derail my art. He didn't do that to me. I did it to myself."

Her sister didn't look convinced.

"No, really. He was a creep who didn't deserve me, but I'm the one who let his rejection keep me from working. I promise you that will never happen again."

Georgie studied her for several seconds. "You know, I believe you."

"You do?" She was surprised and pleased.

"I don't think bravado is making you say that. It's confidence."

"Oh, Georgie." Her throat tightened. "That means a lot to me. Thanks."

"You can handle Mac, but I also think he has issues."

"Oh, I'm sure of it."

"He's told you?"

Anastasia shook her head. "He's hinted. Something in his past spooked him, but I don't know what."

"Knowing you, you'll find out."

"Yep." Anastasia gave her a quick hug. "I'm lucky to have you in my corner."

"Always."

"I just want to warn you that I feel the urge to break some rules. I'm an artist. We're supposed to be unconventional."

"Gonna dye your hair pink and purple?"

"Not today."

"Body piercings?"

"That doesn't appeal to me." She was positioned so that she could see the door to Sadie's. "But I'll tell you what does appeal to me."

"What?"

She nodded in the direction of the door. "Him."

Georgie turned around as Mac walked in. "He's an eyeful, all right."

"Uh-huh."

"Don't tell Vince I said that."

"Never." She sighed. "Wow, that cowboy sure cleans up good." His black Western shirt had a silver design embroidered on the yoke and his black jeans were crisply pleated. She could eat him up with a spoon. "If you'll excuse me?"

"Go for it, little sis."

She walked across the empty dance floor straight toward him. He'd obviously spotted her, too, because he held her gaze as she approached. "I want the first dance, Mac."

"The name's Macario."

She did a double take. "What?"

His mouth twitched with amusement. "It's what Mac

stands for. My full name is Macario. I've decided to start letting people know, and you're the first."

"Macario." She rolled it over her tongue. "I like it. It's different."

"I thought you might. That's why I decided to tell you first."

That made her pulse leap. "Really? I'm the first to hear your real name?"

"Well, not quite. Let me qualify that. Vince has known it for years and never said anything. The other day Travis thought to ask the question and when Vince and I wouldn't tell him, he threatened to turn the mystery into a three-act play. So I told him."

"And you assume within a couple of days it'll be all over town."

"Only because he'll tell one person, maybe Ida, and that's all it takes. It's like touching a match to a long fuse. Eventually the flame will reach the dynamite and everything will be blown to hell."

She smiled. "That's pretty much how it works in Bickford. Which means if I drag you out on the dance floor for the first number, which I plan to do, we'll light another fuse." *In more ways than one.*

"You'll drag me? Really?"

"Actually I was hoping you'd come willingly. I've been hearing about your dancing skills for years, and I want to see what the commotion is all about. But if I end up dragging you out there by your ear, that will feed the gossip mill for weeks."

He regarded her with interest. "Do you like to dance?"

"Love it."

"Are you any good?"

"Dance with me and find out, cowboy."

His easy grin made her heart race and her stomach flutter. She knew he could ride like a dream. She was about to discover if he could dance like one, too. Assuming he made love like a dream was completely logical.

Maybe she'd find out eventually. But not tonight. She wasn't going to rush into anything. First she had to unearth the skeletons in his closet, and that would take time. Even after she knew why he was so adamant about not getting involved with her, he might stubbornly cling to his position.

But that was a problem for another day. The band launched into a spirited two-step and Mac whirled her onto the floor. He challenged her with one tricky move after another and she met the challenge, laughing breathlessly as they cleared the floor.

Although they were surrounded by people clapping to the beat, she saw only Mac, his dark eyes sparkling with fun and admiration. His touch was sure and his footwork perfect. She'd always loved dancing, but she'd never danced like this, as if she'd been sprinkled with fairy dust and couldn't make a wrong move. Like so many things connected with this man, it was magical.

The music ended and they stood there laughing and trying to catch their breath as everyone cheered and whistled.

"You should go pro!" someone called out.

"They should film you guys for the documentary!" someone else said.

"Nah." Mac glanced at Anastasia with a smile. "That would take all the fun out of it."

She took a ragged breath. "Right."

He continued to gaze at her as he rested a hand lightly on her shoulder. "Can I buy you a beer, Twinkle Toes?"

"Absolutely." His hand on her shoulder was warmer than sunshine and made her tingle all over. He'd never touched her for no reason before. He kept his hand there as they walked over to the bar.

Sure, the tavern was crowded, but it wasn't as if he'd lose track of her in such a small place. Instead it seemed as if he didn't want to break the connection they'd had on the dance floor. She didn't want to break it, either.

Only one stool was available and he gestured for her to take it. "I'll stand." When Ike came over, Mac ordered them each a beer. He ordered her favorite without having to ask, too. Apparently he'd paid attention to that.

Swiveling her stool away from the bar, she gazed up at him. "That was fun." Understatement of the year.

"It sure was. You surprised the hell out of me. I had no idea you could dance like that."

"We used to go dancing every weekend while I was in art school. It also helps to have a good partner." She smiled. "You more than lived up to your reputation."

Eyes twinkling, he touched the brim of his hat. "Thank you, ma'am. I have to admit I was showing off a little. But you kept up with me."

"Hey, my reputation was at stake, too."

"How come I've never heard that you were so good?"

"Why would you? We haven't had live music in Sadie's since I came home from school."

"Guess so." He glanced past her to the bar. "Our beer's arrived." He picked up the lighter colored one and handed it to her before taking his. Then he touched his glass gently to hers. "A toast to the best dancer I've ever partnered with."

"Oh, I doubt that."

"It's true. Drink up."

"Okay, and thanks for the compliment." She sipped her beer but she didn't need alcohol to get a buzz. The way Mac was looking at her would make any girl high.

"I am confused about something, though."

"What's that?"

"I wonder why— Hang on, you have some foam." He

leaned down and gently swiped his finger over her upper lip. "Got it." Then he held her gaze for a long, heart-pounding moment. "You do tempt me, Anastasia."

Her chest was so tight she could barely breathe. "Is that the question: You wonder why I tempt you?"

"Oh, no, I know exactly why you tempt me. It's a good thing that we're surrounded by all these people," he murmured, "or I swear I'd forget myself."

"I know what we said before, but honestly, would that be so terrible?"

He looked into her eyes as if weighing his answer. Then he straightened. "Yeah, it would." He took another swallow of his beer.

She could ask him to explain that, but he wouldn't do it now. Sadie's was jumping tonight, which was good news for the town and for Steve and Myra. But a noisy saloon wasn't the place for confidences. She'd have more opportunities to talk with him privately as the week progressed.

"My question has to do with your dancing." He had to stand close so they could hear each other.

That was fine with her. She loved admiring the way his shirt emphasized the width of his shoulders. From this angle they seemed a mile wide. As a matter of self-preservation, she didn't let her glance move down as far as his belt, though. They'd had the crotch conversation and this wasn't the place to rehash it.

She glanced into his eyes, another feature she could enjoy without blushing. "What about my dancing?"

"I didn't expect that level of skill after all the talk about you being a klutz. So what's the deal? How come you're perfectly coordinated on the dance floor?"

The man sitting on her left was talking really loud so she missed a little of Mac's question but she filled in the gaps by reading his lips. His beautiful lips. "It's the music."

"Music makes you more coordinated?"

"Yep. I took an exercise course once and it was the same thing. For some reason music flips a switch in my brain. I focus on it and that seems to cancel out the clumsy tendencies."

"Hmm." He took another sip of his beer. "Do you have music loaded on your phone?"

"Sure."

"Then what if you tried riding a trot using earbuds?"

She thought about that for a minute. "Interesting idea. I don't know if it would work or not, but if I'm listening to music I couldn't hear you."

"That's okay. I'd rather have you find a way to tune in to the movements of the horse than to listen to me yelling instructions."

"We can try it in the morning and see what happens."

"It's definitely worth a shot." He lifted the beer glass to his lips and drank.

She'd never tried to draw him actually drinking a beer. She should, because the way his lower lip curved under the rim of the glass was very erotic. She also liked how strong the tanned column of his neck looked when he lifted his chin.

That would make an interesting study, his neck, a bit of his shirt collar, the underside of his chin, and his lip curved around the beer glass.

Kissing him along the curve of his throat would be a pleasure, too. She could imagine how his skin would feel against her mouth—smooth except where his beard grew, and there she might find a hint of stubble. Right now he'd taste salty because he'd worked up a little sweat on the dance floor.

He lowered the glass abruptly and leaned down so his face was inches from hers. "What are you doing?"

Her cheeks grew warm. "I . . . um . . . had an idea for a drawing. . . ."

"Of what, for God's sake? You were staring at my neck like a vampire looking for a meal."

"You have a nice neck."

"So what? You want to suck my blood?"

"No, I want to . . . draw your neck and chin." *Then I want to kiss it and lick it. And while we're on the subject, that goes for the rest of you, too.*

He gazed at her as if she'd gone crazy. "Give me your beer." He set it on the bar and put his next to it. "We need to dance." He lifted her neatly off the stool, laid his hat on it, and led her into the throng of dancers swaying to a slow tune. Then he pulled her in close.

With almost no room to move they would have been forced together, anyway. But judging from the way he'd engineered this situation, he'd intended to hold her close. Thank goodness, because she'd wondered if he'd risk it at all tonight. He had, and she relaxed against him.

Leaning down, he nestled his cheek against hers and put his mouth close to her ear. "I don't know what to do about you," he murmured. "It's becoming a real problem."

"I know." And she wouldn't apologize for it anymore. She could be a good problem to have if he loosened up.

"I keep telling myself to keep my distance, but that's not working out."

"Are you upset?"

"Definitely. You've turned me upside down and sideways. I feel like I'm on the Tilt-A-Wheel at the carnival."

She had a disturbing thought. "Please don't cancel the lessons." She needed them for many reasons.

"I won't do that. Maybe it's ego, but I feel as if I'm the one person who can help you."

"You are."

"But the more we're together, the more I want you. We shouldn't be dancing this way but here we are."

She wound both arms around his neck and leaned back to look into his eyes. "I can't speak for you, but I like it."

"I like it too much." He settled both hands at the small of her back. "But it's safer than being together in the barn. I'm not about to kiss you with the whole town of Bickford watching."

"But you want to?"

"Oh, yeah." His gaze drifted down to her mouth. "I want to."

Her pulse rate had been in the red zone but now the needle was over the line. "How do you know they're watching? Maybe you could kiss me and nobody would notice."

"Considering how I'd like to kiss you, they'd notice all right."

"And how would that be?"

"You're flirting with me." He smiled. "In fact, you've been flirting ever since I walked in here tonight. What's that all about? What's changed?"

"My attitude. I know you're worried about Georgie's reaction, but I just talked to her and she wouldn't make trouble for you."

"Unless I break your heart. Then she'll come down on me like a blacksmith's anvil. She sent a message to that effect through Vince today."

"You can't break my heart if I won't let you. You can't interfere with my work if I don't let you. I'm the one in charge of my reactions. I finally figured that out. So the only thing standing between us is whatever blockade you throw up."

"I see." He pulled her in a little tighter. "Not going to make it easy on me, are you?"

"Nope."

"Okay." He released her and gently unhooked her arms from around his neck. "Then come with me."

For one wild moment she thought he was about to take her upstairs to one of the hotel rooms. Instead he grasped her hand and ran interference through the crowd before ushering her through the door that opened onto the street. After the heat of the dance floor, the cold air made her gasp. "Mac, you left your hat in—"

"I'll get it later. Come over here." He led her around the end of the building into the shadows. "We have something to discuss and we need privacy."

"All right." A slight breeze made her shiver.

"But first I have to do this." He drew her into his arms.

So like dancing, and so not. Heart racing, she nestled against him. "I think I'm going to like this part."

"I hope so, because I'm going crazy, and if I don't kiss you, I'll go completely insane."

"Can't have that." She lifted her mouth to his and he met her halfway. Heaven.

CHAPTER 15

Ever since Mac had noticed Anastasia watching him from across the saloon, the urge to drag her into his arms and kiss the living daylights out of her had simmered like a hot bed of coals. Kissing her ignited the flames. Her mouth welcomed him, teased and taunted him with what he could have if only he'd let go. He was damn close.

Yesterday morning he'd only cradled her face in his hands while he'd delved deep and sampled the lush taste of her. But after molding his body against hers for that slow dance, he had to have more.

Her plump breasts yielded as he pulled her in tight. His fevered brain pictured the rich promise of her hips and thighs as he stroked downward. Shoving his hands in the back pockets of her jeans, he cupped the sweetest little ass to ever grace a saddle.

She moaned as he pulled her against his rapidly stiffening cock. Clutching his shoulders, she arched against him, inviting him to take what he so desperately wanted. The muted sound of the band playing another two-step filtered through the wall of the saloon. He wondered if she liked making love to music. He wanted to find out.

As the red haze of lust saturated his brain, he imagined pushing her deeper into the shadows and bracing her against the side of the weathered building. He could take her hard and fast. The music and crowd noise would drown out their cries. No one would ever know.

The heat of that vision nearly made him come. Shaking with the effort to control the urgent demands of his body, he slowly released her and stepped back. He could barely breathe and his heart was pounding like the hooves of a runaway.

Vince had told him to carry condoms. He'd deliberately left them at home tonight. But in his aroused state, he seriously considered going there with her now. He could say *Come home with me* and she'd do it.

She was breathing as hard as he was, and her kiss . . . My God, the woman was a volcano ready to blow. The noise from the saloon might not be enough to drown out their cries, after all. If he did take her home, they might break the bed.

"Mac." She took a step toward him.

"Hang on." He ran a trembling hand through his hair. "I haven't recovered."

"Do you need to? Can't we just—"

"No. We have to talk."

"Oh. Is this about the blockade?"

"Yes, ma'am, it is."

She sighed. "I had a feeling. Lay it on me, cowboy."

He let out a strangled laugh. "You have no idea how much I'd love to do that very thing."

"You think not? I was on the receiving end of that kiss and I was fully aware of . . . other indications. If I had my sketchbook, I could draw an accurate representation of what was going on with your—"

"Never mind." She had a smart mouth in more ways than one. "You need to know something about me. I'm divorced."

It took her a split second to respond. "*That's* the blockade?"

"Yes."

"Then I don't get it. Is your ex a psycho who'll murder any woman who tries to take her place?"

"No."

"Are there kids involved?"

"No."

"How long were you married to this person?"

"Less than a year."

"Less than a *year*?" She blew out a breath. "So you made a mistake and married the wrong person. No big deal. Happens all the time. At least the two of you figured it out early on, before you had kids and things got complicated."

He could let her believe that sanitized version and his image would remain untarnished. He'd really enjoyed being the object of her admiration and lust. Giving that up wouldn't be fun, but honesty made him tell her the rest of it.

"The thing is, we didn't come to the decision together. She left me after less than a year because I wasn't making her happy. She said I was lousy at relationships and didn't understand her at all."

Anastasia met that with silence, which he took to mean his shiny image now had raw egg all over it. He'd expected that to happen, but he still didn't have to like it. This moment had to come, though.

He scrubbed his hands through his hair again. Usually during moments like this he fooled with his hat, but he'd left it inside. "Anyway, now that you know the story, you'll probably want to go on back inside and enjoy your evening. I'm thinking of heading home." The hat was for special occasions so he didn't need it immediately. He could pick it up tomorrow.

But instead of walking away, she kept standing there gazing at him. "Did you love her?"

"Does it matter?"

"It always matters."

"I sure thought I did. But it's possible I don't understand love, either."

"Do you still love her?"

He knew the answer to that one. "No. If I did I'd think of her a lot and want her back. I don't. But I sure learned my lesson about marriage. I'm not cut out for it. I mean, if she was sick of me in less than a year, what does that say about my skill as a husband?"

Anastasia stepped closer. "So you got married, spent a few months together, and then she got fed up and walked out. Is that what you're telling me?"

"Pretty sad, huh?"

"Pretty confusing! Did she complain about your behavior but you refused to change?"

"Well, no. I thought we were rocking along okay."

"Did she suggest the two of you go to counseling?"

"I asked her about that and she said it was no use. I didn't understand her and I wasn't going to. When I asked her what she meant, she said that if I really loved her I'd know what she meant. She wouldn't have to explain anything."

"Oh, Mac." She moved right in on him and cupped his face in both hands.

"Look, I didn't tell you so I could get your sympathy." He shouldn't put his arms around her again, but he did, anyway.

"Too late. You have it. And I want to strangle that stupid girl."

"You want to strangle Sophie?"

"If that's her name, yes, I do. Did she think you were

supposed to be some sort of mind reader? She's the one with the problem, not you."

He smiled. "Now you sound like Vince."

"And Vince is right! Who else have you talked to about this Sophie person?"

"Nobody, not even my folks, although my mom tried. I was embarrassed that I married somebody who left me so quick. I mean, who wants to talk about that? I gave Sophie all the wedding presents and decided it was an episode best forgotten."

"Except you haven't forgotten it." She wound her arms around his neck and tilted her face up to his. "That *episode* is what's keeping you from getting involved with me."

"Which it should. That's why I'm telling you all this, so you'll understand there's no future with a guy like me."

"No future? A guy like you? What does that mean?"

"Just that. I'm a dead-end street."

"As opposed to what? A main thoroughfare that leads to the altar?"

"Eventually, yes." She was within kissing range again, but he tamped down the urge to take advantage of that. They should get this issue resolved, and kissing wouldn't help.

"Where the hell did you get that ridiculous idea?"

"From Vince."

"Now I feel like strangling Vince. Did he say that in so many words?"

"Not exactly. But he said you believed in the fantasy, the knight on a white horse and all that. And from what I've seen, he's got it right. You're a dreamer, which is one of the things that makes you such a great artist."

"I'll admit I'm a dreamer, but my dreams are a lot more X-rated than my dear brother-in-law-to-be thinks.

Sure, I wouldn't mind ending up with a guy who loves me more than life itself. Who wouldn't want that? But—"

"See what I mean? You crave the happily-ever-after, just like he said."

"Yeah, *eventually*. But I don't plan to lock myself in an ivory tower until that prince rides up on a white horse to rescue me and pledge his undying love. I'm an artist. I need to sow some wild oats." She wiggled against him. "Want to help me?"

He groaned. She was making this far more difficult than he'd thought she would. "Vince knows my history. He's worried about a matchup between you and me."

"Vince needs to mind his own business. And for the record, Georgie thinks I can handle you just fine."

"I'm not sure Georgie knows all the details of my divorce. And maybe she's giving me the benefit of the doubt. But the fact is that I broke Sophie's heart, and I didn't even realize I was doing it."

"Because she has the communication skills of a fence post, that's why. Or maybe she thrives on drama. Who knows? But she sounds whacked."

"Well, you're not. You're incredible, and if I messed you up somehow I'd never forgive myself. That's the bottom line. So the best thing to do is call a halt before that happens."

Her eyes narrowed. "I think you actually believe that bullshit."

"Well *you* should believe it. For your own good."

"I see." Her jaw tightened and her voice had an edge to it that hadn't been there before. "So you think you know what's good for me?"

He could tell she was getting mad, but he couldn't back down now. "In this case, yes."

Angry spots of color bloomed on her cheeks. "And if I tell you that I'm plenty strong enough to have a hot, juicy affair with you and not end up an emotional wreck, you won't believe me?"

He sensed a trap. Whichever way he answered was liable to get him in even more trouble. Besides that, her description of a *hot, juicy affair* was interfering with his ability to think clearly. "I'm not sure."

She backed out of his arms. "Well, let me give you my bottom line, Mac Foster. I'm tougher than you think." She poked him in the chest with her finger. "Ironically, you're the one who helped me see that." She poked him again. "So if you choose to view me as some fragile flower that you could unknowingly crush under the heel of your boot, that's your loss, buster!"

With that she whirled away and stomped back around the building. He heard the swell of music as she opened the door, and then it was muted again when she closed it.

Somehow in the process of trying to do the right thing, he'd managed to insult her. She was upset with him, but not for the reasons he'd expected. His revelation was supposed to destroy her illusions about him. Instead she'd taken his comments all wrong, as if he'd implied that she was too weak to deal with the likes of him.

Well, hadn't he implied that? She'd been clear about her intentions. She wanted him. And how had he responded? He'd rejected her on the grounds that it was for her own good.

He massaged the back of his neck as he considered what to do. In essence, he'd achieved his goal. She wasn't likely to make advances to him now that she considered him a patronizing jerk who didn't respect her as an adult capable of making her own decisions.

So if he really believed he was bad for her, and deep down he still felt that way, then he should do nothing. He'd taken care of the problem. The riding lessons wouldn't be much fun anymore, but she'd show up because she needed his expertise.

Maybe being her instructor had made him think he had the right to make other decisions for her, too. If so, shame on him. He'd never appreciated people telling him what he should and shouldn't do. Anastasia was no different.

He considered going back in there so he could at least apologize, but that didn't seem like a good idea, either. Too crowded and too noisy to make a decent job of it. As he stood there debating, he heard the music swell up again as if somebody was coming out. Maybe it was her.

His heart pumping, he hurried around to the front of the building. He didn't know what he'd say, but somehow he'd make her understand that he was sorry.

Instead of Anastasia, Vince came out carrying Mac's hat. "I thought you might still be hanging around stewing in your juice."

"Did she send you out here with my hat so I wouldn't have a reason to come back in?"

"No, she did not. I brought it out here to eliminate the possibility she'd turn it into a chip-and-dip bowl." He handed over the hat.

"Thanks. It's my good hat."

"I know that. But more significantly, she knows that, which was why it was in jeopardy."

"What's she doing now? Besides threatening my hat, I mean."

"Dancing with whoever's available, mostly Travis."

Jealousy churned in his gut.

"I can also report that she's not happy with either of us."

"I screwed it up." He put on the hat and tugged the brim down. He didn't feel like making eye contact at the moment. "I made it sound like she doesn't know what's good for her."

"Oh, boy."

"Yeah, I know. Not smooth. But she was coming on strong and so I decided to tell her about the divorce and the reason for it. I thought that would scare her off."

"When she took me over in a corner for my private tongue-lashing, she mentioned that you thought the divorce was your fault when it clearly was not. For the record, I agree with her on that point."

"The fact remains that the marriage was a disaster. I didn't know what I was doing then, and I'm not convinced I have a clue now. She doesn't need to get mixed up with me. You told me she believes in the fantasy, but I don't anymore."

"Oh, yeah, she said you mentioned my comment on that subject. I was guilty of making some assumptions, but she's set me straight. I'm no longer allowed to say such things about her."

"Sorry. I didn't intend to get you in trouble, too."

"That's okay. No permanent damage done." Vince took a deep breath and let it out. "Look, are you positive that Anastasia is the person you're worried about?"

"Of course she is. Who else?"

"You."

"What?"

"I know you don't want to talk about Sophie, and I don't blame you. It's a depressing subject. And you probably don't want to admit this, either, but she hurt you when she walked out."

His chest tightened. "It wasn't pleasant, but like I told Anastasia, I never think about her. It's not as if I still love her or anything."

"I believe you. It's hard to keep loving somebody who

doesn't know how to love you back. She was damaged, Mac."

"Okay! So maybe that's true. But I was stupid enough not to see that. Or blinded by lust. When I'm attracted to somebody sexually, that sometimes takes over and I miss other parts of her personality. That's a failing."

"That's testosterone. We've all been there. You're not the first guy to convince himself that a hot time in the sack equals true love."

"I know, but I don't want to make that mistake with Anastasia and she really gets me—" He stopped abruptly. "I probably shouldn't talk like this. You're about to be related to her."

"Hey, I'm well aware of your obsession. We almost ended up getting soaked today because you were daydreaming about her. But you think having sex with her is going to mess her up emotionally, right?

"Right."

"But what if she's not worried? What if she isn't going to let you mess her up? Because that's what she told me."

"She'd be foolish to take a chance that it might happen. It's not worth the risk."

"How about you? Are you willing to take a risk?"

His chest tightened another notch. "I don't know what you're talking about."

"I think you do. She's getting to you."

He met Vince's gaze. "Not to the point where it's a problem."

"So says you. I'm highly qualified to recognize the signs because I just went through this. I watched you dancing with her. She's getting to you, and you're scared to death that she'll walk away."

"Of course she will! She's going places." He wished

breathing hadn't become so damn difficult. "She has a bright future. Someday we'll all be able to say we knew her when."

"That's not what I mean and you know it. But I won't belabor the point. Are you coming back inside?"

"I don't think it's a good idea."

"Probably not. Give her a chance to cool down before you start groveling."

"Groveling? I plan to apologize, but I don't think I need to—"

"If you'd seen the gleam in her eye when she picked up your hat and asked for a bowl of salsa, you might re-think your position on that."

"She's really mad at me, isn't she?"

"She is, but you could take that as a good sign. My guess is she's upset because she's still into you. Fortu-nately, she'll be at Ed's in the morning because she's mo-tivated to get good enough for the trail ride. You'll have the perfect opportunity to grovel."

"I'll have to think about that."

"I'm just saying that if you play your cards right, this could work out for you, after all."

"Are you telling me I should have an affair with your future sister-in-law? Is that what I'm hearing?"

"Absolutely not. I would never suggest such a thing. But I'll leave you with this question. Are you a man or a mouse?"

CHAPTER 16

Anastasia went to bed mad and woke up mad. At least she told herself that was the situation. Being mad allowed her to skip the cute mug and the extra coffee. She was through making gestures of friendship or any other type of gesture toward Macario Foster.

Anger accelerated her routine so much that she had time to eat her P B and J and drink her coffee before she walked over to the stable. She started to put her hair in a ponytail and then remembered she couldn't do that because she had a hat. Quickly braiding it the way she used to when she was nine, she crammed the borrowed hat on her head and left the house.

The pigtails appealed to her quirky sense of humor. He'd wanted to treat her like a child, so she'd play the part and look like one. No way was she going to wear her hair down the way he liked it. She brought her phone and earbuds, though, because although he was a jerk, he had good ideas.

He had some other good things about him, too. She grudgingly admitted that as she walked into the barn and watched him loading hay into the feeders. For some reason he was alone this morning. Maybe Ed had other stuff to do and so Mac was helping out. He was that sort of person.

Once again they were alone in the barn. She wasn't going to turn that into a romantic opportunity after last night's conversation. Even so, there was something about a man in a well-worn Stetson and a denim jacket earnestly doing his job.

Mac was one of the good guys, which made it hard to stay mad at him. He thought he was doing the right thing, even though he was taking blame where he shouldn't and treating her as if she didn't know her own mind. Also—this was superficial but she noticed—his jeans fit him like a glove, a fact she'd recorded in more than one sketch.

She'd been awake enough this morning to leave her messenger bag at home. Hauling it over here was a silly habit when she never took time to sketch anything. But if she had it now, she'd want to draw Mac the way he looked as he walked down the aisle toward her.

He moved with such grace. There were times she'd wished for a video camera to record that ease of movement, but she wasn't a videographer and never intended to be. Instead she'd freeze that loose stride in a sketch, suggesting it with the subtle tightening of the fabric encasing one thigh while the other remained loose. It would be tricky, but worth the effort.

Yesterday he'd smiled at her. Today he did not. He was probably remembering their last discussion. She'd expected to spend the night dreaming about their heated interchange, but after dancing until eleven, she'd conked out and couldn't remember a single dream.

"You're early."

"Am I?" She could be. Come to think of it, she hadn't paid much attention to the clock as she'd gathered up the phone and earbuds before leaving the house.

"Only by a few minutes. I'm glad you're here, though. I have something to say." His dark gaze was resolute.

"Did you practice it? You look as if you practiced it."

The corners of his mouth twitched as if he wanted to laugh but wouldn't let himself. "Yes, as a matter of fact, I did."

"Then by all means, let's hear it." She folded her arms and waited.

"Why the pigtails?"

"Is that part of your speech?"

"No, but I've never seen you in pigtails. I just wondered."

"They're practical and they make a statement. Double duty."

He sighed. "Yeah, I figured it was something like that. And I get it. I was treating you like a kid last night."

"Well, not *all* the time." Apparently she had a small urge to flirt, despite everything.

His determined expression changed subtly. His eyes became a shade darker as if he'd just recalled the adults-only part of their evening together. Glancing away, he cleared his throat. "In any case, my attitude left a lot to be desired."

"Boy, howdy, did it ever." She couldn't help grinning. "I can't speak for you, but I desired so much more on so many levels."

"I didn't mean it like that."

"Horizontal, vertical, perpendic—"

"I can see you're fully awake."

"I'm sorry. Am I ruining your speech?"

"Pretty much. Maybe I should just say I'm sorry I treated you like a child and leave it at that."

"No, no! I like the idea that you practiced a speech to give me when I showed up at this ungodly hour. Please go on."

"By the way, why are you early? And where's your thermos and Spider-Man lunchbox?"

"I ate before I came over here."

"I'll be damned. You're adjusting."

"I seem to be. Now please give me the speech you practiced. I really want to hear it."

He eyed her as if he'd prefer to forget the whole thing.

"Please."

"Okay." He took a deep breath. "My response to you last night implied that I don't think you're capable of making your own decisions, running your own life, and accepting the consequences of your actions."

"You did imply that."

"But it's actually the opposite of what I think about you."

"It is?" That startled her. She'd expected an excuse based on the same premise—something along the lines of how he was older, he'd been around more, and he knew better.

"I think you're extremely capable."

"Except on the back of a horse."

He waved that away. "You'll have that down in no time." He took a step closer. "Vince said a few things last night that got me to thinking. And I realized that you're not only capable, Anastasia. You're brave as a lion."

Her throat tightened. "Thank you."

"The coward is me."

Too stunned to speak, she just looked at him. She tried to remember if any man had ever admitted such a thing to her. Nope. That put Mac in a whole new category.

"You're beautiful and talented, and deep in my heart I have to ask why you'd be interested in an ordinary guy like me."

She had so many answers for that. "Because—"

"That's okay. I wasn't asking you to stroke my ego."

"But—"

"Seriously, I don't want you to answer the question. I'm just explaining why I've been such an asshole about everything. Sophie was . . . She had a great body and I was into great bodies at that stage in my life." He hesitated. "I guess I still am, come to think of it."

She held back a smile. He was being adorably serious and she didn't want him to think she found that amusing.

"Anyway, subconsciously I probably knew that Sophie and I had nothing in common besides sex, and the relationship was doomed from the get-go."

Her stomach suddenly felt hollow. "Do you think that's all we have in common?"

"No. At least I hope not. But . . . the chemistry's strong."

"Yes. I still think there's more than just sex there, though. We can talk, for one thing."

He looked into her eyes. "Or we used to. It's not as easy now. And more is at stake. I'm working for your sister. My best friend is about to become your brother-in-law. If we become lovers and it doesn't work out, then it'll be awkward for everybody."

She took a shaky breath. "I know all that. But it's not the main issue, is it?"

"No, not really. They'll do what they have to do. If I become a liability, they'll fire me. Vince won't want to, but his loyalty belongs to Georgie and Wild Horse Canyon Adventures, as it should. I'm expendable."

"I disagree. You've become a lynchpin of the operation. I'm just the little sister who draws things, and I could do that anywhere. If push comes to shove, you should stay and I should leave."

"No. You love it here."

"So do you. You have a house. I don't. In some ways, you're more rooted here than I am."

He smiled and shook his head. "Are you hearing this conversation? We haven't even decided whether to have an affair and we're already dividing up the assets. Doesn't that tell you that it's too risky?"

"It tells me that we're two responsible people who know that things don't happen in a vacuum." She searched his expression. "But we haven't reached the bottom of this barrel of issues. I think I know what's down there, though. Or rather, who."

"Yeah, so do I." He rubbed the back of his neck and glanced away.

She didn't blame him for wanting to abandon the subject. He'd put a lot of energy into convincing himself that he'd solved the problem created by Sophie. He'd sworn off marriage by declaring he wasn't good at it. That way he'd never again have to risk being emotionally vulnerable to a woman.

So he'd made do with shallow affairs that he probably ended rather than allowing another woman to dump him. But that wouldn't work with her. Their affair wouldn't be shallow, and if he ended it, he'd risk incurring the wrath of Georgie and Vince. Travis, too, come to think of it.

She presented a dilemma that he didn't know how to handle. Of the two of them, she was likely more resilient than he was. She couldn't imagine being the one to walk away if they became involved, but was she ready to promise she wouldn't? Not really. Not yet, anyway.

Maybe instead of him toying with her heart, she'd be toying with his. That put a new spin on things. What right did she have to insist he get involved with her, knowing what he was risking? No right at all.

He met her gaze and tension radiated from him. "Anastasia, I—"

"You know what? We should probably give the subject a rest."

Relief flooded his expression. "Thank you."

"I brought my phone and my earbuds. What do you say we test out your theory about music helping me ride a trot?"

"Good plan."

"I'll get the lead rope and bring ol' Jasper out to the hitching post."

"Are you okay with doing that by yourself? I need to check on Skeeter. The horses got new shoes yesterday and he seems to be favoring his right front hoof."

"I can do it." Her stomach did one little flip, but that was so much better than the day before, when it had been performing an entire gymnastics routine at the thought of taking Jasper out of his stall by herself.

When she approached his stall with the lead rope, he made a funny little neighing sound.

"I heard that!" Mac called out from the far end of the barn. "He's saying good morning to you."

She was charmed. "Good morning to you, too, Jasper. Did you have a good night's sleep?" She couldn't resist a question just to get him to nod. Unfastening the stall door, she lowered her voice. "Am I in over my head with Mac?"

Jasper nodded again.

"Thought so." She stepped into the stall and clipped the lead rope to the gelding's halter. "I'm going to concentrate on learning to ride you this morning and stop thinking about that gorgeous cowboy. If I'm not careful, I'm liable to create a real mess."

Jasper gazed at her with his large brown eyes.

"I'll bet you've seen your share of crazy humans doing dumb things." She walked him out of the stall. "I don't need to be adding to the confusion around here. We have a wedding coming up and a film crew will be here the weekend after that. I'm going to cool my jets."

Jasper walked quietly along. Once he blew air through his nose, but she was used to that now. "You're an excellent listener, Jasper. That's a good quality in a friend, and that's what I think we are now, friends."

She considered herself Mac's friend, too, and a friend wouldn't put an unnecessary burden on him or place him in a difficult position. He might be incredible to look at and even better to kiss, but if she caused him anxiety, that was bad.

With no clouds in the sky this morning, the sunrise was a different kind of beautiful, a deep glow of peach that gradually paled until it was the color of a strawberry shake. She and Jasper stood for a moment to admire it before she led him over to the hitching post and looped the lead rope around it. "I'll be right back." She left him there and went to get the plastic tote full of grooming supplies.

Mac was already in the tack room reaching for it. He glanced over his shoulder. "It wasn't the new shoes bothering Skeeter." Grabbing the tote from a shelf, he turned around. "He'd picked up a stone. I got it out and now he's . . ." He stood there looking at her as a smile tugged at his mouth.

"What?"

"Those pigtails. They make you look cuter than a border collie pup."

"I think you just called me a dog."

"No, I didn't. I compared you to a border collie pup, and if you'd ever seen one, you'd know it's a compliment."

"I'm going to Google it and find out." She pulled out

her phone and in a few seconds she'd found several pictures of black-and-white puppies with floppy ears. "Awww."

"Told you." He came around behind her and peered over her shoulder. "They're great dogs. Really smart and easily bored so you have to give them plenty to do, and . . . damn, you smell good."

She stood very still, her heart beating fast. His breath tickled the back of her neck. All she had to do was turn around and they'd be in each other's arms. "See, this is the problem."

"I know." He wasn't moving, either. "I thought I could just look at pictures on your phone, no big deal."

"Here's an idea. Carry the tote outside. I'll be along in a minute."

"All right." He left.

She closed her eyes and took a deep breath. Why did this have to be so complicated? She could partially solve the issue if she discontinued her riding lessons.

But thinking of that option filled her with sadness. She was making rapid progress and he was a great instructor who intuitively seemed to know how to work with her. In another few days she'd be ready to head out to see the Ghost. After all this, she wanted Mac to be with her when that happened.

He'd want to be there, too. He and Georgie might be the only two people who understood why seeing the Ghost was so important to her. Then she had another thought.

Walking back to the hitching post, she found Mac briskly rubbing Jasper with the grooming mitt. "I thought that was my job."

He didn't look at her. "You can take over whenever you're ready. I thought we should get this program started."

"We definitely should, but I have to ask this. When I first mentioned wanting you to give me riding lessons, did you have any idea what might happen between you and me as a result?"

"Sure I did." He kept working, his back muscles flexing rhythmically under his denim jacket. "Didn't you?"

"Not consciously. Then later, when I realized the attraction might cause a problem, I figured I'd be so scared all the time, not to mention sleepy, that it wouldn't matter."

"So you're saying you miscalculated." He rounded the back of the horse and started on the other side, neatly putting the horse between them.

"Apparently. But you anticipated this all along. Why didn't you just tell me no?"

"I couldn't do that." He didn't pause or look at her, even though now he was facing in her direction.

"Why not? Why put yourself through it?"

"Because I believe in your art, and if seeing the Ghost is important to your creativity, then I'll do my damnedest to make that happen."

So he'd sacrificed for her. Her heart ached. "Did you ever consider having someone else teach me?"

"No."

"Why not?"

Finally he stopped working, tilted back his hat and leaned his forearms on Jasper's back. His gaze was steady as it met hers. "You confided in me, Anastasia. You revealed a fear that nobody else knew about except Georgie, and you didn't want her to teach you. You chose me and that was an honor I didn't take lightly. I still don't. I told myself I could handle the situation. I'm not doing that very well, and I apologize."

She cleared the lump from her throat. "You're doing great. Fabulously. I feel like a selfish little bitch because

I've flirted with you and taunted you and made everything worse for you. I'm the one who should apologize. And I do. I'm sorry, Mac."

"Don't beat yourself up. You didn't know what was going on with me. You saw what everybody else sees, a happy-go-lucky guy."

"No, I saw a kind man with a lot more depth than people give him credit for. I saw a trustworthy man with the ability to put himself in someone else's shoes. My shoes."

"Yeah, until last night."

"You were scared. But when you had a chance to think about it, what did you do? You put yourself in my shoes and practiced a speech apologizing for your attitude. It was a good speech."

"I don't know about that."

"It was! And now I discover you took on these lessons knowing they could cause problems for you. But you did it because you believe in my art and you want to protect my secret. That's nobility of spirit. And you wonder what I see in you?"

He regarded her in silence for several long moments. When he finally spoke, his voice was husky. "Thank you."

"You're welcome. I mean every word."

"I know you do. I hope I can live up to your high opinion of me. And speaking of that, I'll turn the grooming over to you while I go fetch the tack." He rounded the back of the horse and tossed the grooming mitt in her direction. "Catch."

She missed and had to pick it up off the ground. "See? Klutz."

He smiled. "Good thing you brought your earbuds, Twinkle Toes." Then he turned and walked into the barn.

She was guilty of watching him leave instead of tend-

ing to her job of brushing Jasper. He'd called her Twinkle
Toes, just like he had after their two-step performance
last night. She wondered if they'd ever dance that way
again, if they'd even dare. Maybe not, and that made her
sad.

CHAPTER 17

Mac leaned against the rail as Anastasia walked Jasper around the perimeter. She looked pretty confident up there this morning, although the next few minutes would tell the tale. She had her earbuds in and they'd gone through her music selection until he'd found a rhythm that seemed to go with a trot.

Right now she was listening to the one before it, which happened to be a slower tune not unlike the one the band had played during their slow dance last night. He pushed that memory away. It would only distract him, and he needed to focus in case the music didn't work the way he hoped.

If it did, though, that could be the key to some really fast progress. And the quicker she progressed, the sooner she wouldn't need him anymore. Without the daily riding lessons, they wouldn't have to see that much of each other. When they did, like at Sadie's, they'd be in a crowd.

He'd pull back, and if he did, so would she. That would be for the best. Although the truth hurt like hell, he couldn't duck it any longer. He was afraid to be with her because there was an excellent chance she'd leave him.

She'd said it herself—he was more rooted here than

she was. With the talent she had, she could end up any-where in the world. Any day now, her career could ex-pand until it was too big to fit in this tiny town, and he'd never expect her to stay because of him.

He appreciated what she'd said about him a little while ago. He'd been blown away by it, actually. But no matter how much she admired him, and ironically she still did, she'd follow wherever her art led her. And she should do that. She had a gift and he wanted her to share it with as many people as possible.

So he'd cherish moments like this as he watched her ride around and around, listening to a waltz through her earbuds, her cute little pigtails bobbing with the motion of the horse. Aha. Her body language told him the waltz was coming to an end.

They'd agreed that when the faster music started, she'd nudge Jasper and attempt the trot. He held his breath and mentally crossed his fingers. She wanted suc-cess and he wanted it for her.

She took hold of the saddle horn and squeezed with her legs. Jasper changed his gait. She bounced a couple of times but then she seemed to look inward, as if con-centrating on the music. Gradually she began moving with the trot instead of against it.

It was working. Yesterday she'd flopped around like a ragdoll. Now she was tuned in, both to the music and Jasper. When she let go of the horn and rode holding only the reins, he felt like cheering, but he stayed com-pletely still. He didn't want anything he did to change the dynamic.

She wasn't perfect by a long shot. Her back could be straighter and her heels weren't down where they should be. She could afford to loosen up on the reins a little. But she was doing it and hardly bouncing at all. He grinned with pride. *Way to go, Twinkle Toes.*

The music was a crutch, but he could wean her off of it. Once she had muscle memory of how to ride a trot, she wouldn't need the music. Or if she did need it, she could play it in her head after she linked the tune to the gait.

The song must have ended, because she pulled back on the reins and brought Jasper to a halt. Then she took out the earbuds and rode toward him with a megawatt smile that made his chest hurt. God, she was beautiful.

"Congratulations." He couldn't stop smiling, either. He was so happy for her. "This is a huge breakthrough."

"I know." Her voice quavered with excitement. "I can't believe how the music changed everything. I imagined I was dancing with Jasper and he was leading, so all I had to do was follow his lead."

Her description of the process charmed him. "Is he a good dancer?"

"Not as good as you."

He had to treat her comment as a joke or things would get mushy. "I should hope not. After all, he has two left feet."

"True." She flashed him another brilliant smile. "Mac, thank you. If you hadn't come up with this after our dance last night, I can't imagine how long it would have taken me to learn to ride a trot."

"I'm glad it worked. And now that it has, here's my plan. You can practice some more in the corral today. When you get here tomorrow morning, I'll have both Cinder and Jasper saddled and ready to go so we can ride partway into the canyon." Today he'd go out with loppers and trim a few of those overhanging branches he'd noticed yesterday.

"Only partway?"

"I don't want to push you."

She hesitated. "Well, I was planning to tell you this

later, assuming everything went well with the lessons, but I should probably tell you now."

"Probably." He couldn't imagine what new thing she'd spring on him, but he shouldn't be surprised by anything when it came to Anastasia.

"Three weeks ago, as I was debating whether I'd ask you to give me lessons, I looked online for strengthening exercises for horseback riders. I thought it would help if I came into it with at least some physical preparation. I've been doing those exercises and I might be more prepared than you think."

"That's great. Terrific. Excellent foresight on your part." Her ability to ride a trot today made even more sense, now. Her thigh and calf muscles were somewhat conditioned.

"Does that mean we could ride all the way into the canyon tomorrow morning?"

"Let's see how it goes. I really don't want to push it."

"The next morning?"

"Georgie and Vince will be there with the trail riders."

"Oh, that's right. I don't know why I thought we had the weekend and the canyon to ourselves. Of course they'll be out there, and I don't want to show up in the middle of their deal."

"There are other trails. You won't get to see the Ghost, but you can test your skills."

"Monday morning, then?"

"Let me clear it with Georgie and make sure she doesn't need me for anything that morning. If she doesn't, and you're not stove-up from the next three days of trail riding, then, yes, we probably could make the full circuit on Monday."

"Georgie will be fine with it. She's the one with the wedding I need to be ready for."

"Good point. I'll check with Georgie to make sure,

but I guess you can plan on Monday for your first trip to look for the Ghost."

"I'm taking my sketchbook."

"I figured you would."

"I'm going to see him on Monday. I feel it in my bones."

With the kind of energy she projected, he didn't doubt it, but he wasn't going to make promises. "Let's hope you do. But before then we have more work to do. Are you ready to turn on your music and show me you can do that a second time?"

She laughed. "Yeah, baby."

How he longed to haul her down off that horse and kiss her. "A few things. Try to keep your back in line with your hips and watch your heels. They should be down."

Her expression turned serious as she nodded. "I'll remember that. I know I still have a lot to learn." And off she went.

He was impressed by how earnestly she attempted to follow his directions. She had a lot to think about at this stage, and he could see whenever she remembered his instructions. Her heels would suddenly go down and her back would straighten. Then she'd forget.

After she finished the song, he sent her out again. And again. Now that he knew she'd been doing exercises for three weeks he was more optimistic than ever about this project. Obviously her request last Sunday hadn't been a spur-of-the-moment thing if she'd started preliminary exercises long before asking him. He wondered what she would have done if he'd refused. As determined as she was, she would have found a way.

He had to assume her next candidate would have been Travis. The guy was one of his two best friends, and yet the idea of Travis teaching her to ride made him crazy. Travis might even do a halfway decent job, but

Mac shuddered at the thought of Travis standing here instead of him.

When she'd asked if he'd considered turning her over to another riding instructor, he'd made it all about the confidentiality aspect. That was important, but it wasn't the reason. He hadn't wanted to let anyone else, especially not any other guy, handle this. She'd come to him, and he would do it. End of story.

When he was thinking logically, he knew that was stupid. He'd already established that she belonged to the whole world and he had no claim whatsoever. But this riding thing was his area of expertise and he didn't trust anyone else to do it right.

Figuring out about the music had been a happy accident, but even without that, he would have taught her to ride a trot. It might have taken longer, like she said, but he'd have accomplished the task. Failure had not been an option.

After the third time around with the earbuds in, he asked if she'd like to try it without them and imagine the music playing instead.

"You want to take away my pacifier?"

"Or your training wheels, however you'd rather think of it. I doubt you want to be wearing earbuds when you're the maid of honor at Georgie and Vince's wedding."

"Guess not." But she was obviously reluctant to give up what had worked so well.

"Using them on a trail ride isn't a good idea, either. For one thing, you'll miss all the sounds of birds and other creatures. You'll miss the sound of the wind in the trees. For another thing, you might miss something critical that would be good to know when you're out there in what is essentially a wilderness."

She regarded him with an expression he couldn't interpret.

"Did that last part scare you?"

"No. You're making me realize how much my fear of horses has cost me and I'm stunned by what I've lost. In this country, riding is the way to experience wild things. I've essentially cut myself off from whatever's out there. The Ghost, yeah, but what about the rest? What about bobcats and coyotes and wild turkeys? And the scenery? Georgie says the waterfall in the box canyon is breathtaking."

"It is. I thought of you when I was there yesterday. You'll love it."

"I know I will." The light in her eyes said she'd love seeing it with him, too.

He realized that every time he'd imagined taking her to see that waterfall, they weren't riding toward it the way he and Vince had. They were walking toward it hand in hand, and when they felt the mist on their faces, he'd kiss her. But that was pure fantasy and he needed to get over it before they made the trip.

"Ready to give up the earbuds this time around? You can sing if you want."

"Maybe I'll hum. I sometimes do that when I draw, especially when I'm alone."

"You know, I thought I heard a little humming going on when you were doing Jasper's portrait, but it was soft."

"I probably was humming, but I don't do it while I'm sketching portraits anymore. It makes my subjects uncomfortable."

"I suppose it could for some people, although I wouldn't care. What do you hum?"

"My favorites are 'Amazing Grace,' 'Danny Boy,' and 'Streets of Laredo.'"

"Songs about death and dying?"

"It helps me remember there are worse things than drawing a lousy picture. But they seem to depress the hell out of most clients. Well, except for Ida. She plans to use one of my sketches for her obituary, so she says funeral songs are appropriate in her case."

"I don't have anything against sad songs now and then, but they're too slow for a trot. How about humming the song you have on your phone, the one you've been using? It's peppy. Cheerful."

"Sure, I can do that. Might as well leave my stuff with you." She unhooked her earbuds from around her neck and reached into the front pocket of her jeans for the phone.

He glanced down. She hadn't meant it as a provocative gesture, but that didn't keep him from remembering how she'd felt when he'd pulled her close last night.

He looked up in time to take the phone, its case warmed by the heat from her body. "Start off with a walk like before. Then, when you're ready, go into a trot."

"Okay." Clicking her tongue the way he'd taught her, she nudged Jasper's flanks and started around the corral humming "Amazing Grace."

If there was a funnier, sexier, or more endearing woman in the world than Anastasia Bickford, he'd never met her. Just when he'd convinced himself that he could get through these lessons and then back away, she revealed another part of her quirky personality and he was hooked again.

Her funeral dirges made perfect sense when she explained why she hummed them. With death looming as a possibility, who could get upset about an imperfect sketch? Brilliant.

By the time she was across the corral from him, he couldn't hear her humming anymore, but he knew when she switched over to pop music because Jasper broke into a trot. Anastasia stayed with him, following his lead as if they were dancing, just as she'd said.

He shouldn't be surprised that music inspired her. It was another art form, after all. The band from last night had appeared to be a hit, so chances were they'd play again tonight. He wondered if she'd be there. He'd be home working on his floors. Safer that way.

Looking extremely pleased with herself, she trotted Jasper around the corral several times. With each circuit she appeared more relaxed. She began to glance at her surroundings instead of staring straight ahead.

He leaned against the fence, arms folded, and enjoyed the view. As her instructor, he had an excuse to watch her, a special perk of the job. She'd come a long way in a short time, but as Vince had said, when she was motivated she was unstoppable. It was a trait that could take her far in her career as an artist.

He could stand there and watch her all morning, but he thought she should quit while she was feeling strong and successful. He waved her over. "That's enough for today."

"I could go a little longer."

"I know you could, but I want to make sure we end on a high note. Then you'll be eager to come back tomorrow and hang out some more with ol' Jasper."

"You don't have to worry about that anymore. Jasper and I are buddies." She reached down and patted his neck.

"I'm really glad to hear you say that." He opened the corral gate. "Riding skills are great, but if you don't feel bonded to the horse, then it becomes a technical exercise."

"That's true in art. If you aren't bonded with your subject, it shows in the work. You kept telling me to look at things from Jasper's point of view. When I do that, it changes everything."

"Yeah, it does." He gestured toward the open gate. "After you."

She walked Jasper out of the corral. The gelding would have kept on walking toward the hitching post because he knew the routine, but her soft *whoa* and a tug on the reins kept him there while Mac latched the gate. She was starting to act like a rider, not a scared woman clinging to the back of an animal she didn't trust.

"That was good what you did right there." Mac started over toward the hitching post and she clicked her tongue so Jasper would follow along. "You didn't let him go wherever he wanted. You made him wait for me."

She laughed. "I think what he wants is to get this saddle off. That cinch must feel like a corset."

"I wouldn't know. Never worn one."

"I have, and it's no fun. I've heard that men think it's sexy, especially the black lace ones, but I don't get it."

"What can I say? It's a guy thing." Of course now he was imagining her wearing nothing but a black lacy corset and a smile.

"They should try one sometime and see how they like it. What good is a tiny waist and amazing cleavage if you can't breathe?"

"I'd have to say breathing is more important than cleavage." He was fascinated by the ease between them considering the topic. This was how they used to talk to each other all the time. Maybe they hadn't lost that, after all.

"I know, right?" She reached the hitching post and dismounted with the cute little hop she'd perfected. "And it's fake cleavage, anyway. Once you take off the corset, everything goes back the way it was before."

Mac grinned. "Good point." That comment was so Anastasia. He briefly allowed himself to imagine a life in which they were together in every sense of the word. Fun conversation and fun sex. No doubts, no barriers. Friends and lovers. He didn't trust himself to pull it off.

"Okay, bridle off, halter on, then saddle and saddle blanket off. Do I have that right?"

"You do." Before they'd gone out to the corral, he'd had her practice unbridling and putting on the halter. She'd caught on fast. With her fear greatly reduced, she could concentrate more on his instructions.

"Don't tell me anything unless I start screwing up."

"I won't."

She started humming "Danny Boy" as she cautiously went through the steps he'd shown her. When she was finished, she stepped back, the bridle looped over her shoulder exactly as he'd suggested. "How's that?"

"Excellent. I'll take the bridle while you start unsaddling."

"I should probably go hang it up myself."

"Let's not carry this self-sufficiency business to extremes. I'm right here, so I can hang up the bridle."

"All right. Thank you. But I'm carrying the saddle into the barn. It's a point of honor not to expect some big strong man to do the heavy lifting."

He smiled. "Understood." When he came back out, she nearly had Jasper unsaddled.

She huffed and puffed a little getting it off such a tall horse but eventually she carried it proudly toward the barn door.

"Will you be offended if I take off the saddle blanket?"

"Go for it."

As he laid it over the hitching post to air out, he thought of calling out to remind her to bring the tote with the grooming supplies. Then he decided to wait and see if she remembered on her own.

Moments later she appeared, tote in hand. "I'm starting to get the hang of this."

"You definitely are."

"I just rub him down this time, right?"

"That should do it. We didn't work him very hard this morning. After a trail ride we might need to be more thorough."

"I've been thinking about that." She moved the cloth over Jasper's neck. "You said you'd have both horses ready to go, but I want to help tack them up."

"Listen to you using horse lingo."

"I know! Anyway, I'll be here early in the morning so I can saddle and bridle Jasper. Is five thirty good enough?"

"It is, but—"

"Then expect me at five thirty. Case closed."

"All right. But don't eat breakfast. I'm bringing it. We'll stop somewhere on the trail to eat."

"A breakfast ride." She rounded Jasper's hindquarters to finish the job. "That sounds perfect. Would you mind if I brought my sketch pad, just in case? I know we're not going all the way into the canyon, but I'd like to have it, anyway."

"By all means. We won't be in any hurry. I don't have anything else scheduled for tomorrow morning."

She paused and glanced at him across Jasper's back. "This is sounding like an event!"

"It's your first trail ride, so it's definitely an event."

She hesitated. "Just so you know, the band's playing again tonight, but I'm going to skip going down there. Not that it should matter to you whether I go or not, but—"

"Of course it matters to me. And for what it's worth, I'd decided to stay home tonight, too."

"I sort of figured you would. For one thing, Sadie's will be even more crowded tonight. Some of the trail riders will already be in town."

"Right." That wasn't his reason for not going, but it worked as an excuse. "I used to be all about hanging out in a noisy, crowded bar, but I realized last night it's not as much my thing anymore."

"I know what you mean. I'd dance the night away in college, but I'm over it."

And then he had the crazy idea that it would be fun to invite her to his place for dinner. He could show her what he was doing with the house and they could sit on his front porch, drink a beer, and watch the sunset. He'd cook something simple for dinner, and then . . . Well, he knew what he'd want to do after dinner.

"Mac? Are you okay?"

Startled out of his little daydream, he cleared his throat. "Yeah, sorry. Got distracted for a minute."

"No kidding. You were a million miles away."

He smiled. "Not quite that far." He wouldn't ask her to dinner, of course. That would take them down a road he wasn't prepared to travel. But it had been fun to think about.

CHAPTER 18

Anastasia was so excited she had the shivers. In order to make it over to the stable by five thirty, she'd had to get up at a time when she'd been known to go to bed. But the prospect of a trail ride into Wild Horse Canyon with Mac, even if they didn't go far enough to catch a glimpse of the Ghost, made climbing out of bed easy.

He'd told her not to eat breakfast, so she hadn't, but she'd made a cup of coffee that was pure sludge to tide her over. Getting up had been a breeze. Staying awake now that she was up would take some dedication and caffeine.

Once she'd arrived, she'd helped with the saddling and bridling rather than insisting on doing everything for Jasper herself. The job went faster that way and she didn't want to slow them down with her fumbling. And now, here they were, heading out the gate of the stable yard before sunup.

Mac led, but they'd barely cleared the gate before he turned in his saddle to check on her. "How're you doing back there?"

"I feel like a kid on Christmas morning."

He smiled. "I sort of do, too. Travis and I take greenhorns into the canyon every weekend, but this is the first time I've been able to show it off to someone I know, and an artist, at that."

"I'm glad you're excited, too, then." The pace was slow along the paved road and there was no traffic at this hour. The steady clop of their horses' hooves reassured her, but she took her greatest comfort from Mac. He rode with such confidence that he inspired it in her. "What's your favorite thing about the canyon?"

"I'd have to say the waterfall, but Sing-Song Creek is also pretty. I like watching the morning sunlight moving up the canyon walls. We won't see any wildflowers this late, but the cottonwoods are turning. You'll see those on Monday when we make the complete trip."

"Do I remember right that you don't have anything you need to do this morning?"

"Not really. I told Ed I'd help him get ready for this weekend's ride, but he doesn't need me until around two." He swiveled around toward her. "If you want to stop and sketch something, we have time."

"Good. I just might." Too bad she couldn't sketch and ride at the same time, or she'd do one of Mac leading her down the trail. Somehow he achieved a relaxed posture without slouching.

She used what art school had taught her about muscle structure to figure out that he kept his lower back flexible so he could move with the horse. Breaking it down that way helped her copy him, although it didn't feel natural yet. He looked as if he could maintain his position all day.

The trail wound through a grove of mesquite trees, and the sky was light enough now that she noticed spots where branches had recently been cut. As they continued on, she saw a few lying on the ground near the trail. "Has someone been out here trimming trees?"

"Yeah, me. I hauled some of the branches back to my house. If I have time today I'll get the rest so I can cut them up. By next winter they'll make great kindling."

"When were you out here?"

"Yesterday."

As she passed another tree with a branch that had been cut, she realized why. He'd spent part of yesterday removing anything that could pose a hazard for a passing rider. "Do you trim often?"

"When it needs doing."

"So you cleaned things up for the trail ride this weekend?"

"That, too."

"You did this mostly for me, though, didn't you?"

He chuckled. "Yeah, pretty much."

"Thank you. That was so considerate."

"Can't have you getting all scratched up on your first trail ride. I didn't go clear to the creek, though, because we won't be out that far today. This particular grove was the most overgrown, anyway."

"Well, I really appreciate it." The sweet gesture warmed her in places she hadn't known were cold. He obviously cared about her even if he didn't think they could make a go of it.

They continued to mosey along, the saddles creaking and the horses' hooves thudding softly in the dirt. But now she was watching for those cut branches, and every one they passed felt as special as if he'd given her a long-stemmed rose. They were only about twenty minutes into the ride and already it had been special.

"Hold up a minute." He brought his horse to a halt. "Come alongside me. There's room."

She nudged Jasper. He drew abreast of Cinder and stopped the second she pulled back gently on the reins.

Close quarters. Her right stirrup was only inches from Mac's left one.

"Turkeys," he murmured. "About fifteen yards ahead. Let's give them a chance to cross."

She peered into the shadows. She heard their soft gobbling first, and then she saw them meandering across the trail. As if showing off for her, one paused and spread his tail.

Mac's camera phone clicked. He'd promised to take pictures because she didn't feel confident enough yet to mess with her phone while riding a horse.

"Thanks for taking that. I've never drawn a wild turkey. Now I want to try."

"I don't know if the picture will be any good. The light's still pretty dim."

"But it could be fine for a reference photo, so send it to me, anyway. Poor turkeys. The canyon used to be named for them and now it's not. No respect."

"Face it, wild turkeys aren't sexy. Wild horses are."

And so was the cowboy sitting next to her astride the big black horse. Without these riding lessons, she'd never have shared this experience with him. He was in his element out here far more than he was on a barstool at Sadie's.

He tucked the phone away and glanced at her. "Everything okay? Any issues so far?"

"Nope. Doing fine." Except at this moment she had a fierce urge to lean over and kiss him. She wouldn't have to worry about falling because he'd hang on to her. But kissing wasn't part of the program.

"Then we'll keep going, but if you start getting tired, let me know right away."

"I will." But she'd have to be bordering on exhaustion before she'd say a word, because ultimately she wanted to get to the creek this morning. She didn't plan to tell him that. No doubt he'd put up an argument.

But she'd listened to Georgie describe the Ghost's habits, and if they made it to the creek within the next hour or so, the stallion might be there with his herd. Early morning and late afternoon were prime times for spotting the wild horses in that area. No reason to put off until Monday what could be accomplished now.

The walls of what was now called Wild Horse Canyon loomed ahead and her pulse rate picked up. Unless the Ghost had taken his band into another area, unlikely without some threat, they'd be at the creek right about now. The grass wasn't abundant in the meadow this time of year, according to Georgie, but enough still grew along the creek to keep them coming back.

Anastasia wanted to see the Ghost so much she could taste it. Now that Mac had taught her to look at things from the horse's point of view, she understood that the stallion would be more afraid of her than she could ever be of him. If he had a choice, he'd run away.

She wanted to get a really good look at him before he did that. Georgie had told her about quietly sitting on a rock near the stream when the Ghost just showed up. Georgie hadn't moved a muscle while the horse had taken a long drink. And then he was gone.

An encounter like that would thrill Anastasia's artistic soul, but she didn't want to be greedy. Even a brief glimpse of the stallion would be special. If that didn't happen, she had a backup plan.

She could ride now. Georgie had already mentioned loaning her Prince, her old nemesis, so they could ride together. She and Georgie could ride into the canyon together, and Georgie was a whiz at anticipating the stallion's habits. She had a connection with the Ghost.

Anastasia did, too, but it was through all the sketches

she'd done. Her connection was one step removed from reality. She was determined to change that this morning.

In the meantime, she didn't want to focus so intently on seeing the Ghost that she ignored the wonders of the canyon at sunrise. Besides her terror of horses, she'd also been imprisoned by her habit of staying up late and sleeping even later the next morning.

And oh, what she'd missed. The chatter and chirping of what sounded like a million birds echoed off the canyon walls. Sunlight gilded the rim of the canyon before sliding slowly down its sculptured cliffs. The shadowed patterns it created as it descended mesmerized her. When she could tear her gaze from that light show, she saw bunnies with flirty white tails and amazing ears charting a zigzag course as they bounded away through the tall grass.

"There's a grove of oak trees up ahead where we can stop for breakfast," Mac called over his shoulder. "Then we can head back."

"Breakfast sounds good." But she had no intention of heading back so soon. "How far into the canyon are we?"

"About halfway."

"Good to know." Her exercises were paying off. She might be a little sore if they made the full circuit, but that's what sports creams were for. She didn't have any, but Georgie did and would be happy to loan her a tube. She'd be ready to go again first thing in the morning.

The oak grove Mac had mentioned was a natural picnic spot, a clearing circled by trees sporting fall colors and several large rocks in the middle that provided makeshift seating. He guided Cinder off the path, quickly dismounted, and let the reins drop to the ground.

She watched that with interest. "Don't you have to tie him to something?'

"Not anymore. He used to be a flight risk, but now I can ground tie him."

"He'll just stay there even if he's not anchored to anything?"

"He will. You can do the same with Jasper. It's quick and easy when you're on a trail ride, so Travis, Vince, and I have trained all the horses to ground tie. It simplifies our life during the day. At night, though, we still tie them the old-fashioned way. We can't afford to let one of Wild Horse Canyon Adventures' horses wander off into the canyon."

"And become part of the Ghost's herd."

"Could happen." He walked toward her. "Ready to get down and have some breakfast catered by yours truly?"

"I am." She took her right foot out of the stirrup, swung her leg over, and dropped to the ground as she normally did. Except her right foot didn't support her as well as she'd expected and she stumbled.

He grabbed her arm to steady her, but once she had both feet planted, he let go and backed away. "All right, now?"

"Yeah, thanks. I don't know why that happened. My right ankle just sort of collapsed on me."

"You've been in an unfamiliar position for a while. It's common for first-time trail riders to be a little wobbly when they dismount."

She remembered how he'd casually walked in her direction and invited her to get down. "So that's why you came over, just in case?"

"Yep."

"Thank you. I probably would have landed on my butt if you hadn't been there." She was disappointed in herself, too. She was shaky from riding what couldn't have been much more than a half hour.

"Have a seat on a rock and I'll serve you breakfast."

She took his advice instead of trying to help organize the meal. Here she'd thought he'd grossly underestimated her tolerance for a long ride. Maybe not.

"Do you want me to bring your sketchbook over?"

"Not just yet, thanks." Sinking down onto the cool rock, she stretched her legs out in front of her. She was far from exhausted, but that stumble getting off had been sort of embarrassing.

What if she talked Mac into going all the way into the canyon and then was even shakier? She wouldn't have the option of resting overnight like the trail riders did. When Charmaine had made the trip, she'd had hours to recover before starting back.

Plus Charmaine worked out at a gym every day in order to maintain her size two figure. And her job as a personal shopper had her on the go constantly.

Anastasia, on the other hand, worked sitting down, except for those few times she stood when using an easel. Even then she sometimes sat. Dancing at Sadie's the other night had left her breathing hard.

All things considered, maybe she should follow Mac's plan instead of trying to expand on it. She'd tried to stay relaxed during the ride, but she grudgingly admitted to being a little tense. Maybe her body still held some residual fear, a problem Charmaine hadn't had to deal with.

"I thought you'd want this first." Mac walked over with a deep blue pottery mug and handed it to her.

She accepted the coffee gratefully. "Perfect." She also recognized the mug. Inez Abbott, the mayor's wife, was an excellent potter and this looked like her work. "I'll bet Inez made this."

"She did." He poured coffee from a thermos into a second mug that was similar, although Inez never made two exactly alike. "I bought six at the craft shop this summer."

The mug's rounded contours fit smoothly into her

cupped hands as she lifted it for her first sip. Closing her eyes, she sighed in appreciation. "You sure know how to take care of a girl, Mac."

"It's easy when the girl is you."

She looked up to find him watching her, his expression tender. Her heart beat faster. "The way I see it, I've been a royal pain in the ass."

"Sometimes." His smile was as warm as the light in his eyes. "But you make up for it in other ways."

"Good to know." She wasn't sure what to think about how he was looking at her. It wasn't the gaze of somebody who'd decided to keep her at arm's length. It was more along the lines of *I want to kiss you all over.*

She'd just about decided he was going to close the distance between them and start doing that when he glanced away and cleared his throat. "Let me get the food."

"Okay." She stared after him in confusion. *What the heck?*

"Sure you don't want your sketchbook?" he called over his shoulder.

"No, I'd rather sit here and relax."

He returned with two wrapped sandwiches and handed her one. "You got room on that rock?"

"Sure." She scooted over and he sat next to her with only a couple of inches between his hip and hers. There was another flat rock a few feet away and he could have taken that, but he hadn't. Instead he was right there, within kissing range.

"You've done great so far today." He unwrapped his sandwich. "And I figure you're hoping to talk me into taking you all the way to the creek, but that would be a mistake."

"Believe it or not, I agree with you." She took out half of her sandwich, which looked like a P B and J, but the bread smelled more heavenly than any she usually ate.

"You do? I thought for sure you'd want to go on."

"That was my plan, but I've reconsidered." She bit into the sandwich and the flavors were so wonderful she moaned.

He gave her a startled glance. "Something wrong?"

She shook her head as she chewed and swallowed. "What's in this sandwich? It's fabulous!"

"I went over to Sadie's to see Henry yesterday. He gave me the ingredients and I put the sandwiches together this morning. He's started baking his own bread, and he had some gourmet almond butter he picked up in Amarillo and a jar of homemade peach preserves from somewhere, maybe from one of the ladies in town."

"You got Henry's help on the sandwiches for this trail ride?"

He shrugged. "Henry's the foodie around here, so when I told him I wanted something special, he came up with this."

"And when did you talk to Henry? I was at Sadie's by about eleven thirty yesterday morning and I didn't see you all day."

"I went over earlier because I wanted to surprise you with something special. P B and J is still the best thing if you don't want to cook on the trail, so this is essentially a fancy P B and J."

"I love it. It's amazing." She took another generous bite and thought about the significance of the coffee in beautiful mugs and a sandwich that had required Henry's assistance.

The care Mac had taken with breakfast, combined with the way he'd looked at her a moment ago made her wonder if he'd reevaluated his position on certain things. And here he was sitting right next to her, as if he preferred to be close.

"How come you're giving up on riding out to the

creek today?" He picked up his mug from the spot on the ground where he'd left it. "I thought for sure you'd push for that."

"I might have except for that part where I almost fell getting off. I thought for sure I could ride out and back because Charmaine did it."

"Yeah, but she rode out one day and back the next. That's not the same as a round-trip in one morning."

"Exactly. Plus she's not afraid of horses. Mentally, I'm not anymore, but I'm not sure my muscles got the word and they're still kind of tight."

He nodded. "Not surprising. The more you ride, the looser you'll get, but it takes time to learn to relax, especially if you were afraid."

"I understand that better after this morning. Oh, and another thing that's different about Charmaine and me that I didn't take into account—she works out every day. Except for those exercises I've been doing, I'm basically a couch potato."

He glanced at her. "You don't look like one."

"Appearances are deceiving. Charmaine has a hard body. I don't."

"I know you don't." He sipped his coffee and stared straight ahead. Then abruptly he stood. "Take your time finishing your sandwich. I'll go check the horses."

"What do you need to check?"

"Their feet. They might have picked up a rock."

It could be true. On the other hand he could be making an excuse to move away from her before he grabbed her and started in on those kisses she was certain he'd been thinking about earlier.

One thing she knew for sure. He still wanted her. But he seemed to be having trouble deciding what to do about that. She had suggestions, but she'd keep them to herself. This time it was his call.

CHAPTER 19

Planning the special breakfast had been the beginning of Mac's mental shift. He'd had fun getting Henry to help him come up with something similar but different to what he might ordinarily have served. Then as he'd ridden the trail trimming stray tree branches, he'd thought about the invitation to dinner he'd never issued.

That night, sitting alone on his porch drinking a beer, he'd wondered why the hell he was rejecting the chance to spend quality time with Anastasia. He wasn't her knight in shining armor, and she wouldn't stick around and play house with him. So what? They could have fun together for as long as it lasted.

But he'd have to go into the situation knowing that he couldn't end it. Ever since Sophie, he'd made sure he was the first one out the door. He'd promised Vince he wouldn't break Anastasia's heart, though, so this time he had to let her walk away when it was over.

Last night as he'd polished off his second beer, he'd decided he was okay with that. Given the choice between never making love to her and being the one left holding the bag, he'd take Option B. No woman up to this point had inspired him to take that kind of hit, but she did.

Once he was clear on all of that, he'd thought about what should come next. He'd concluded that her first trail ride wasn't the time to say or do anything different. Yet she could tell his attitude had changed. He could see it in her eyes.

She was confused, as well she should be after the way he'd carried on about not trusting himself to get involved. He'd been hung up on not being good enough for her. Simple answer—he wasn't. Consequently he'd just be himself, knowing that eventually she'd move on.

In the meantime, though, he'd have the extreme privilege of making love to her. He didn't doubt for a minute that she'd let him. He'd been the one holding up the program. And yet . . . when should he broadcast his intentions?

He debated that as they headed back up the trail. He'd put her in front because she'd been over this part once and leading was a confidence builder. Besides that, he loved watching her ride Jasper. She might not be totally comfortable yet, but she'd get there.

Although he'd claim some credit for the transformation in her since Monday, so much of it was her doing. When she'd first asked for his help, she'd had no idea that he'd ask her to change her sleep patterns. She probably hadn't expected that he'd require all the grooming, saddling and bridling chores, either.

But she'd accepted the challenge and now she and Jasper were buddies. A different horse might make her nervous, but eventually she'd be fine with that, too. Tomorrow they'd take a slightly longer ride, and Sunday a longer one, yet. By Monday she'd be relaxed enough to manage the ride out and back.

Then he had another thought. If this weekend turned out the way he hoped, they could change Monday's plan. Instead of leaving first thing in the morning, they could ride out when she finished at Sadie's and spend the night in the box canyon.

Doing that would announce to several people that they were more than friends, but he didn't think it would come as a shock. Georgie and Vince were already somewhat prepared for it to happen.

When they were within ten minutes of the stable, she put up her hand like a scout in an old Western movie as she pulled Jasper to a halt. He allowed himself a smile because she couldn't see him. "What's up?"

"Coyotes," she murmured. "Jasper heard them. I was watching his ears."

"That's smart of you. He would hear them. They're predators." He saw one member of the pack dash across the trail. Movement in the bushes indicated the presence of more.

"Wow, that first one was beautiful. Is a pack any sort of threat to the horses?"

"Not to a couple of strong geldings like these, especially when we're riding them. An older horse or a foal might be at risk. But Jasper and Cinder can take care of themselves."

Jasper danced nervously as another coyote trotted across about ten yards in front of them. "I can tell my horse is not a fan."

"I wouldn't expect him to be." He loved that she'd referred to Jasper as *my horse*. Maybe someday he would be. "But he's trained not to react, so you don't have to worry."

"I was only worried for him. Coyotes don't scare me. This reminds me I want to sketch one."

"Oh, right." He pulled out his phone. "I forgot I'm the official photographer."

"Tomorrow I'll probably be confident enough to take

pictures. Plus I really like the view from up here. You can see so much more."

"Yeah, you can." All he cared to see was Anastasia perched in the saddle and looking quite pleased with herself. She was concentrating so intently on the trail and the bushes beside it that she might not be aware that she was smiling. But a little indentation in her smooth cheek and the tilt at the corner of her mouth told him she was.

She'd left her hair down today—no braids to make him think of Dorothy in *The Wizard of Oz*. And God, how he loved the hat she'd borrowed from Vivian. She'd been born to wear a hat like that.

Today she had on a dark green T-shirt that she'd tucked into the waistband of her jeans. She'd taken off her jacket back at the breakfast stop and tied it around her waist. No, she definitely didn't have a hard body. She was all soft, yielding curves.

"Oh! Coyote!"

He turned but missed the shot. "Sorry. Didn't get it. I think that was the last one in the pack, too."

"That's okay. We'll see more tomorrow or the next day. I'm going to sketch something tomorrow, too. It's good we have three days before we come back out here on Monday so I'll be used to everything." She turned toward him with a wide smile. "Ready?"

She had no idea how ready. He'd been an idiot to pass up the chance to be with her. If he only had a week—hell, if he only had a day, it would be worth the price of eventually saying good-bye. In that moment, he knew what he wanted to do. "Do you have anything else going on this morning?"

"Nope. Just need to be at Sadie's before noon. Why?"

He glanced at his phone. Plenty of time. "Then let's take a different route back. I'd like to show you my house."

Her eyes widened. "Now?"

"Yes." As he looked into her eyes, he gave up any attempt to play it cool. "I want you to come home with me, Anastasia."

Gradually the surprise in her expression was replaced by understanding.

He held his breath. Maybe he'd misjudged. Maybe after the way he'd behaved, she'd changed her mind about wanting him.

She held his gaze as a flicker of heat appeared in the depths of her amazing eyes. The flame grew stronger and a slow smile touched her full lips. "I should probably ask what changed your mind."

"Well, I—"

"But I really don't care. I would love to come home with you, Mac."

The breath whooshed out of his lungs. "Thank God. I'll lead." He unconsciously nudged Cinder into a trot but immediately reined him in. "Sorry." The way he was feeling, it was a miracle he hadn't taken off at a gallop. But leaving her in the dust wouldn't achieve the results he was hoping for.

"We can trot if you want."

He turned in the saddle to look back at her. "We don't have to. Walking is fine."

"How much time will we save by trotting?"

"We'd get there about twice as fast."

"Then what are you waiting for, cowboy?" She gave him a saucy grin. "I'm as eager to get there as you are."

Lust slammed into him so hard that if he'd been carrying a condom like Vince had told him to, they'd be off the horses and making love on a saddle blanket somewhere in the bushes in no time flat. Good thing he'd had sense enough to ignore Vince's rules.

"Okay." He urged Cinder into a trot but kept checking on Anastasia to make sure she was all right.

She was more than all right. She owned that gait now that she'd discovered the musical connection. He caught snatches of the pop tune she'd used yesterday as she hummed in time to Jasper's rhythmic hoofbeats.

Trotting cut down the time from ten minutes to five, but it was still the longest five minutes in the history of the world. He wouldn't chance a canter, though. She'd only ridden it once with him holding her in the saddle.

He left the main path for a lesser one he'd discovered earlier this summer. They were getting close. He slowed Cinder to a walk and swiveled in the saddle. "Almost there."

"You bought the Anderson place, didn't you?"

"I did."

"They were nice people."

"So I heard." He rounded a bend in the trail and there was his house shaded by two large mesquite trees that dropped bean pods on his roof and all over his front yard. He didn't care. The trees made the house look as if it belonged right there, tucked in under the branches.

"You're nice, too, though." There was a smile in her voice.

"Glad you think so. We'll just put the horses in that little corral out back."

"Okay."

He headed over to the corral and jumped down to open the gate. He'd never used the corral for anything, but today he was really glad it was there. If he bought a horse someday, then he'd build a small barn. The metal-roofed ramada shading a portion of the corral wasn't enough shelter from the elements, in his estimation.

As he quickly took off Cinder's bridle and hung it on the gate, Anastasia rode through on Jasper. Mac walked over to her. "Let me help you off. Just take your feet out of the stirrups and I'll do the rest."

She shook her head. "I'm okay. I know I almost fell last time, but I'll be ready for that. You don't have to baby me."

Tipping his hat back, he gazed up at her. "Believe me, I'm not babying you."

She looked into his eyes. "I see." With a knowing smile, she kicked her feet free and turned toward him. "You just can't wait to get your hands on me."

"You've got that right." Lifting her down this time was a breeze because she knew what to do. And so did he, once her feet touched the ground. He gathered her close, tilted her hat to give him access and claimed that smiling mouth.

She kissed him right back, wrapping her arms around his neck and rising up on her toes as if to get closer yet. With a groan he pulled her in tight. The feel of her warm, supple body drove him a little crazy.

Maybe he should have waited to kiss her until they'd made it into the house, but she tasted so good and he'd been thinking about this kiss for a long time. Before he knew it, his tongue was in her mouth and his hands were cupping her sweet little ass.

Flexing his fingers against the seat of her jeans, he wished them gone. He craved her silky smooth skin. He wanted to explore, to lick and nibble his way over every moist, delicious inch of her.

She moaned and he brought her hips in line with his, fitting them together as he thrust deep with his tongue. Dimly he realized that if he wanted more than this, he had to get them both out of the middle of the corral and into the house. And he wanted more than this, much more.

Focusing on the ultimate goal, he slowly released her and stepped back. Gasping for air, he realized he was shaking, too. He'd better get a grip or their first encounter would be over way too soon.

Her hat was in the dirt and she was breathing as hard as he was. "We . . . We should probably . . ."

"Yeah." The denim was severely strained over his crotch, but he managed to shove his hand into his pocket and come up with his house key. "Go on in. I'll take care of the horses."

"But I should help you."

"If you don't get out of this corral, I'm liable to grab you again." He scooped up her hat. "See you in a minute, Twinkle Toes."

She took the hat and left.

He resisted the urge to watch her go. That would waste time. Instead he turned to Jasper, who was eyeing him as if he'd lost his mind.

He sighed. "I have lost my mind, horse. That woman has fried every brain cell in my head." He fumbled with the throat latch as he unbuckled Jasper's bridle, but eventually he made himself focus on the task at hand instead of the reward waiting for him.

Yet that reward remained in the back of his mind as he quickly unsaddled both horses and propped the saddles on the top rail of the corral. He hung the bridles there, too and filled the water trough. He'd started out the gate when he realized how fast his heart was pumping. Pausing, he took a steadying breath. Better.

As he approached the house, he noticed Anastasia sitting on the front porch swing, her hat lying beside her. "You didn't go in?"

"I unlocked the door, but I waited for you. You said you wanted to show me the house, so it felt wrong to go in before you had a chance to do that."

His heart rate sped up again as he climbed the steps. "I don't think I have the patience to show you the whole house right now."

"No?" She stood and the swing rocked gently.

"No." He took off his hat and tossed it on the swing. "But I'd be glad to show you the bedroom."

Her eyes darkened. "That's fine with me. Some people think the bedroom is the most important room in the house."

"It is now." He held out his hand and she laced her fingers through his. He was more in control than he'd been in the corral, but his heart still pounded as he led her through the front door. He nudged it closed with his foot before continuing on through the living room.

"Nice sofa. And that lamp is pretty. I see you have most of the carpet ripped up in here."

"Later." He pulled her down the short hallway so fast that she started laughing, and that was perfect. Whatever this was between them—an affair, a fling, an adventure—it should be filled with laughter and joy.

Making love to her for the first time in daylight was perfect, too. Secret trysts in the dark weren't their style. His east-facing bedroom windows weren't shaded by the mesquite trees, so his king-sized bed was flooded with sunshine.

He'd splurged on a massive four-poster and it dominated the small room. At times he'd wondered why he'd felt the need to buy it. The reason had just walked in.

She surveyed the room. "Looks like you refinished the bedroom floor, first."

"Had to before I could bring in the bed."

"And my, what a big bed you have." Her voice sounded husky.

"The better to make love to you." Taking her other hand, he turned her to face him. He still couldn't believe she was here. Her back was to the window, so the golden light surrounding her made her seem not quite of this earth. "You're beautiful."

"I could say the same about you."

"Men aren't beautiful."

"That's where you're wrong." Her gaze traveled over him as if cataloging every detail.

Knowing her, she probably was. He'd finally figured out that she had a photographic memory. The pictures on her phone were just for backup, but she could study something and sketch it exactly later on.

Slipping her hands free, she stepped closer and traced the line of snaps down the front of his shirt. "Mac, I want . . . Will you let me undress you?"

"You bet." He slid both hands under the hem of her T-shirt and caressed the warm, silky skin at the small of her back. "I fully intend to return the favor."

"And you can do that when I'm finished. But I've sketched you so many times and I always wanted . . . I want to see you, really *see* you."

He considered the implications of what she'd just said. "Are you thinking you'll do a sketch of me later?"

"I might. Would you mind?"

He tried to sort through his feelings. "I'm flattered and everything, but . . . what would you do with it?"

"It would be just for me. Except if you want to take a look at it, of course."

"I'm not sure if I'd want to or not." He hadn't thought about this aspect. Of course she'd want to draw him naked. Not right this minute, but eventually. She'd probably taken a class in that kind of art.

All right, then. He was already making himself vulnerable in so many ways just by bringing her into his house and his bedroom. If she wanted to memorize his naked body and draw a picture of it, so what? Letting go of her, he sat on the edge of the bed. "I can at least take off my boots."

"No, I want to do that, too. I want to do all of it." She dropped to her knees in front of him. "This is part of my fantasy, revealing you a little at a time so I can concentrate on the details instead of suddenly being confronted with you in all your glory."

He laughed. "Anastasia, I'm an ordinary guy. I guarantee there's not a lot of glory going on under my clothes."

"That's what you think." She grabbed the heel of his boot and tugged it off. Then she pulled off his sock. "See there? Glorious toes."

"Good Lord. If you're impressed with my toes, then I can't wait to find out what you think of my—"

"Exactly." She smiled up at him. "I'm saving that for last."

CHAPTER 20

Anastasia felt like a kid unwrapping a birthday present. She pulled off his other boot and sock. "I've never seen your bare feet before. They're quite elegant."

Mac braced his hands on his knees and studied her, his expression bewildered. "I'm glad to hear you like my feet, but couldn't you admire them later?"

"I could. That's how it's gone in the past." She cupped his heel and began a slow massage of his foot. "But I'm hoping this time with you will be different. Better. I want to learn about your body *before* we make love."

"You'll learn quite a lot about it during. Just sayin'."

"Not your feet."

"Well, no. But there they are." He gestured toward his feet. "You've investigated them. I promise the rest of me will be fully involved. Certain parts more than others, but pretty much all of me will make contact."

She switched to his other foot. "And that's when you'll be trying to give me an orgasm, right?"

He swallowed. "That's the general idea."

"See, at that point, I'll be too distracted to take proper visual notice of your body. I'll be too involved with the tactile experience we're having touching and stroking each other. I'll be busy responding to whatever you're doing, especially when you start thrusting."

"Uh . . ." He seemed a little shell-shocked by her statement.

"But we can forget my plan if you're desperate."

He cleared his throat. "I'm trying not to be."

"You look desperate, though."

"The thing is, nobody's ever massaged my feet and now we're discussing orgasms and stroking and thrusting, and . . . Yeah, I'm getting a little desperate."

She was at a good angle to see what he was talking about. "Then why don't I unfasten your jeans?"

"Good idea. While you're doing that I'll unsnap my shirt. Speed things up a little."

"I guess you can." She unbuckled his belt. "But I'll bet the end result won't be as good if you take your clothes off too fast."

"How do you know?" His voice sounded as tight as the denim stretched across his crotch.

"I don't." Unfastening the metal button at his waist, she pulled down the zipper. Oh, my. Now she wondered if *she'd* be able to follow the plan. Underneath his cotton briefs it was obvious that he was richly endowed. "All I've experienced is tearing off each other's clothes and then going at it."

He sucked in a breath. "Uh-huh." He looked quite ready for that program.

"I'm a very visual person."

"I'm aware of that."

"If I take time to look at you first, then the visual of your naked body will add to the pleasure of having sex with you. I won't be going into it blind, so to speak. At least that's my theory."

He scrubbed a hand over his face. "Wow."

"I've never had the nerve to explain my theory to a

man I was about to have sex with. I think that's why the first time has always been a dud."

"Oh?" He perked up at that. "A dud, huh?"

"For me, at least. No climax. But later, after I had a mental picture, then I could. Well, mostly."

"You just sold me on the concept."

"Yeah?"

"Yeah. I'm declaring this a no-dud zone. Just tell me what to do."

"Nothing." His willingness to make love her way was so arousing that she couldn't imagine having dud-level sex with him even if she couldn't visualize every inch of his body. But now that she had his full cooperation, she was determined to test her theory.

From where she knelt in front of him, she could reach the snaps on the cuffs of his shirt. She undid one and rolled back the sleeve to his elbow. Although she'd watched him do the same thing, being the person doing the uncovering of that muscled forearm was completely different. Because he'd turned his sleeves back often this past summer, he was tanned there and the soft hair was lightened by the sun.

She examined his large hand with its blunt-tipped fingers, fingers that would soon be exploring her the way she was exploring him. Her body hummed at the thought of where he would touch her. He had a scar on the back of his hand she'd never noticed before and she ran her finger over it.

"Barbed wire." His voice was low and thick, as if his imagination was working overtime, too.

She glanced up at him. "Battle scar."

"I guess." His dark eyes were intently focused on her. "I have a few of those."

Inside and out. But she wouldn't say that aloud and remind him of things best forgotten right now. Moving to his other arm, she rolled back that sleeve. And he didn't think he was beautiful. She had the urge to lean down and kiss the sculpted contours, but that wouldn't be fair.

Uncovering was one thing. Kissing and licking was a whole other method of exploration. She anticipated the pleasure of that eventually, but she'd wait until later, after they'd worn each other out a little.

Reaching up, she unsnapped the front of his shirt and gradually unveiled his lightly furred chest. It heaved as she made her way to the last snap. "Are you okay?"

"I'm on fire and my balls ache. Other than that . . . yeah."

His comment made her aware of a similar insistent throbbing. As she stood so she could take off his shirt, she realized her panties were damp. Apparently this was her kind of foreplay, because she was also trembling enough that she wasn't doing a good job of getting his shirt off.

"Want some help?"

"No, and I love that you asked instead of just doing it. There. Got it." She stepped back to get a better view of Mac, shirtless, and let out a long sigh. Perfect shoulders, perfect pecs, perfect abs.

If she had her way, he'd never wear a shirt again. She'd seen classic marble statues that didn't look this good. Plus she loved a man with some chest hair, and statues didn't have any.

His voice broke her concentration. "I have an idea."

"What?"

"If you took off a few things, too, then after your visual tour, we could . . . proceed."

The plan had merit. The more she revealed of his gorgeous body, the more she wanted to experience that restrained power. "Okay."

"There's a chair right behind you if you want to sit down and pull off your boots."

She had to drag her attention from his magnificent chest, but she managed to accomplish that long enough to locate the wooden chair. After she'd removed her boots and socks, she stood.

"How about your shirt?"

She saw no reason not to. She stripped it off and tossed it on the chair behind her. Then she figured the bra could go, as well.

"Might as well ditch the jeans, too." He made it sound like a casual suggestion, but there was nothing casual about the way he was looking at her.

"You're not going to grab me when I come back over there, are you?"

"Nope. I'm following your plan to the letter."

She unbuttoned her jeans and slid them down her thighs, which were a hundred times more sensitive than they had been a few minutes ago.

His breathing changed as he followed her movements, and his eyes grew so dark they were almost black. Then his gaze traveled slowly back up. It lingered on her white lace panties, caressed her midriff, and settled on her breasts.

She could almost feel the brush of his fingers along her inner thighs and the teasing pressure of his hand against the damp crotch of her panties. Under his intense stare, her breasts tingled and her nipples grew taut.

He took a shaky breath. "How about—"

"No. Not yet."

He groaned softly. "Have mercy, Anastasia."

"I'm almost done." She quivered as she walked back to the bed. "You've been a good sport."

"This could backfire, you know."

"How?"

"All this waiting. One thrust and game over."

She hadn't figured on that possibility. "That would be unfortunate."

"You're telling me. I'm the one who promised this was a dud-free zone."

"Are you beyond hope?"

"Not yet." His jaw clenched. "Getting there."

"Where do you keep your condoms?"

"Here." He leaned over, yanked on the bedside table drawer, and pulled it right off its moorings. It clattered to the floor, along with a box of condoms.

She snatched up the box. "Take off the rest. I'll get one of these."

"Have you visualized enough?" He stood and shucked his jeans and briefs.

"I think so." She was in the process of digging a foil packet out of the box when she came to a full stop. From the corner of her eye she glimpsed the most impressive package she'd ever seen in her life. She turned to stare. "Oh, Mac."

"Give me that. You can memorize me later." He took the packet and ripped it open. "Better get rid of your panties because I would hate to tear them to shreds."

His urgent tone galvanized her into action. By the time he'd rolled the condom on that amazing penis, she'd taken off her panties. He caught her hand and they tumbled onto the bed, laughing like crazy people.

But he quickly pinned her to the mattress and moved between her thighs. Then he paused and leaned down to drop a gentle kiss on her mouth. "Got your slide show ready?"

She ran her hands up and down his sturdy back. "I didn't get this part."

"Take my word for it." He nibbled on her lower lip. "It's decent."

"I'm sure."

"Then we're good to go."

Her heart raced as he sought her entrance and slid partway in.

He put his lips next to her ear. "No duds, Twinkle Toes." He eased in a little more. "I'll wait for you. Take all the time you want."

Breathing fast, she clutched his hips. Her theory was right! She knew this man from his head to his elegant toes and her body rejoiced at making the ultimate connection. "More," she whispered.

"Gladly." He pushed deep.

And she came, much to her surprise and even more to his. Gasping and crying out with wonder, she reveled in the sensuality of an orgasm that had required no thought and no effort.

His hot breath touched her ear. "That was too easy. We're going for two." And he began to pump, slowly at first, and then more vigorously.

"Oh, Mac!" She rose to meet him as the pressure of a second climax bore down on her.

His low chuckle was sex personified. "I knew it. I knew it would be like this. Come for me, Anastasia."

And she did, her body spiraling out of control a second time.

"My turn." Lifting his head, he gazed into her eyes as he pounded into her. "Can you come again?"

"I don't know."

"I think you can." He shifted his angle. "How's that?"

"Good. So good. So . . ." And she surrendered to a third climax at the same moment he drove home one last time and shuddered in her arms, the pulsing of his orgasm keeping time with hers.

For several long minutes they lay there, panting and plastered together in the kind of sensual bliss created by a mutual climax, or in her case, three. *Three*. First-time sex with a man had never been even remotely like this.

He was the first to stir. "Don't go away." He aimed for her mouth and kissed her nose, instead.

"I just had a record three orgasms in a row. I can't move from this spot, let alone leave the room."

"Good. That was part of my evil plan." He eased away from her and climbed out of the bed.

When he was gone she opened her eyes and stared up at the ceiling. It had beams up there. Who knew? She'd been concentrating on the most incredible sexual experience of her life.

Maybe her theory had something to do with her response, but she thought maybe some of the credit belonged to Mac. Mac and his awesome equipment. His lovemaking hadn't been fancy but it had been assured. He'd learned how to use what he'd been given to the best advantage.

He walked back into the bedroom and instantly she imagined a pencil drawing of his sketch-worthy body. But he'd been hesitant about letting her create that. He'd wanted to be okay with it, but she'd heard the reservations he hadn't voiced. Paid models were one thing, but Mac was her friend and now her lover. She didn't want to invade his privacy.

She propped her head on her hand and watched as he came over to the side of the bed and picked up the drawer he'd yanked out in his eagerness to find a condom. "Just to put your mind at ease, I won't draw you if you'd rather I didn't."

He slid the drawer into place and glanced at her. "But you want to, right?"

"More than you can even guess. I've sketched male models before, but they were . . . I don't know . . . anemic compared to you. You're so vibrant." *And well endowed.* "My fingers itch for a pencil."

Smiling, he picked up his briefs and his jeans and started putting them on.

"Yikes, did I scare you with that comment? I promise I won't draw a single line if you don't want me to. Please don't cover up. I know you're a private guy, and I—"

"You didn't scare me. I'm going out to get your sketch pad and pencils from your saddlebag." He walked over to his closet and pulled out some flip-flips.

"Flip-flops? What kind of cowboy wears flip-flops?"

"I do." He shoved his feet into them. "Shows off my elegant toes." Laughing, he left the room.

She flopped back on the bed. The guy was blowing her away. First he'd helped her get over her fear of horses. Then he'd given her the most satisfying sex ever. Now, even though he'd been clearly hesitant about having her create nude sketches, he was fetching her paper and pencils so she could begin.

When she'd asked him to teach her to ride, she'd had no clue the issues that she would be stirring up for him. She'd thought it was all about her fears, but he'd had a few of his own to conquer. Judging from the evidence—her presence in his bed and his willingness to pose nude for her—he seemed to have done a fair job of that. And she admired the hell out of him for it.

She sat up when the front door opened and his flip-flops slapped along the wood floor. Mac Foster in flip-flops. It made her laugh. She wondered if anybody knew about them besides her.

Sketchbook and pencils in hand, he walked in. "What's so funny?"

"Your footwear. It cracks me up. Have you always worn them or is this something new?"

"Sort of old and new, I guess." He handed over her drawing supplies and slid his feet out of the flip-flops. "I used to have some when I was a kid. Then I grew up to be a big, bad cowboy and wouldn't be caught dead in anything but boots. But I have my own house, now, and so I got some to wear around here."

"Do Vince and Travis know about this?"

"I don't think so, but I don't care if they do." He unfastened his jeans. "I have some shorts and sweatpants, too. And gym shoes. I don't feel the need to put on cowboy clothes all the time."

"I'll bet you've never worn shorts and flip-flops into town, though."

"No. Whenever I'm in town I need to project an image that fits with Wild Horse Canyon Adventures. We're selling a type of fantasy, and I get that." He shoved his jeans down and stepped out of them.

And speaking of fantasies . . . the flexing muscles of his powerful thighs and calves made her catch her breath.

"Something wrong?"

"Not at all." She shouldn't be ogling him now. She'd have plenty of time to do that while he posed for her. When he stuck his thumbs in the waistband of his briefs in preparation for stripping those off, she forced herself to look up.

He was looking right back at her, a knowing smile on his face. "I've been watching you, too, you know."

"You have?" She'd been too busy studying him to notice.

"I think you're onto something with this visual appreciation business. I hope you're planning to stay naked while you sketch."

"Well, sure. There's no reason to put on my clothes."

"You're not painting naked, but you'll be drawing naked. Maybe now you'll tell me what the difference is when you do that."

She thought about the mug she'd brought to the stable. Maybe she'd subconsciously chosen it, after all. "My work's more elemental, more passionate."

"I figured." He took off his briefs and he was already semi-aroused. "How do you want me?"

She laid her sketch pad aside. Some things were more important than drawing a picture. "Anyway I can get you."

CHAPTER 21

Mac wasn't about to argue. If Anastasia would rather make love than draw, he'd take it as a huge compliment, considering how much she enjoyed drawing. He was in no condition to be immortalized, anyway. The gleam in those hazel eyes had brought an instant reaction from his cock.

When she did finally record his naked self in her sketch pad, and he knew she would sooner or later, he certainly didn't want it to be when he was stiff as a broom handle. On the other hand, if she was naked while she sketched, would he be able to control himself? Maybe if they'd had sex three or four times in a row prior to the modeling gig he'd be able to manage it.

At the moment, the prospect of crawling back into bed with her was the single most exciting thing he could imagine doing and his cock was well aware of that. The first round had taken the edge off, so now he could linger over the gift that was Anastasia. She scooted over and he climbed in next to her.

When she stretched out on her side facing him, he mirrored her position and lay there for a moment gazing into her eyes. Reaching over, he cupped her soft cheek. "I want to take it slower this time."

Her lazy smile and her smoldering glance taunted him. "Good luck with that." She trailed her fingertips across his chest and began a leisurely journey south.

He caught her wrist. "Uh-uh."

"But I want—"

"Next time." Still holding her wrist, he guided her to her back and moved over her.

Her eyebrows arched. "Next time?" Her other hand began exploring.

He'd love to have her touch him there, but not right now. He had plans. He caught her other wrist and drew her hands over her head. "After I fix you dinner tonight."

"I'm coming to dinner?"

He chuckled. "You're coming to dinner and you're coming after dinner. At least you are if I have anything to say about it."

"Oh, you have a great deal to say about it, Macario."

"I like when you call me that." He imprisoned both wrists with one hand and cradled her breast with the other.

"I like when you touch me like that." She arched into his caress. "And when you get all macho and assertive."

"You called the shots the first time." He gently squeezed her plump breast as he leaned down and brushed his mouth over hers. "Now I get to be in charge."

"I feel as if I could come right this minute."

"Good to know." Levering himself up so that he had room to maneuver, he slipped his free hand between her thighs and discovered that she was very hot and very wet. "I think we should do something about that, don't you?"

She gasped as he thrust his fingers deep. "Maybe . . . maybe so."

His mouth hovered over hers as he found her G-spot and began to stroke her there. "Does that work?"

Her soft moan told him all he needed to know.

"I'm going to find all the ways I can make you come," he murmured as he increased the pace.

"This is ... definitely ... one." Her breathing grew rough.

"Tonight I'll see how you like the feel of my mouth."

She whimpered. "Oh, Mac ..."

"I want you to think about that while you're sitting in your corner at Sadie's." When he felt her contract around his fingers, he bore down. "Think about my head between your thighs and my tongue driving you crazy."

"You're a devil, Mac Foster!" She lifted her hips and cried out as her climax rolled over his pumping fingers.

When she finally relaxed against the mattress, still shuddering from the aftershocks, he gave her a long, slow kiss with lots of tongue to remind her of what he'd said. Then he moved away long enough to grab a condom and roll it on.

Sliding into her was pure luxury. She was slick, hot, and totally open. A few orgasmic tremors remained, and that gentle squeezing motion was almost enough to make him explode. But he held back.

The first time he'd been here lust had set the pace, and it had been hard and fast. But this—gliding in and out in an easy rhythm that he imagined he could keep up forever—this was heaven. He gazed down at her and discovered she was looking up at him.

She seemed ... dazzled. Maybe it was egotistical of him to think that, but it was the only way he could describe the light in her eyes. She looked happy, too. Making her happy had turned into one of his goals, and if having sex with him did that, he was one lucky son of a gun.

Her voice was breathless. "It's never been like this."

"For me, either."

"Really?"

"No one's like you." He thrust slowly, not wanting the moment to end. But the pressure was building.

She clutched his hips and began rising to meet him. "I've . . . always been different." Her eyes darkened.

"That's good." He sucked in a breath and shoved deep, locking them together.

"This?" Her body quivered. "Or being different?"

"Both." Looking into her eyes, he held very still. "Don't move."

But she did. Her first contraction became his tipping point, and gasping her name, he let go. Then he shuddered in reaction as her climax bathed him in such pleasure that he closed his eyes to savor it.

When he opened them again, he was greeted by the most beautiful smile. His world shifted. He'd never felt this close to a woman after making love to her. Gazing into eyes that sparkled in emerald and gold, he knew that something wonderful and dangerous had happened.

It had probably started months ago when she'd drawn his portrait for the first time. Ever since then he'd refused to believe he was falling in love because that was such a bad idea. It still wasn't a particularly good idea, but that was irrelevant. The process was complete. He was in love with Anastasia Bickford.

She wound her arms around his neck. "That was spectacular."

"Sure was from my vantage point. But you didn't get your sketching done and now we both have places to go and things to do."

"I seem to remember a dinner invitation." She combed her fingers through his hair.

He thought of all the art those fingers had created and

how lucky he was to have such a talented woman lying here looking up at him as if he'd hung the moon. "It still stands. I'm not as good a cook as Henry, so if I really wanted to treat you right, I'd take you to Sadie's."

"Except then we'd have all those other people around and I wouldn't be able to give you sultry glances across the table."

He laughed. "Is that what you're planning to do?"

"I'm going to try. I can't guarantee whether I'm any good at it."

"You wouldn't have to be. Just having you sitting at my kitchen table will be enough to do the trick." Reluctantly he eased away from her, climbed out of bed and headed for the bathroom. "Be right back."

"I'll get dressed," she called out to him. "I just looked at your bedside table clock and we really do have to get going. I'm surprised nobody's tried to call either one of us."

"I turned off my cell." When he walked back in she had her panties on and was reaching behind her back to fasten her bra. Funny how this didn't feel like an affair. Her being here was so natural, as if this was where she was supposed to be.

"And mine is . . ." She paused to glance around. "You know what? It's still in my saddlebag." She grinned at him. "No wonder I didn't hear it."

"Is that a problem?" He began putting on his clothes, too.

"Nah. I have a reputation for turning off my cell when I'm sketching. But I don't know what excuse you're planning to give for not answering."

He shrugged. "I turned it off when we were out riding and forgot to turn it back on." He fastened his jeans and located his shirt. "But that brings up another subject. Are we keeping this whole deal a secret?"

"Are you kidding?" She tugged her shirt over her head. "There are no secrets in Bickford, at least not for long." Popping her head through the opening, she glanced at him. "But if you're worried about fallout, we can try."

"That only makes it seem as if we're ashamed of what we're doing. I'd like to be up-front about our relationship. That doesn't mean I'm not worried about fallout. If you and I get crossways . . ." Because she was using the chair to put on her boots, he perched on the edge of the bed to put on his.

"We won't get crossways." She put on her second boot and stood. "I know what's at stake for you. You love it here and hope to stay. I'm not going to let our situation mess with that."

He was touched by her determination. "Relationships can get complicated. Differences can crop up that neither one anticipated. Then, before they know what happened, the two people involved have issues."

"I'm not saying that's impossible. But I am promising you that I won't let whatever goes on between us jeopardize your job or your place in this community." She turned around to straighten the sheets and comforter.

If he hadn't already fallen, he would have dived headlong into love after hearing that little speech. She was one of the least selfish people he'd ever met. On top of that, she instinctively wanted to tidy up after herself instead of leaving chaos in her wake.

He'd married someone who had constantly created a disaster zone and then had sailed out the door. Blinded by lust, he hadn't paid attention, but he did now. He lusted after Anastasia, but that didn't mean he was blind, deaf, and dumb. Sometimes it was the little things that gave clues about who a person was.

He walked to the other side of the bed and helped her

make it up. "How soon can you get away from Sadie's tonight?"

"I promised to stay through happy hour, so is seven too late?"

"Nope. I'll pick you up."

She smiled at him across the broad expanse of the bed. "That will start tongues wagging."

"No doubt, but between now and then, I'll have a talk with Vince. I think Travis has already left for New Mexico, but I'll fill him in when he gets back. I don't want any significant people in our lives to be surprised."

"Neither do I. And I'll talk to Georgie."

"Okay." Despite his outward confidence as to how they should proceed, that made him nervous. "What if she's upset?" He'd tasted paradise, and he wasn't ready to give it up just yet.

"I doubt she will be, especially if she's convinced our being together won't hurt me in any way."

"I'd die first." The comment surprised him, but it was true. He'd sooner die than hurt her.

She seemed even more surprised to hear it. "I hope that won't be necessary." But her gaze was assessing. "I'm not that fragile, Mac. Please promise me you won't treat me like some delicate porcelain figurine."

"I certainly didn't this morning."

She smiled. "No."

"I know you're not fragile, but I cherish you and want the best for you. Maybe that statement came across as overly dramatic, but hurting you is so beyond my comprehension that I can't imagine it. I would do anything to avoid that."

"Just don't go hurling yourself off a bridge."

"That's difficult to pull off in West Texas. Unless you time it to the rainy season, you end up eating a mouthful of dust."

She laughed. "So true. It's tough to make a dramatic exit around here, so you might as well stick it out."

He walked around the foot of the bed and drew her into his arms. "Then we're agreed. No drama."

She lifted her face to his. "I pretty much hate drama."

"Then let's not have any." He allowed himself one last kiss, but when it threatened to get out of hand, as kisses involving Anastasia tended to do, he released her and backed away. "Let's go climb on those horses and get back over to the stable."

"Easy for you to say."

Instantly he was concerned. "Are you sore?"

"Maybe a little. I haven't had this much sex in quite a while."

"Then forget about sex after dinner. We'll—"

"Hold on there, cowboy! Don't go ruining my evening! As I recall, you made reference earlier to oral sex."

He laughed. Trust her to be direct. "So I did."

"Then might I suggest we put that on the menu along with whatever you're preparing for dinner?"

"Absolutely." The thought of that sent urgent messages to his groin.

"Good. And after we've explored those options, I'll get out my sketch pad."

"Right."

"Unless you'd rather I didn't? I sense some anxiety."

"Once we've had a chance to romp around for a while, I'll be fine about that. I just don't want you drawing me when I'm . . ."

"Aroused?"

"Exactly."

She gazed at him with those incredible eyes. "I wouldn't do that to you, Mac. Drawing your magnificent body is about beauty, not titillation. Besides, I don't want to share that image of arousal with the world. It's private and special."

"Thank you." She'd said something similar before, but it hadn't completely registered. He felt safe now. He'd never believed that she'd exploit him in the name of art, but now he knew that for sure.

"I should be thanking you. In spite of being reluctant, you've agreed that I can sketch you in the nude. You're trusting me not to do anything with those pictures that would embarrass you. I don't take that trust lightly."

"I know." He pulled her close. "Forgive me for being jumpy. Now that we've talked it to death, I'm eager to find out how you'd depict me when my cock is determinedly limp. You've mostly seen it the other way."

She traced the line of his mouth with her forefinger. "Which has made me very happy."

"And me. I've never had a better morning." With a sigh of resignation, he stepped back. "But we need to get back to the corral. After you." He ushered her down the hallway.

"What's involved with preparing for the trail ride?"

"We'll clean the tack. Then we'll spiffy up the horses. Vince likes to use the wash rack on all of them so they sparkle."

"I'd love to see that."

"Wish you could, too, but today should be lucrative for you with the trail riders in town."

"It will be. And this is the last time I'll feel like a fraud every time I sell a rendering of the Ghost."

"Anastasia, I can't promise that we'll see him."

"We will."

He hoped to hell they did. If he had it in his power to command the Ghost to appear, he'd do it.

She glanced back at him as she opened the door. "Just

think, if I hadn't broken my pattern of sleeping late, I'd have less chance to see him."

"Do you think you'll start sleeping in after the riding lessons are over?" He followed her out the door.

"I don't know." She laughed. "That might depend on who I'm sleeping with."

"I see." His pulse rate kicked up. He'd asked her to dinner and he'd suggested some after-dinner entertainment, but that was the extent of his long-range planning. He'd toyed with the idea of going out Sunday night instead of Monday morning, but he hadn't committed to it in his mind. If she packed a bag and spent the weekend with him, that would simplify everything.

Or complicate everything. If he woke at dawn tomorrow with Anastasia in his bed, he might not be so eager to crawl out of it and go for a horseback ride. He'd probably have other activities in mind.

But that wasn't the only issue that occurred to him as they walked out to the corral. Except for the apartment he'd shared with Sophie during their brief marriage, he'd lived in bunkhouses his entire adult life. By default, then, he'd mostly had sex at the woman's house or apartment.

He wasn't in the habit of staying over, either, especially after his divorce. That would remind him too much of life with Sophie. When it came to actually *sleeping* with a woman, as opposed to having sex with her, he was woefully out of practice. Not to say he didn't want Anastasia to spend the weekend, but he had to think about it.

He helped her catch Jasper and made sure the big roan didn't go anywhere while she saddled and bridled him. She was getting great at the process, though. He loved how intently she applied herself and the obvious bond that was growing between her and Jasper.

She mounted up all by herself and gazed down at him. "You've gone into strong, silent mode, there, cowboy.

Was it my comment about sleeping with you that caused that to happen?"

"Yes." He saw no point in dodging the question. "But—"

"I didn't mean to be pushy. I certainly won't stay over if that would be a problem."

"I want you to." The statement rang true the minute he said it. So what if he was out of practice? Considering the lack of eligible males in Bickford the last few years, she'd be out of practice, too.

"In fact, I'd like you to stay all weekend." Nudging back his hat, he rested his hand on her thigh as he looked up at her. "I can't think of anything more wonderful than waking up next to you in the morning."

She flushed. "I'm still not a morning person, you know. So I won't be—"

"Oh, yes, you will." He caressed her thigh. "You might be blurry-eyed and fuzzy-headed, but you'll also be cute and tempting. That's partly why I hesitated. We have trail rides we need to take, and I might . . . get distracted."

"Oh. I hadn't thought of that." Her eyes got all sparkly again. "Well, tomorrow will be different because of the Wild Horse Canyon ride going out. We can either rush to beat them to the stable or . . . not."

"Hmm. Good point." His groin tightened.

"As for Sunday, would it matter so much if we start our trail ride slightly later than usual?"

He grinned. "Guess not."

"Monday morning is the critical one for an early start, right?"

"It is, unless. . . . Listen, is there any chance you'd want to skip your happy hour sketching time at Sadie's on Sunday?"

"Why?"

"Once the trail riders are back and the coast is clear,

we could ride out late in the afternoon and camp in the box canyon. That would give you two chances to see the Ghost, in the evening and first thing in the morning."

Excitement flashed in her eyes. "I love that plan! Let's do it."

"Ever camped before?"

"Nope, but you have. You can show me the ropes."

"It's easy." Damn, this was going to be fun. "Just zip two sleeping bags together and you're all set."

She smiled. "We're going to have sex in the great outdoors, aren't we?"

"Yes, ma'am, we are."

"Excellent. I've always wanted to." She grew thoughtful. "We just have to figure out how I can get my clothes and stuff to your house tonight. I'm not going to roll a suitcase down Main Street on my way to Sadie's."

"No, you're not. Maybe we aren't keeping this a secret, but there's such a thing as being too obvious. I'll pick you up at Sadie's in my truck and we'll fetch your suitcase from your house."

"Perfect."

"Yeah, I do believe it will be." He'd avoided this kind of entanglement for so long that he should probably be worried about whether spending the weekend with her was a good idea. Maybe the great sex had scrambled his brain, because he wasn't worried at all.

CHAPTER 22

As Mac had predicted, Anastasia had plenty of customers wanting portraits done that afternoon. She had to put an OUT TO LUNCH sign on her table so that she could grab a quick sandwich. She didn't want to arrive at Mac's house starving, at least not starving for food. She might arrive famished for his brand of lovemaking, though.

She couldn't stop thinking about him and all those wonderful orgasms. Either her theory about establishing a good visual beforehand had worked spectacularly, or Mac was the best lover she'd ever had. She suspected it was a little of both.

About halfway through the afternoon, she made another sign that read BACK SOON so she could call Georgie. The next challenge was finding a private spot to make that call. She'd rather not be overheard telling her big sister that Mac had asked her to spend the weekend with him.

At last she remembered the hotel breakfast room, which wasn't used for much else. She walked across the lobby and through the double doors. Sure enough, the eight tables sat empty and the room was deserted.

She chose to stand, though. This was the kind of call where she might need to pace a little. She didn't like having to contact Georgie at the general store, but if she didn't do it now, the afternoon could get away from her. Georgie wouldn't like hearing this news from someone else.

When Georgie answered her cell, she sounded busy. "Hi. Can you hold on a sec? I'm ringing up a big order."

"Sure." Anastasia walked over to the bay window, which looked out on Main Street. At last the town was the way she remembered it from when she'd been a kid growing up here. Her mother and Charmaine had complained that they lived in Podunksville, but she'd always loved it.

She could walk everywhere and knew everyone. Yeah, the Bickford kids had to be bused to school in Amarillo, but she'd used that time to draw. After the bus let them off in the afternoon at the end of Main Street, she'd stop at the ice-cream parlor for a sundae if the weather was nice, and for a cup of hot chocolate if it wasn't. Good memories.

"Hey, sis, what's up?" Georgie's voice snapped her out of her reverie.

"I'll make it quick." She kept her voice down even though she doubted anyone could hear her. "I'm spending the weekend at Mac's house and I wanted you to—"

"Spending the weekend?" She said it pretty loud.

"Georgie, is anybody in the store?"

"Um, yeah." This time her sister's voice was much softer. "Sorry about that. Maybe she won't make the connection."

"Who won't?"

"Ida."

"Georgie!"

Her sister said something else, but now she was talking

so faintly Anastasia couldn't make out the words. "You're overcompensating. Now I can barely hear you."

"I'll step into the back room. There, that's better. I said you took me by surprise. I've been expecting something to happen, but I didn't think you'd go from nothing at all to spending the entire weekend with him."

"Well, I'm not going from nothing at all, exactly."

"You're not? Seriously? So when did you—"

"This morning, after our ride. We went over to his house."

"Nice! Must have been pretty special if you're committing to an entire weekend with him."

Anastasia's cheeks grew warm. "It was *amazing.*"

"Oh, I'm glad." George laughed softly. "So very glad for you, sis. You deserve amazing."

"Thanks." She debated saying something about Georgie's pregnancy, which couldn't be much of a secret anymore, considering the immediacy of the wedding plans and Georgie's new habit of ordering club soda at Sadie's instead of her usual red wine. But the phone didn't seem the right venue for discussing it.

"Can't wait to talk to you when I get back from the trail ride. Oops, gotta go. Ida's calling for me. She must have finally decided which sparkly T-shirt she wants. Have fun this weekend." Georgie disconnected.

Anastasia turned off her phone. Ida's sharp ears and keen powers of observation would probably lead her to the right conclusion about the person Georgie had been talking to and what the topic had been. But now that Georgie had been informed, it really didn't matter who else knew. Mac was a great guy and she was proud to be romantically linked with him.

When she returned to her table at Sadie's, a woman paced nearby, clearly waiting for her. She wore beige slacks, a white silk blouse, and fashionable high-heeled boots. Her dark hair was cut in an asymmetrical style that was both sleek and sophisticated.

She glanced at Anastasia and brightened. "Great! You're back."

"Sorry if I kept you waiting. I had to make a phone call." She couldn't judge the woman's age, but she was probably somewhere between midthirties and midforties.

"No worries. I've been hanging around Sadie's watching you work, and just when I decided to come over and talk to you, you ducked out."

"Were you interested in a portrait?"

"Actually, no, although that might be fun sometime." She adjusted the shoulder strap on her purse and held out her hand. "I'm Kathryn Abernathy. Ryan Nesbitt's my boss and he sent me over here."

She sure remembered Ryan Nesbitt, the guy who'd borrowed Travis's hat to have his portrait done. "That's really nice of him. Word of mouth is the best kind of advertising. Have you been up to the gallery in Amarillo?"

"Yes, but I'm not here to buy your art, although I may end up doing that, too. Can we sit down?"

"Of course." She gestured to the chair where her clients usually sat and she took the one catty-corner from it.

Once she was seated, Kathryn reached in her shoulder bag and pulled out a card. "Let's start here."

Anastasia studied the card and recognized the production company name as one she'd seen a few times in the credits of some movies she'd liked. Travis had guessed right that Ryan was connected to Hollywood. Apparently Kathryn Abernathy was the artistic director who worked for him.

But that didn't explain what she was doing in Bickford. Anastasia glanced up, puzzled. "Ryan sent you to see me?"

"Yes. He thinks you have the kind of nimble talent we're looking for, and after seeing your work in Amarillo and watching you create on-the-spot portraits, I agree with him. I'd like you to come out to California, take a look around, and see if a job with our company would be a good fit for you."

Anastasia stared at her in astonishment. Snippets of class notes from art school scrolled through her mind. One of her professors had lectured on the artistic opportunities available in the film industry—storyboarding, graphics, concept art—the list was pretty long, but the competition was supposed to be fierce. She'd never considered it as an option.

"I realize this is sudden," Kathryn said, "but I wasn't sure what I'd find when I got here, so I didn't know if I'd be offering you this opportunity or not. I'm taking the red-eye back tonight, but that doesn't mean you have to decide immediately. Monday would be soon enough."

"This Monday? Two days from now?" The offer was startling enough to speed up her pulse. Add in an immediate deadline, and she was in danger of hyperventilating.

"Or Tuesday. The thing is, we have an opening and we need to fill it ASAP. The sooner you can fly out and get a feel for whether this is what you want, the better. If you're not excited about it after seeing the setup, then we'll look for someone else. But I seriously doubt that will happen."

"Why? You don't even know me."

Kathryn smiled. "Yes, I do. You prefer charcoal, pencil, and watercolors, all mediums that require a quick, deft touch. I've just spent a couple of hours watching how you handle the rapid-fire nature of these cute portraits. You have the kind of artistic flexibility that would be perfect for us."

As the shock began wearing off, Anastasia felt excitement rush in to fill its place. The thought of working for a film company in Hollywood was scary as hell, but everything Kathryn had said about her work rang true. If that was the kind of artist they were looking for, she was their girl.

"I should probably also mention the starting salary." Kathryn named a figure.

Anastasia blinked and barely managed to stop herself from asking if Kathryn was joking. Even with the higher living expenses in L.A. that was a lot of money. She didn't need money, so it wasn't a deciding factor in her mind, but she probably shouldn't say that out loud.

"Of course it's negotiable," Kathryn said quickly, as if interpreting Anastasia's silence as hesitation because it wasn't enough. "I'm asking you to uproot yourself, too, so of course we'd help with that. When you fly out to see the situation, we'll cover all your expenses."

They were rolling out the red carpet for her. Astounding. Plus the job could be a fun challenge, except that she'd have to live in California. A week ago she would have been a lot more eager to experience that. Now there was Mac.

"Obviously I'm surprised," she said at last, "and pleased that you think so highly of my work. But even if I considered flying out there, my sister's getting married next weekend, so that's a priority for me."

"That's wonderful! I wouldn't want to interfere with something so important. How about the following week?"

"A film crew is coming to town to do a documentary on Wild Horse Canyon Adventures. I want to be here for that."

"I understand. I'm sure your art has helped sell the

trail-ride concept. That was another factor in your favor. You instinctively sense what will be commercially successful. Exactly when will they start shooting?"

"Thursday."

"Let's look at the dates." Kathryn pulled out her phone and consulted her calendar. "And your sister's wedding is?"

"The previous Saturday."

"So if you flew out Sunday and flew back here Wednesday night, is that doable? Then if you decide to take the job, we'll bring you out to California after the documentary wraps."

"I guess that would be okay, but I really do need to think about it before I say yes or no." Her head was spinning with a million thoughts, but her overriding emotion was exhilaration. This could be so cool, except for . . . Mac. "It's a big decision."

"It is." Kathryn gazed at her with compassion. "A potentially life-changing one. Normally I'd give you more time to mull it over, and then maybe a couple of weeks in California before we finalize everything. But we really do need someone now so I'm abbreviating the process, mostly because I'm sure this is the right thing for you and for us."

"And I appreciate that confidence." It could so easily have been flattery designed to manipulate her, but as she looked into Kathryn's gray eyes, she saw honesty there. The woman was giving it to her straight. They had a need and she was a good candidate to fill it. The rest was up to her.

"I have to go." Kathryn pushed back her chair and stood. "I promised Ryan's friend in Amarillo I'd take him to dinner. He loaned me his car and offered to drive me to the airport tonight."

Leaving her chair, Anastasia held out her hand. "Regardless of how this turns out, you've made my day with this offer. I never expected such a thing."

"You should have." Kathryn's grip was warm. "You have incredible talent, but then again, the good ones never believe how good they actually are. I hope to see you in L.A. My cell number's on that card."

"I'll let you know this weekend."

"Great." Kathryn flashed her one more smile before walking out of Sadie's.

As Anastasia watched her leave, she felt a tug on her elbow and looked over to see Ida standing there, her eyes huge behind her thick glasses.

Ida gestured toward the doorway Kathryn had just walked through. "And who was *that*?"

"Someone interested in my art."

"She didn't leave with any of it and she didn't ask you to draw her portrait, either. Did she commission something?"

"Um, yes." Anastasia thought it was close enough to the truth that her nose wouldn't grow.

"Good. I hope you charged her an arm and a leg. She looks as if she could afford it."

"She can."

"Ha. Your stock is going up, sweetheart, as I knew it would. But what's the deal with you and Mac Foster? Unless I miss my guess, my prediction about you two is playing out the way I expected."

Anastasia smiled and shook her head. "I'll neither confirm nor deny."

"You do realize that when someone says that, it's understood they're confirming it." She squeezed Anastasia's arm. "And I'm tickled pink. You're exactly right for each other."

Before Kathryn had made her offer, Anastasia would

have enjoyed Ida's teasing. Now it made her uneasy. What was she going to do? "What makes you say so?"

"He's a big strong cowboy with a sensitive side. You're an artistic soul who has more backbone than most people realize. Perfect combination."

"I'm glad you approve."

"I do. Enjoy your weekend." She gave Anastasia's arm another squeeze and walked over to the bar. In a voice that carried throughout the saloon she asked Ike to serve her some "Sex on the Beach."

That made Anastasia laugh along with the rest of the patrons, but she felt a tug at her heart, too. She wouldn't only be giving up Mac if she moved to California. Georgie was here, and Vince and Travis. She'd miss Ike and his wife, Raina, plus all the senior citizens who'd watched her grow up and encouraged her artistic ambitions.

Not surprisingly, she wouldn't miss her mother all that much. Getting out of that house would be something of a relief. If she made really good money, she could save it in case Georgie needed it later to help buy her precious Victorian.

This offer from Kathryn validated her using family resources to go to art school because she might have a chance to help Georgie. She'd thought settling down in Bickford would satisfy her, but now that something spectacular had been dangled in front of her, she wasn't sure anymore. She hadn't acknowledged that she craved a bigger canvas, but there it was. She had ambition, after all.

Yet every time she thought about explaining that to Mac, her chest ached. She wanted to talk to Georgie and get her opinion, but a stream of people wanting portraits prevented her from escaping to make a phone call. Before she knew it, Mac walked into Sadie's and straight over to her table.

His smile was tender. "How's it going?"

"Busy." She looked into his warm gaze and couldn't imagine ever leaving. "And we have to talk."

Instantly his expression grew alert. "Okay. Ready to go?"

"Sure." She quickly packed up her things and walked out with him as curious stares followed their progress. She could feel it. But that wasn't her biggest concern now. She had more to worry about than public opinion.

He helped her into his truck and started the engine. "What's up?"

"Let's get my suitcase and head to your house first."

"You still want to do that?"

"Yes, I do." She wanted his counsel and his strong arms. Ironically, she was thinking of giving up both, so he had a right to know that before they fell into bed again.

When she went in to get her suitcase, she stopped in the doorway to the parlor.

As usual, her mother was watching the big-screen TV and eating her microwaved dinner, but she glanced up at Anastasia. "Where are you going?"

"I'm spending the weekend with Mac Foster."

Her mother frowned in disapproval. "From what I gather, he doesn't have much to offer."

"As a matter of fact, he has a whole lot to offer, but for now we're just enjoying each other's company. Nothing serious."

"Let's hope not." And her mother returned her attention to the television.

At one time Anastasia would have challenged that dismissive statement, but these days she realized how deep her mother's prejudices ran. For whatever reason, Evelyn Bickford was extremely damaged and narcissistic, and nothing would change her at this stage. "See you later, then."

Her mother waved absently.

Nothing to lose there if she moved to California, she thought as she rolled the suitcase out the doorway. Mac had climbed the porch steps and took it from her. She hoped he hadn't heard that interchange.

He stowed the suitcase behind her seat and helped her back in. "Your mother doesn't approve of me."

So he'd heard it. "She doesn't approve of anyone who doesn't earn seven figures."

He paused before closing the door. "That doesn't bother me in the least, but just so you know, I've never considered myself your ideal match. Earning seven figures has nothing to do with that, though. Buckle up." He swung the door closed.

After he climbed into the driver's seat, she turned to him. "Why don't you consider yourself my ideal match? Ida does."

"She does, huh?" Smiling, he started the engine and pulled away from the house. "When did she make this particular statement?"

"This afternoon. Word leaked out, as we both knew it would, that I was staying with you this weekend, so she had to let me know what a great idea that was. Disloyal as this may seem, I put more faith in Ida's opinion than in my mother's."

He laughed. "Thanks, but Ida's a starry-eyed idealist. Your mother is right. You can do a lot better than me."

"I disagree."

"Is that what we need to talk about? Ida's opinion versus your mother's? Because I can think of better ways to spend our time."

Heat surged through her. "So can I, and, no, that's not the issue on the table."

"How long do I have to wait for this discussion?"

"I figured we could talk about it over dinner."

"The meal's in the oven but it won't be done for a little bit. How about if we grab a couple of beers and sit on the porch swing for a while?"

"That sounds great." As she glanced over at his strong profile, she realized how tough this decision was going to be. Sitting on the porch swing with Mac on a fall evening sounded cozy. She couldn't expect porch swings if she moved to L.A. Maybe it wouldn't matter. She wouldn't have Mac to share them with, either.

CHAPTER 23

Mac had an uneasy feeling about this news of Anastasia's, but he told himself he was being paranoid as they settled into the porch swing with their beers. He wrapped his free arm around her to pull her close against his hip, and she nestled against him. "I'd kiss you hello," he said, "except I know where that would lead. We'd never get around to this thing we need to talk about."

"Probably not." She sighed. "So here's what happened. A woman came into Sadie's today. She works for Ryan Nesbitt, the one who borrowed Travis's hat to have his portrait done. She offered me a job as an artist with their production company. In Hollywood."

The bottom dropped out of his world. And damn it, he couldn't, *wouldn't* let on. "That's fantastic!" He turned so he was facing her. "What an opportunity! You're taking it, right?"

She met his gaze, her expression solemn. "I don't know."

"Sure you do. This is your big chance and you'll set that town on its ear. I'll have to start going to the movies more often so I can see your name scroll past in the credits." He'd known this moment would come. He just hadn't expected it to happen the very day they'd made love for the first time, the day he'd discovered he was *in* love.

"I know it's a great opportunity and I knew you'd re-act this way because you've always been so supportive of me and my career. But . . . I don't know if I can give up my peaceful life here. I don't know if I can give up . . ." She swallowed. "You."

"Anastasia." Taking her beer and his, he set them on the porch floor. Then he took her hands in his and looked into her eyes. "You have an incredible talent and this is added proof. My God, Hollywood came to your door."

"I know, but—"

"That's huge. We both know you're not destined to hide away in Bickford while you sketch portraits in the corner of a saloon and draw posters for your sister's trail-riding business. Over there you'll make so many good contacts. You'll be hanging out with people like you—well, in your league, anyway. There is no one *like* you."

She took another breath. "I do feel kind of excited when I think about working over there, but there's Geor-gie, who's going to have a baby, and you and I . . . We just got started." She glanced down at their joined hands. "It's so wonderful being with you." She laced her fingers through his and looked up at him. "I don't want to go to L.A. if it means you and I . . . that we . . ."

Misery created by selfish emotions squeezed his chest, but he refused to give in to them. "I'm flattered more than I can say, but let's put this into perspective. When I showed up, datable guys weren't thick on the ground, so I probably looked pretty good to you, but I've never kid-ded myself that I'm your be-all and end-all. Your future isn't in Bickford."

"If you asked me to stay, I would."

She'd never know how tempting that was. "I won't ask. It wouldn't be fair to you." And he wouldn't try to hold on to her through some kind of long-distance relationship, either. She could meet her artistic soul mate in L.A. and he didn't want her to turn away from anybody because she'd made a commitment to him.

Her gaze searched his. "So you really think I should take the job?"

"Of course. Have you told Georgie?"

"Not yet. There really wasn't time to call her."

"I know you want to be around when her baby's born, but I can guarantee she'll be eager for you to accept the offer. How soon would you start?" He braced himself for the answer.

"First I need to visit, get a feel for the place, and meet the people I'd be working with. Obviously I can't go this week because of all the preparations for Vince and Georgie's wedding. Kathryn offered to fly me over next Sunday and then fly me back here Wednesday night so I'll be here when the film crew arrives. After that's over . . . I'd leave for L.A."

Theoretically he had mere days left with her. "That's her name? Kathryn?"

"Kathryn Abernathy. She arrived in Texas early this morning and is leaving tonight on the red-eye."

"All so she could make you a job offer." He picked up her hand and kissed her fingers. "I'll bet they don't usually take that much trouble."

"I don't know. Apparently she and Ryan were impressed with my *nimble talent*, whatever that means."

"I know exactly what it means. You're like a sunbeam that dances around and makes everything you touch look brighter and more beautiful."

She smiled. "That's very poetic."

"Nah. Just the truth."

"I don't know how a girl's supposed to walk away from a guy who describes her as a sunbeam. Nobody's ever said something like that to me before."

He couldn't let her go down that road. "That's because you've spent most of your time in Bickford. See what happens when you get to Tinsel Town. Guys will come up with way better compliments than that."

"But they might not mean them as sincerely as you do." Warmth shone in her eyes.

"Oh, I think they will. You're a charmer, Anastasia Bickford." He looked at her in the soft glow of twilight and knew he was going to remember this bittersweet moment for a long time. "And the world's waiting for you."

"Why do you have to be so noble?"

Because I love you. "It's not noble. It's realistic. If I tried to keep you from leaving, you'd eventually get restless and might resent the fact I'd encouraged you to stay. There's not enough of a challenge for you here."

"Mac, I—"

"I think the food's ready." Another few seconds and he was liable to kiss her, which wouldn't help the situation. Giving her hand a squeeze, he released it so he could pick up their beer bottles. "We might as well take these in and drink them with dinner." He ushered her back into the house.

"I'm trying to remember if a man has ever made me dinner." She walked into the living room. "I mean, besides Henry, and that's his job. I think this is a first."

"But no pressure, right?"

"None. I'm not a picky eater."

"Good thing. Go straight ahead and you'll end up in my kitchen. I don't have a dining room."

"You don't need one. I like this house, Mac. It has good bones, as they say."

"I'll like it better once the carpet's gone." He'd be working a *lot* on his house this winter. It could well be his saving grace after she left town.

She gestured around the living room. "Just look at this! You have a great rock fireplace and awesome beamed ceilings. Your house has an Old West feel that speaks to me."

"Me, too." He realized that she was his first official guest, and she was reacting exactly the way he had to the house when he'd first looked at it. "I'm a cowboy, after all."

"Yes, you are, and I like that in a guy." She walked into his kitchen and sniffed. "Lasagna?"

"Bingo."

She turned to him. "You must have noticed me ordering it a lot at Sadie's."

Of course he had. He'd noticed everything about her. "Fortunately it's something I know how to fix and I could put it in the oven before picking you up." It was one of his favorite meals.

As closely as he'd observed her over the past few months, he'd never admitted to himself how often they agreed on things. He had to encourage her to take that job, but damn, she was everything he'd ever dreamed of. He couldn't assume that he was everything she'd ever dreamed of, though. Some guy in L.A. might be perfect for her.

"Can I do anything?"

"Nope. Just take a seat." He brought over the lasagna pan and a bowl of tossed salad with bottled dressing and set them on the small wooden table. He only had two chairs, but that was enough. "Want some water?"

"No, this is great. Sit down." She took a deep breath. "The food smells delicious and I'm starving."

The simple act of breathing, which lifted her breasts

and made him aware of her cleavage, was all it took. He was ready to abandon the meal and drag her into his bedroom. He would not. As she'd instructed, he sat down and picked up his beer. "We should toast your job offer."

"Maybe I'll hate L.A. and come straight home."

"No, you won't." He lifted his bottle. "To doors opening."

She touched her bottle to his. "To everything that's made that possible." She drank and put down her beer. "If you three hadn't come to town last spring, we wouldn't have a revitalized economy, and I wouldn't have started drawing again. You were my first inspiration, the portrait I simply had to get down on paper."

He sipped his beer. "Right place, right time."

"You think I'll go off to Hollywood and forget all about you, but I won't."

"Okay."

"You don't believe me, but it's the truth. I won't forget you." Breaking eye contact, she tucked into the lasagna and moaned in appreciation.

Predictably, that moan had an effect on him, so he concentrated on his meal and controlled his reaction. "We should probably talk about our planned ride into the canyon Sunday afternoon. Do you still want to? Is it important anymore?"

She swallowed quickly. "Damn right it is. Do you think this changes my focus?"

"Of course it does. Georgie's wedding is a priority, but maybe going out to see a wild stallion doesn't make so much sense now."

"Are you kidding? I've changed my sleep patterns and fought my demons so that I can ride Jasper into the canyon to see the Ghost. Hollywood or no Hollywood, I'll by God have a personal sighting with the sketches to prove it!"

He smiled. "Good to know."

"In fact, if I take this job, I don't want to abandon Wild Horse Canyon Adventures. I won't be able to do the portraits in Sadie's anymore, but I'd like to keep supplying sketches of the Ghost if I have time."

"You might not have time. How about signed and numbered prints?"

She paused, her fork in midair. "Prints. That's the obvious answer, and I didn't think of it because only well-known artists sell numbered prints. I didn't put myself in that category."

"You'd better start putting yourself there." Her comment told him what he'd suspected all along. She didn't yet grasp how her life had changed. She definitely needed to go into this job with nothing and nobody tying her down.

"If I'm going to consider doing prints, the trip to see the Ghost is even more important. I'm not making multiple copies of work I consider fraudulent. But the sketch I do after I've seen him—that one will be worth making into a numbered print."

"Then I'm glad we're going out there on Sunday." He glanced at her empty plate. "More lasagna?"

"It was delicious, but I'm saving room for dessert."

He groaned. "That's what I forgot. I'm sorry, but I don't have anything for dessert."

She gave him the smoldering look she'd promised earlier in the day. "That's what you think, cowboy."

Good thing he could take a hint. He left the dishes on the table. He'd deal with them later. Right now he had the great privilege of sharing his bed with Anastasia and that took precedence over everything else.

In the soft light of his bedside lamps, they undressed each other eagerly. They'd made love only hours ago, and yet it seemed so much longer than that. This morning he'd thought they were beginning something special. Now he had to face an ending that was already in sight.

He'd imagined they'd take it slower tonight, but after her announcement about the job, slow wasn't working for him. His heartbeat thundered in his ears and he was hot and tight with desire. As the last articles of clothing hit the floor, he pulled her into his arms. "Forgive me, but I just need—"

"Me, too." Winding her arms around his neck, she pressed against him. "You get the condom. I'll pull back the covers."

"A woman after my own heart."

"And a man after mine." She kissed him hard on the mouth before wiggling out of his arms.

He wasn't after her heart, not really. He didn't want her to fall in love with him because that would make her life more difficult. But as he finished rolling on the condom and climbed into bed with her, he looked into her eyes and discovered an emotion that made his breath hitch.

She didn't try to hide it, either. Apparently she didn't care if he knew. By all rights he should glance away. A smart man would break the connection before she caught on that he was in the same boat. But he couldn't seem to do that.

Instead he held her gaze as he moved over her and nestled between her thighs. Poised for that first thrust, he took a steadying breath. Her expression grew even more radiant and her smile trembled as she caressed the tense muscles of his back.

Somehow he knew she wouldn't say the words, just as he wouldn't. But they were there in her eyes and surely in his, too. Slowly he eased forward, saying with his body what he dared not speak out loud.

She rose to meet him in a gesture of sweet welcome.

Dear God, how he loved her. The words pushed at his throat, but he swallowed them. Not now. Maybe not ever.

At least he was here, moving in tandem with her as they created a rhythm that was ageless yet uniquely theirs. It had to be enough. He watched her eyes darken and heard her breathing change. Her fingertips flexed against his skin and deep within her moist body, her muscles clenched.

Taking his cue, he stroked faster. Her lips parted and she began to pant, yet her gaze never left his. Another spasm rippled over his cock. She was about to come. And so . . . ah, yes . . . so was he.

"Mac!"

"I'm here." He pumped faster. "I'm here!"

Arching against him, she came in a glorious rush. He pushed deeper, bellowing in triumph as he surrendered to the pulsing heat, the incredible joy . . . and the love.

Oh, yeah, it was love, all right. As the orgasmic haze cleared from his brain and he could see straight, he gazed into her eyes. The glow he'd seen before was even stronger. No doubt his expression was a lot like hers.

Leaning down, he kissed her softly. Then he lifted his head a fraction. "I really want you to take the job."

She chuckled. "Interesting pillow talk."

"You know why I'm saying that, right?"

"You're afraid I'll hang around Bickford so I can be with you."

"Right. If spending time with me will make that more likely, then I'll back off."

"You can't. You promised to take me into the canyon Sunday evening."

She had him there. He had promised and he was a man of his word. Plus he knew how important that trip was to her. He also knew they weren't capable of spending an entire night together without getting friendly. Not anymore.

He needed to think, and he found that extremely difficult while locked tight against her yielding body. "I'll be right back." Leaving the bed, he went into the bathroom and took care of the condom.

When he returned, she was on her knees, still naked, rummaging through her suitcase. "Need something?"

"My sketch pad."

Right. He'd agreed to pose for her tonight. He might want to stop saying yes whenever she asked him to do something. Except he couldn't imagine denying her anything, especially when she was all pink and tousled from making love, like now.

"Just stretch out on the bed on your side and prop your head on your hand. That shouldn't be too difficult a position to hold for a while. I promise to be quick."

She wouldn't be quick enough to keep him from becoming self-conscious, but he'd already said he'd do this. "And nobody will see this except you and me."

"Absolutely." She sat cross-legged on the bed, the sketch pad in her lap. Then she paused. "But if you're worried about it, I won't draw you."

"I'm a little worried, but then, so were you when you showed up at the barn that first morning."

"More than a little worried. But I put my trust in you, and that worked out."

"Then I'll put my trust in you."

"Good." And she started humming "Streets of Laredo" as she worked.

That made him smile. "Are you afraid that it'll be a bad sketch?"

"I'm afraid I won't do you justice. You're impressive, Macario."

His cheeks warmed with embarrassment. "I'm not."

"You are, but I can tell that makes you uncomfortable so I'll shut up about it." Her pencil moved across the page in rhythmic strokes.

He needed a distraction so he wouldn't think about the fact that a sketch of his naked body would soon exist. "Getting back to our discussion, I promised to take you into the canyon, as you reminded me, but after that, maybe I should fade into the background and leave you free to make a decision without taking me into consideration."

"That won't work, either. I'm the maid of honor for the wedding and you're the best man." She kept glancing at him, but it was with an assessing eye as she continued working.

"True, but that doesn't mean you have to come home with me after the rehearsal dinner and the reception."

She glanced up. "But what if I want to?"

He had no response to that because he was too busy imagining them frolicking in his big bed.

"Here's the thing." She tapped the pencil on her sketch pad. "Unless I hate the work setup or L.A. itself when I go over there, I probably will take this job because you're right that it's an amazing opportunity."

"I'm glad to hear you say that."

"But giving you up won't be easy."

"No, but necessary."

She paused in her sketching. "Is it? Or is there some way we could work it out to see each other?"

"Maybe, but . . ." He blew out a breath. "You're going to want to give a hundred percent to this job, which means you won't have time to be hopping back home much at all."

She held his gaze. "You're right. So it won't matter if we end it now or the day I leave for good. I'm already into you, so it'll hurt no matter what we do between now and then."

Guilt swamped him. "I'm sorry. I should never have suggested that we come back here this morning."

"Mac! Get over yourself! If you hadn't made a move on me, I would have made one on you. I'm not into you because we've had great sex recently, although that's been wonderful. I've been into you since the day I sketched you the first time. Leaving Bickford was always going to be sucky if it meant leaving you."

"Oh." He didn't like the idea that she'd suffer no matter what, but he felt a little less responsible for that suffering.

"So what about you? Should I back off so you won't be miserable if and when I leave town?"

"No." He didn't even have to think about it. "I never expected we'd be a long-term thing. I'll take whatever time I can get and be grateful."

That telltale emotion flashed in her eyes again. "Me, too. Now I need to get this sketch finished before you end up with a muscle cramp." She returned her attention to her sketch pad and began humming "Danny Boy."

Muscle cramps were nothing. He watched her work and realized he could put up with muscle cramps all day if it meant being with her. But that wasn't going to happen, so instead of muscle cramps, he'd have to deal with heartbreak. And he'd do that, too, because leaving Bickford would be the best thing she could possibly do for herself.

CHAPTER 24

Spending the weekend with Mac taught Anastasia many things about herself. She learned that his little house felt more like home than the large Victorian where she'd lived most of her life. Economic use of space, clean architectural lines, and sturdy furniture appealed to her far more than gingerbread trim and delicate silk upholstery.

Sharing living space with a man instead of her mother felt strange at first, but she adapted quickly because Mac was the most easygoing person in the world. He'd accepted her obsession with capturing him on paper and he'd let her sit on the edge of the bathtub and sketch him while he shaved. That portrait would go in her private portfolio, along with his nude and the one of him wearing only shorts and flip-flops while he cooked breakfast.

He'd insisted on driving her to Sadie's both days for her stint at the portrait table and she'd appreciated the gallantry of that even though she was perfectly capable of walking there. Word had spread about their weekend arrangement, so no one was surprised. In fact, they seemed pleased that she and Mac were a couple.

They'd taken a trail ride Saturday morning but had

decided to skip it on Sunday because they'd be riding into the canyon in the late afternoon. During a break between portraits on Sunday, Anastasia texted Georgie and asked her to stop by Sadie's once she was home from the trail ride. Her sister needed to know about the camping trip, but mostly Anastasia wanted to tell her about the job offer.

In spite of Mac's enthusiastic support, she still hadn't decided for sure what to do. Talking about it with Georgie would help. Like Mac, Georgie had her best interests at heart.

Georgie showed up in the middle of the afternoon, looking tired and dusty but very happy, too. She picked up a tall glass of water Ike handed her on her way over to Anastasia's table. Fortunately the portrait chair was vacant and she settled into it.

"Good ride?" Anastasia could tell it had been from Georgie's expression, but she wanted to hear all about it, anyway.

"The best. We saw him."

"You did? Awesome!" She didn't have to ask who. "Morning or evening?"

"Both. We settled everyone in the box canyon and then at dusk we led them back down the trail to the meadow where he usually takes his band." Georgie grinned. "There they were. He looks great. They all do. They'll be fine through the winter, I think. No ribs sticking out, no dull coats. They're in good health, near as I can tell."

"I'm so glad. I don't know if you heard, but Mac and I are riding out there tonight. We're going to camp."

"Ed mentioned that." Georgie gave her a sly look. "So? Does that mean the weekend's gone well?"

She couldn't help smiling. She'd been doing that a lot lately. "Very well."

"No complaints?"

"Not a one. Mac's great." Her smile faded. "But something's happened, and it could change everything." She filled Georgie in on Kathryn's Friday afternoon visit.

"But that's *wonderful.* I'm only sorry my wedding is holding up the works! Not that I'm sorry about the wedding, because I've been anticipating that all summer, but the timing sucks for you. Maybe we can figure it out so you can fly to L.A. this week and come home Friday night before the wedding."

"Nope. I don't want to mess up the plans we have in place. Besides, it wouldn't help anything because I'd still want to come back for the shooting of the documentary. Kathryn's fine postponing my preliminary visit until next Sunday. The only real glitch is Mac."

"Mac?" Georgie frowned. "If he's trying to talk you out of—"

"Oh, no. He wants me to take it. He thinks it's a fabulous opportunity. I'm the problem." She sighed. "I like him a lot."

Georgie's militant expression disappeared. "Aw, sweetie." She gazed at Anastasia with compassion. "It doesn't seem fair, does it?"

"No." Her throat tightened. "I finally find a really nice guy and along comes a chance of a lifetime that will take me away from him. What would you do?"

"That doesn't matter. This decision is unique to you and you'll have to make it. I would hate to see you turn away from something so exciting, though. I can tell you think it is, too, from the way you described it to me."

"I can't lie. It sounds incredible. Mac says if I stayed because of him I might come to resent him for it."

Georgie nodded. "Wise words. If you care about someone, you never want to be the reason they don't grow, even if you don't mean to hold them back."

"And he cares about me." The lump in her throat grew bigger. "We would love to see each other, but we both know it's unrealistic to think I'll have time to visit when I'm committed to doing well in the new job." She swallowed. "Maybe I'm being really selfish to go on this camping trip if I'm planning to leave. Wouldn't it be easier on Mac if I canceled?"

"No, it wouldn't." Mac's deep voice made both women jump. He glanced at Georgie. "Hi, Georgie."

"Hi, Mac."

He turned his attention to Anastasia. "What's this talk about canceling? I thought going out there was important to you?"

She looked into his dark eyes. The last time his gaze had been this intense, he'd been deep inside her. She shivered in response to the hot memory. "It is important, but so are you."

"Then you need to know I'd be deeply disappointed if you cancel on me. We've both put time and effort into this project and I, for one, want to see it through. The gear's in the truck. I stopped by early to see if you wanted to take off now and maximize our chances. Vince says the Ghost and his band are out there."

"They are," Georgie said. "We had no trouble seeing them. They seemed almost unconcerned about our presence."

"That's good to know." He turned back to Anastasia. "So? Ready to leave?"

"Yes." She started packing up her sketching materials. "Yes, I am."

"It's beautiful in the canyon right now." Georgie stood. "You'll love it."

"I know I will." She hooked her messenger bag over her shoulder. "Do you need a ride home?"

"Nope. Vince is supposed to meet me here. He gave

me a head start because he thought you and I might have some girl talk to get out of the way."

"Thanks, sis." She hugged her.

"Anytime. Say hello to the Ghost for me."

"I will." As she turned and walked with Mac through the saloon to the outside entrance, she thought about the bond she shared with her sister. Georgie wanted her to go to L.A., but that wouldn't make it any easier.

Mac reached out a long arm, pushed the door open, and held it for her. "I still can't believe you were willing to cancel to spare my feelings."

She stepped onto the sidewalk and turned to face him. "We're getting close to each other, and this will just bring us closer. That seems unfair to you."

"It would also be unfair to deprive me of the joy of watching you see the Ghost for the first time. Besides, if you didn't go out there, you've wasted your efforts and mine."

"You're angry."

"Hell, yes, I'm angry. I thought we had an understanding that we'd make the most of our time together before you left. Then I walk into Sadie's and hear you telling Georgie you should probably cancel our camping trip."

"Because I was thinking of you!"

"Well, don't. Think of yourself. That's what will make me happy. I want you to do what is best for you, and that means riding into the canyon so you can finally catch a glimpse of that stallion." He took a deep breath. "It also means moving to L.A."

She thought of what Georgie had said a little while ago, that if someone cared for you, they'd want you to grow. Mac wouldn't be grateful and happy if she turned down that job offer. He'd be mad as hell. Georgie wouldn't be mad, but she'd be upset. Staying here wouldn't make Georgie happy, either.

"Okay, I get it, now." She met his gaze. "If I do what's right for me, it'll be right for the people who care about me."

"Yes."

"Then it's time to saddle up."

He smiled. "Attagirl."

That morning she'd packed her suitcase in preparation for returning to her mother's house, so he detoured past the Victorian so she could drop it off. Then he parked his truck at the stable.

As they tacked up the horses and loaded the saddlebags, excitement fizzed in her veins. The moment she'd dreamed of was close at hand. She tucked her sketch pad in with a light jacket, a change of underwear and a few toiletries. She was willing to be grubby but not *that* grubby.

She figured Mac was adding condoms to his saddlebag. He was also in charge of the food for dinner and breakfast. Her knowledge of camping could be written on the head of a pin.

He'd promised to bring liners for the sleeping bags, which were already on site. That was standard operating procedure for the trail rides, and this would be similar but more intimate.

Extremely intimate, she thought as they started down the trail with Mac in the lead. The last time she'd ridden into this canyon with him, they hadn't been lovers. Now she knew every detail of his body and he could say the same about her, although he didn't have a sketch to prove it.

She knew about the mole that was about two inches above his navel and that he had an innie. She knew that he had knobby knees and strong thigh muscles. She could picture how he looked fully aroused with his cock jutting proudly and his balls drawn in tight.

Now, as she rode behind him on the trail, she could imagine his naked back and buttocks. She knew how his muscles felt when they bunched during a climax and when they relaxed afterward. She loved touching him and refused to think of what her life would be like when she couldn't do that anymore.

"Coyotes ahead," he called softly.

Amazing what a difference a few days had made. She trusted Jasper to behave himself as she took her phone out of the drawstring bag she'd hung on the saddle horn. Mac made room for her and Jasper on the trail and she managed to get several shots of the coyotes before the pack disappeared into the underbrush.

She smiled at Mac. "Thank you. Great reference photos."

"I'll keep my eyes open."

"I know you will." Resting her hands on the saddle horn, she looked around at the russet canyon walls rising above them and the touches of fall color here and there. It wasn't a spectacular display like the leaves in New England, but she appreciated the subtleties. "Beautiful."

"Yeah."

Glancing over, she discovered he was focused on her, not the landscape. The undisguised warmth in his gaze might have caused her to question the wisdom of this trip, except that he'd pretty much told her that he didn't want to be shut out of it. She'd honor his wish.

He took a deep breath. "We should get going. I want to reach the box canyon and make camp before dark."

"Should we trot?"

"Only if you're up to it."

"I have that pop tune loaded and ready to go in my brain. Move 'em out, cowboy."

"Call out if you need a break." And he was off, trotting his big black horse, Cinder.

She urged Jasper into a trot and started humming. Jasper didn't need any encouragement. He obviously didn't like being left in the dust. Amazingly, the trot felt pretty good, and they were covering ground faster. She was as eager to get there as Mac was, so if that meant trotting, so be it.

Then the trail opened up. Mac turned in the saddle. "We could canter here, but I don't want to push you."

She remembered the magic of cantering around the corral with him. "Let's try it."

"Holler if it isn't working for you." And he was off.

A quick nudge of her booted heels and Jasper followed. For one heart-stopping moment she was afraid. And then she wasn't. She matched Jasper's fluid movement and rejoiced in the freedom of it.

"You okay back there?" Mack called over his shoulder.

"Yes! This is great!"

"I knew you'd like it!" He rode with such ease, as if he and Cinder were a single unit.

She couldn't aspire to that. She wasn't one with Jasper by any stretch, but she felt the power of his stride and managed to stay on as he kept up with Cinder. This was another memory she'd store away to take out when she was sitting in her apartment in L.A.

The canter ended and she was ready for that. She'd done well, but much longer and she might have lost that sense of balance and well-being. Riding was a skill, and she didn't kid herself that she'd mastered it.

Mac had, though. Watching him on a horse was an experience that bordered on the erotic. Tonight she'd have all that coordination and power with her in a double sleeping bag. She could hardly wait.

The excitement of camping with Mac and sighting the Ghost carried her almost to the meadow. But when they were within a quarter mile of it, she began to fade. She'd never ridden this far before and she realized that expertise wasn't the same as endurance.

On top of that, Mac had slowed the pace. She struggled to sit upright in the saddle and began to long for the end of the ride. Maybe after a meal and some rest she'd be ready to meet the Ghost, but right now she didn't feel capable of sketching anything.

Abruptly he stopped. "He's there. Cinder knows it, and I can vaguely hear them."

Her fatigue melted away. "The Ghost is in the meadow?"

"I'm pretty sure. I heard some nickers, and Cinder is really alert. The wind's blowing in our direction, so they might not have smelled us, but they'll hear us any minute. If we go slowly, we might be able to creep up on them before they bolt."

Her heart pounded with anticipation. The horse she'd been drawing for the past six months was close by. He'd become a mythic figure to her, but at last she'd have a chance to see for herself that he was flesh and blood. "I'll follow your lead."

"Stay close."

"Yep." She marveled at the assured way Mac led them forward. His movements were cautious but focused. She realized that she would trust him to lead her anywhere.

Slowly they proceeded down the trail toward the meadow. She'd never seen it before, but plenty of people had described it. When the tall cottonwoods rose above the mesquites, their golden leaves glowing in the late-afternoon sunshine, she knew they were almost there.

Now she could hear the restless movements of the herd—soft thuds of hooves on moist ground, a snort, a muted whinny. Excitement became a steel band around her chest. Gradually the trees gave way and then . . . she saw them. She counted thirteen, mostly in shades of brown.

Two were light gray like their father. They all stood poised, heads up, obviously on alert.

Mac's voice was a low murmur. "To your right."

She looked over, and there was the Ghost at the edge of the meadow, his nostrils flared, his gaze directed at the spot where they stood in the shadow of the trees. Adrenaline shot through her, enhancing all her senses. "He sees us," she whispered.

"He does. He may take off any second. Activate that photographic memory."

"I will." She concentrated on the stallion. Ah, he was magnificent, more regal than she'd given him credit for. But that kind of presence didn't show up in a photograph. She'd needed to be here to feel it. Now she knew how she'd draw him, not as a wild renegade on the run, but as a king in full command of his domain.

He snorted and pawed the ground.

A thrill of fear generated by an ancient memory ran through her. But that terrified little girl had learned to put herself in the horse's place. When the Ghost shivered, she realized he feared for the safety of his band. He might challenge the humans who'd appeared at the edge of the meadow, but only to protect those in his care.

Lifting his head, he issued a command and the horses leaped into action. The ground shook as they raced across the meadow and splashed through the creek. The Ghost followed, his powerful muscles bunching as he ran.

Anastasia watched until they were out of sight in the trees on the far side of the canyon. Then she slowly let out her breath and turned to Mac. "Thank you."

His grin of triumph was cute as hell. "Pretty cool, huh?"

"You have no idea."

"I have some idea. I've seen that look before and it always means you're really happy."

She could guess when he'd last seen her looking this happy. They'd likely been naked at the time. "Will they be back tonight?"

"Maybe, but Georgie and Vince have decided that after a sighting, we need to leave them alone for a while. We don't want to disturb their pattern too often if we can help it. We'll walk down from the campsite at dawn and should see them again then."

"Even if we don't, I'm ready to start sketching."

"Then let's get a move on." He guided Cinder into the clearing.

She followed on Jasper as they walked the horses to a trail on the other side of the meadow. "Did you take pictures with your phone? I didn't notice."

"Didn't need to this time. You're here."

The significance of that comment didn't register at first. When it did, she blinked in surprise. He hadn't been taking pictures of the Ghost for his benefit all this time. He'd been doing it for her.

She thought back to all the Sunday afternoons he'd walked down to Sadie's after the trail ride to show her the pictures on his phone. She'd been eager to see those pictures, but now she could admit she'd been even more excited to see Mac. She had a hunch he'd felt the same. Damn. They'd probably been in love with each other from the get-go.

Leaving him was going to be the hardest thing she'd ever done, but if she didn't take that job, he'd be disappointed in her. She'd be disappointed in herself, too. In her heart she knew that this was her big chance, a huge turning point in her creative life. But it wouldn't come without sacrifice.

For now, though, she was still here, riding up a narrow trail to a secluded canyon she'd heard about for so long, the place where Vince and Georgie would be married in less than a week. She'd be foolish to let dread of an impending separation from Mac ruin their brief time together.

Because the trail was so narrow he blocked her view of what lay ahead, but she could hear the waterfall. Not being able to see it only added to her anticipation. At last he reached the end of the path and moved forward into the canyon. Her first glimpse stole her breath.

The russet rock seemed to glow in the fading light of the setting sun, and the backdrop of clear sky had never seemed so blue. Silver ribbons of water cascaded hundreds of feet from the rim to the canyon floor and fed into a rippling brook. To her right, a colorful chuck wagon and a stone fire pit marked a cozy campground. No wonder Vince and Georgie wanted to have their ceremony in this canyon.

"You can see why I wanted to show you this."

"It's spectacular." She turned to look at him, a fantasy cowboy astride a gleaming black horse, the perfect addition to the scene. "This might sound crazy, but I'd like to try cantering across that meadow toward the falls."

He smiled. "Like you imagined it would be riding Prince?"

"Yes." She should have expected that he'd understand. "You know what the ground is like. Would it be safe?"

"Should be. Tighten the string on your hat so it'll stay put. We'll start out at a trot and go from there."

"Okay." Her pulse leaped, but Mac would be beside her. She could do this. She *wanted* to do this. "I'm ready." She nudged Jasper forward, and as they began to trot, she was so focused on her surroundings that she forgot to sing. Amazingly, she didn't bounce.

"Here we go!" Mac called out as he pressed his heels against Cinder's ribs.

She did the same and for one tiny moment panic engulfed her again when Jasper took off. But then she caught his rhythm and her panic again faded, this time turning to joy. She was doing it! She was flying across a meadow on a beautiful horse exactly the way her six-year-old self had dreamed she would!

When they were close enough to the waterfall that the mist dampened her face, she pulled gradually back on the reins and brought Jasper to a stop.

"Liked that, did you?"

That's when she realized she was grinning like a fool. "Loved it." She glanced at him. "Thanks for making my dreams come true."

"My pleasure."

"We should move, though, before the moisture starts affecting my sketch pad." She turned Jasper and started back toward the campground.

Mac laughed as he came along beside her. "Some women I've known would be worried about their hair."

"Why, does my hair look bad?"

"No. You look . . . beautiful."

She met his warm gaze. "Thanks." Oh, yes, leaving Mac was going to be very tough.

CHAPTER 25

They unsaddled the horses together, because Anastasia insisted on that. But once the horses were munching on their dinner, Mac took over the chores. He built a fire and unpacked the supplies while she sat on one of the logs grouped around the fire pit, her sketch pad balanced on her knees.

He loved watching her work. He'd become used to the mournful tunes she hummed while she drew, but they still made him smile. She'd offered to help him with the meal, too, but he knew she'd been itching to get her hands on a pencil.

He was itching to get his hands on her, but he controlled that urge. They'd have plenty of time to make love after she'd poured out all the images in her head onto paper. He'd never known someone so filled up with creativity. Hard to believe that she'd ever lost interest in drawing, but apparently she had and he'd inspired her to start again.

That justified his existence right there, because he wondered what would have happened if she hadn't gone back to her art. She never would have realized her potential and the world would be a poorer place as a result. But now she would expand into a whole new area. If he'd contributed to that, he'd consider it a point of pride for the rest of his life.

He'd made some stew this morning so he'd have something he could warm up instead of cooking dinner from scratch. He liked cooking, but he liked kissing better, especially if he could be kissing Anastasia. But that wouldn't last. What did? At least this time he knew when the end would come and he also knew she didn't want to leave. That helped.

Henry usually handled the food preparation for the trail riders, so Mac had all kinds of equipment at his disposal at the campsite, including a heavy pot that he could suspend from an iron tripod. Once he had the stew simmering over the fire, he turned his attention to their sleeping arrangements.

He could do without an air mattress but he wanted her to have one. He inflated two so they'd have a level playing field, so to speak. He'd forgotten to ask her if she wanted him to set up a tent, though.

Because he didn't want to interrupt her, he made an educated guess. Lying outside gazing up at the stars seemed like an Anastasia thing to do. That would be after they'd wrung each other out, of course. He pulled a couple of sleeping bags out of the storage trunks, zipped them together, and secured the liner inside.

He chose a location near the fire but not too near. They'd generate plenty of heat all by themselves. Last of all he inflated a couple of pillows and put on clean pillowcases. He tucked some condoms inside the one on the left side, a habit he'd fallen into because that was the side he usually took when they were in bed.

"You've been busy." Her sketch pad under her arm, she walked over and surveyed the bed he'd created. "Cozy."

"I hope so. Are you going to show me what you've been working on?"

"Yeah." She grinned and flipped open the sketch pad. "I'm willing to make prints of this."

He looked at her new drawing of the Ghost and gave a low whistle. "Amazing."

"I know, right? I had him rearing before, but this is so much better, with him standing proudly, head up, mane blowing in the breeze. He doesn't need to fight because he's the king."

"I love it."

"Good thing, because you get the original for your living room wall. Everyone else gets a signed print."

"You shouldn't do that. You should sell the original for a whole lot of money. Put it in the gallery in Amarillo. Set the price really high, because it's worth it."

"No. It's yours, Mac. You made this sketch possible and it's not for sale. It's my gift to you."

He looked into her eyes and felt a visceral tug that was part lust and a whole lot of something more significant. To hell with the stew. He didn't care if it burned to a crisp if he could only . . . but she might be hungry. "Ready for dinner?"

"Not yet." She closed her sketchbook, put it on the ground, and anchored it with a nearby rock. Then she sat on the closest log and pulled off her boots. After that she began taking off her clothes.

He'd died and gone to heaven. That was the only explanation for being in the presence of a beautiful woman who seemed to read his every thought. She'd caught him by surprise, so she was way ahead of him by the time he started fumbling with his own clothes. Anticipation made him clumsy.

By the time he'd shed everything, she was already in the sleeping bag. She patted the space next to her. "I saved you some room." Then she held up a condom packet. "I also went fishing and found this."

He climbed in and reached for it.

"Nope." She snatched it away. "Lie down, cowboy. You can test the resilience of the air mattress while I test you."

And did she ever test him. She started with oral sex, something he'd never experienced while staring up at the twilight sky. She was wickedly good at it, too. He focused on the evening star and made a wish that he could hold out a little longer, just a little . . . "Okay, stop." Jaw clenched, he fought off his climax.

She kissed the tip of his cock. "You can come, you know. We have all night."

"I know." He gulped for air.

"Then let me." She licked the cleft underneath that was all kinds of sensitive.

Breath hissed out between his teeth. "No. Please. Scoot up here."

She wiggled her way up his body, which was another form of sweet torture. Then she propped herself above him and looked down. "What?"

She was so cute about it that he had to laugh. "Where's the condom?"

"Here." She held it in front of his face.

"Please put it on. Or let me do it. I want . . . I need . . ."

"All right." She smiled. "Me, too, actually."

"Thank God." He battled his climax some more while she rolled on the condom. After what seemed like an hour, she finished the task and he sighed in relief. "Good job. Now—"

"Don't worry. I know what you want." Holding his gaze, she moved over him and began claiming territory. "Better?"

"Much."

"I want to treat you right, Mac."

He sucked in air as she rotated her hips in a slow circle on her way down. "You're doing . . . a terrific job."

"You've been so good to me."

"Like I said, it's easy."

"Because we fit." In one smooth movement, she was there.

"We sure do." He grasped her hips and lifted his to intensify the connection.

"Mmm." Leaning forward, she braced her hands on either side of his shoulders. Her mouth hovered over his. "I'm gonna miss you like crazy."

"Same here."

Keeping the rest of her body still, she kissed him, taking it slow and making generous use of her tongue. Then she angled her head and took the kiss even deeper, as if silently telling him something. He had a pretty good idea what that something was.

And he answered her. Sliding both hands up her warm back, he cradled her head and slackened his jaw. She could have anything she wanted from him. He was completely, absolutely hers.

She made love to him with her mouth while the rest of her body remained completely motionless. Then she moaned softly and her muscles tightened around his cock. Her orgasm rolled through her with a silent power that shook him to his core. His hips rose without conscious effort and his release brought a surge of joy so great that he lost track of where he was.

But he never lost track of who was in his arms. As she ended the kiss and sank against his chest, panting, he held her close and murmured her name. This moment would stay with him forever, even if she couldn't.

Their night together was filled with laughter and lovemaking and very little sleep. Even though Mac knew she wouldn't be leaving permanently for another two weeks, he couldn't help thinking these few hours gave them a chance to say good-bye. He sensed that she felt the same.

At dawn they dressed and crept back to the meadow. The horses were on the far side picking at the scattered tufts of dry grass left from the summer and didn't appear to take notice of them. Mac held Anastasia's hand as they crouched in the shadows and watched.

The stallion moved through the herd as if taking a head count. He seemed relaxed and in charge. Mac had wondered if the trail rides and the increased presence of humans in the area would upset the Ghost's routine, but so far that didn't seem to be happening.

Anastasia put her mouth close to his ear, her breath warm and arousing. "Let's go before we disturb them."

He nodded. As they crept back up the trail, he listened for a whinny of alarm and rapid hoofbeats signaling that the herd was running away, but the meadow remained peaceful. He and Anastasia had managed to slip in and out of the horses' world without being noticed.

Back in camp, all he had to do was look at her and they were in each other's arms again. They made love without words because they no longer needed them. He wouldn't share her future, but he'd had this special week, far more than he'd ever dreamed of. And it was enough.

They cooked breakfast together and he taught her what he knew about frying eggs and bacon over an open fire. He doubted she'd need to know that in L.A., but she'd asked to learn. The chance that they'd ever share breakfast again was slim.

Their weekend was over and she'd go back to the Victorian this morning. Wedding preparations would take up most of her free time for the rest of the week, although he might see her at Sadie's now and then. Things would return to the way they'd been before she'd asked him to teach her to ride. Except nothing would ever be the same, at least not for him.

They sat on a log near the fire to eat the breakfast they'd made. She was halfway through her meal when she put down her fork and turned to him. "I'm going to destroy that nude."

"You are?" That shocked him. "Why?"

"If something ever happened to me, people could go through my stuff and find it." She put her plate on the ground and stood. "Besides, I don't need that sketch to remember how beautiful you are. I can just close my eyes." She took her sketch pad out of her messenger bag, flipped through it, and tore out the drawing she'd made of him on Friday night.

"But you took the time to draw it. I hate to think of you destroying something you created."

She tucked her sketch pad back in her messenger bag and set it down before walking toward him holding the nude. "Do you want it?"

"Uh, no. That would be weird."

"Then it's going away." She leaned down and thrust it on top of the warm coals. Then she returned to the log and continued eating her breakfast.

He watched the paper crinkle and burn with a mixture of sadness and relief. Knowing she'd drawn the picture made it precious just like everything she created. But she was right. It was too personal to keep around.

He glanced over at her. "Thank you."

"You're welcome." She smiled. "Thank you for trusting me to draw it in the first place. I'm keeping the ones of you shaving and cooking because those are adorable, but that one . . ."

"I know." She'd captured his expression perfectly.

Anyone looking at it would recognize that he was a man in love.

And because of that, he didn't want to leave the canyon. She didn't seem in any hurry, either. They had a second cup of coffee and listened to the sound of the waterfall mingled with the chirp of birds. They took their time packing up.

But eventually they couldn't delay the moment any longer. He made sure the fire was out, and then they mounted up. He suggested that Anastasia should lead, figuring she'd take it slow.

Near as he could tell, she did that, but still the trip went faster than he wanted. Part of the time they talked about the wedding. Part of the time they rode in silence, but it was a comfortable one. He didn't know about her state of mind, but he was treasuring every second.

They were almost clear of the canyon walls when his cell phone chimed, indicating an incoming text. He'd noticed before that this was the first place on the way out where he could get reception. Any deeper in was out of range.

He brought Cinder to a halt and pulled out his phone. "Hold up a minute. Let me see what this is about."

"Sure." She paused and turned Jasper slightly so she could look back at him.

"It's from Vince." He scanned the message as a dull ache settled in his chest. "The documentary filming's been postponed. They may try to do it in November, weather permitting, but it might end up being next spring."

"Oh, no! I hope it's November and not spring. Everyone will be so disappointed if they have to wait months."

How like her to consider other people first. He'd selfishly thought of what it would mean to him, personally. "I hope it's November, too. But in any case, you won't have to come back from L.A. next week, after all."

"Yes, I will." Panic laced her words. "I'm only supposed to be going for a preliminary visit. Maybe I won't like it or they won't like me. But if it's all good, then I have to come back for my stuff. I won't take all of it on Sunday, obviously, so I'll need—"

"Georgie can ship it." He was pounding nails in his own coffin, but her future employer would say it if he didn't. "Either you'll come back because you're still not sure and need to think things over, or you'll decide to stay. If you're staying, you'll mostly just need the rest of your clothes, right?"

She hesitated, her expression troubled. "I guess. I'll probably rent a furnished apartment to start with. But I thought . . . we'd have a little more time."

"I know. Me, too." He took a deep breath. "Maybe it's better this way. We've had a wonderful weekend. We were able to relax and enjoy each other. If you had come back for the filming, we wouldn't have had that luxury. Trying to see each other could have been frustrating."

"What are you saying?"

"I think you know. This week will be busy. Georgie needs your help with all the details that go into a wedding, and Charmaine will be coming into town in two days. I'll be on tap for whatever Vince wants me to do. We'll both have lots to do."

"So this is it?"

The ache in his chest grew sharper. "After what we've shared, are we going to be satisfied with a few stolen moments here and there? I think that might be worse than if we just . . ." But he couldn't make himself say it.

"Ended it now?"

"Yeah."

"Oh, Mac."

He swallowed. "We always had a shelf life. It just turned out to be a little shorter than we thought."

"But we'll be seeing each other at Sadie's, and I'll be the maid of honor and you'll be the best man at the wedding. I won't be able to pretend I don't care about you whenever we're together."

"I'm not asking you to. I couldn't do that, either. We'll see each other around town this week and then we'll dance at Georgie and Vince's wedding. After that ... we'll kiss each other good-bye. It's the way it needs to be."

"Is that what you want?"

"Don't ask me that."

"I am asking. Is that what you want?"

He gazed at her. If he said no, then they'd spend the week desperately trying to find time to be together. They might even come to resent Vince and Georgie for making that so difficult. A frantic attempt to re-create what they'd shared this weekend could make their eventual separation tougher for both of them. "Yes," he said. "That's what I want."

"Okay, then." Her jaw firmed. "I'm on board with that program." Pointing Jasper straight ahead, she rode the rest of the way without speaking, but the silence was no longer comfortable.

Unsaddling and grooming the horses at the stable wasn't a lot of fun, either. He offered to take over the chore, but she refused. He'd seen that stubborn light in her eyes before and knew better than to argue.

When they finished, she picked up her messenger bag and a small knapsack that held the few things she'd brought on the camping trip. He'd been impressed with how little she'd chosen to take along. She might not be an experienced camper, but she had the concept of minimal possessions down.

Now that the moment of separation was at hand, he wasn't sure how to handle it. They stood in the stable yard in view of Ed's front porch and the main road. Not a particularly intimate or romantic place to end an affair.

First he thought of practical considerations. "We haven't set up any more rides between now and Saturday. Will you be okay with the ride into the canyon for the ceremony?"

She looked like a person facing a firing squad. "I'll be fine."

"Look, don't be noble just because of what I said back in the canyon. If you need a couple more lessons, we can work that out."

"Nope. I'm good."

"Yes, you are," he said softly. "You've made incredible progress in a short time. I'm not the least bit worried about Saturday."

She met his gaze. "I had a good teacher."

"I had a talented pupil."

"Thank you."

She looked so earnest standing there in that hat. He wanted to kiss her more than he wanted to breathe. But that wouldn't help anything. "See you around."

"Yeah." She gave him a soft smile. "See you around."

He watched her walk out of the stable yard and wondered if he'd survive losing her, after all.

CHAPTER 26

Fortunately for Anastasia, the next five days turned into a mind-numbing blur of activity. Between helping with wedding-related projects and organizing her trip to L.A. on Sunday, she had very little downtime. She caught glimpses of Mac during the week and they only exchanged brief comments.

That was a good thing, because every damn time she felt as if she'd been stabbed with a dull knife. When her sister Charmaine arrived on Wednesday from Dallas, Anastasia gave her a condensed version of her history with Mac and made Charmaine promise not to discuss it again, especially in front of their mother. Evelyn was overjoyed about the opportunity in L.A. and had mentioned several times that Anastasia had dodged a bullet by getting away from that cowboy Mac Foster.

Anastasia didn't feel as if she'd dodged anything. Love had hit her hard. The promise of a new and exciting job was great, but so far it hadn't lessened the pain of giving up Mac. She had to take it on faith that eventually she'd know for sure that she'd made the right decision.

Georgie and Vince's wedding day dawned clear and crisp. Amazingly, Anastasia had been getting up early every morning that week. Without a riding lesson, she'd expected to go right back to her night-owl pattern. Instead she kept waking up at sunrise as if her body rhythm yearned to keep in sync with Mac's.

Georgie had slept in her old bedroom the previous night as a nod to the tradition that the groom shouldn't see the bride until the ceremony. The men were heading out ahead of the ladies, with the exception of Ed, who had volunteered to lead the contingent of women.

The old Victorian wasn't even slightly soundproof, so Anastasia could tell that Georgie was up and Charmaine was not. She decided to walk across the hall and see how Georgie was doing.

Georgie answered her knock looking uncharacteristically flustered. Her honey blond hair was tangled and her bed looked as if she'd been wrestling the sheets all night. She stared at Anastasia. "You're up! I can't believe you're up."

"It seems to be my new thing, greeting the dawn. How are you?"

"Can you believe it?" She moved away from the door to let Anastasia come in. "I'm nervous. I love Vince so much, and I've been living with him since June so I know all his bad habits and he knows mine. We're perfect for each other. Why should I be nervous?"

"Because today you'll give your word, so there's no going back, at least not for a person like you, who takes these things very seriously."

Georgie gazed at her and nodded. "That's it. This is serious."

"And there's the baby to consider."

"You know?" Her eyes widened.

"Georgie, I'm sure everyone knows. You quit drinking wine! You love a glass of red wine with dinner. And then the wedding date is, like, immediately. What else would people think?"

Her sister's grin was sheepish. "I suppose that's true. But nobody's mentioned it."

"They won't. Bickford folks might be nosy but they won't say anything until you decide to make the announcement."

"What announcement?" Charmaine appeared in the doorway rubbing her eyes. Without makeup she looked much younger than twenty-seven. Her salon-lightened hair was the platinum color of a child's and she kept herself skinny so she'd fit into designer clothes.

Georgie gazed at her. "If I tell you, you have to promise not to screech. I don't want Evelyn to know."

"She wears earplugs so she won't hear me, but I promise not to screech if you tell me you're pregnant."

"What? Does everyone in the world know?"

"You are?" Charmaine raced over and gave her a hug. "I was just being a smart-ass! That's awesome! Boy or girl?"

"We've decided not to ask."

Charmaine sighed. "Which means I have to go with yellow baby outfits. Except I predict it'll be a girl. Girls run in the family. I hope it's a girl. Maybe she'll play dolls with me and have tea parties since neither of you losers ever would."

"Speaking of parties," Anastasia said, "it's time to get this one started, especially with only one shower up here."

"I'm first!" Then Charmaine slapped her forehead. "Except I can't be first. The bride should be first."

Georgie laughed. "Go ahead, Charmaine. You can be first."

"Nope, nope, nope. You can be first, but don't dawdle, okay?"

"I never dawdle."

"You're right. Anastasia's the one who can get in there and start sketching in her mind and forget where she is."

"I do not!"

Both Georgie and Charmaine turned to her, eyebrows raised.

"Well, maybe sometimes."

Charmaine nodded. "Often. In any case, I'll be second. What about your dress, Georgie? Does it need ironing?"

"It might."

"I know mine does, and I'll bet Anastasia's does, too. I'll set up the ironing board in my room. Anastasia, go fetch your dress. Chop, chop, everybody! We have a wedding today!"

Smiling, Anastasia went to get her dress out of the closet. Later on she'd have to deal with seeing Mac, which might be difficult. But hanging out with her sisters while they all got ready—that was going to be big fun.

Two hours later as all three of them walked the short distance to Ed's stable, Anastasia longed for her sketch pad. Their outfits were practical yet gorgeously retro. Georgie was in white, while Charmaine and Anastasia had matching outfits in aspen yellow, but the design was virtually the same.

Ankle-length split skirts showed off lace-up riding boots. The bodices of the dresses were flatteringly snug but high-necked, and each sister wore a jaunty hat over her upswept hairdo. Georgie had a veil, which she'd pull forward for the ceremony but left up for the ride into the canyon.

The other women riding with them had assembled in the stable yard and applauded as they approached. Of course Ida was going, and so was the mayor's wife, Inez, along with Ike's wife, Raina. Steve and Myra Jenson had chosen to stay behind and make sure the reception was under control. Sue Bryson would ride out with them, though. She was excited about Georgie's wedding but she also looked forward to watching her husband, Frank, conduct the ceremony.

Ed had spent the week contacting nearby ranches for loaners so he'd have enough mounts for everyone attending the wedding. Technically, either Sue or Frank should have ridden Jasper because they owned him, but they'd graciously allowed Anastasia to do that while they both took borrowed horses. Georgie was on Prince, and Charmaine had been given Skeeter, the horse she'd ridden the first time she'd been out on the trail.

The big bay wasn't the prettiest horse in the group, though. Anastasia wondered if Charmaine, who usually paid great attention to her appearance, would object, especially because each of her sisters had a handsome mount. She didn't say a word, and Anastasia realized how much her previously self-centered sister had evolved.

The ride into the canyon was merry. Some of the women hadn't been on a horse in a while, and no doubt they'd have aches and pains tomorrow, but they all seemed to be having the time of their lives being part of this adventure. They repeatedly thanked Georgie for coming up with such a creative venue, and she gave all the credit to Vince.

For Anastasia, the canyon would always hold memories of Mac. Without his help she wouldn't be part of this wedding procession. Come to think of it, without Mac there wouldn't be a wedding in the box canyon. Georgie would have had the ceremony in Sadie's because of Anastasia's fear.

But he was largely an unsung hero because no one knew that she'd been terrified of horses until Mac had taught her not to be. She and Georgie were the only ones who realized what a miracle he'd accomplished in less than a week. But if she announced it during the reception, an idea that had crossed her mind, he would hate that.

The steady stream of conversation made the ride seem short and Anastasia was surprised when they reached the narrow trail leading up to the box canyon. Half the people in the group had never seen it, although they'd heard descriptions. Obviously they were eagerly anticipating their first glimpse.

"I'm checking off two items on my bucket list today," Ida announced. "I'll see this canyon everyone's talked about, and I'll watch Georgie and Vince get hitched. It's a twofer."

"Same here," Inez said. "Since I'm old enough to be Georgie's grandmother, I've known her since she was a bitty thing. And here I am going to her wedding in a canyon I didn't know existed until six months ago."

"That's right," Sue added. "I know we're all a little bummed about the documentary being postponed, but think of how far we've come, thanks to Vince and his friends. It's about time we celebrated our progress, and this is the perfect occasion."

"And this is the perfect place." Ed had been leading the procession with Anastasia and Georgie bringing up the rear. "Ladies, have you ever seen anything prettier than this?" He moved aside so the women could emerge from the narrow trail into the clearing.

At the chorus of exclamations, Anastasia turned back to Georgie. "I think they like it."

"Vince has good taste."

Anastasia smiled at her sister. "I know he does. He chose you."

"Thanks." Georgie's cheeks turned pink. "Remind me

to do something nice for Mac. He was a huge part of making this possible."

"You know what? I have the perfect thing. I promised him a sketch, and if you'd mat and frame it for me, then—"

"Consider it done."

That was the last private conversation she had with Georgie. They emerged into the open meadow to discover it had been transformed. The guys had outdone themselves.

They'd created an arched trellis large enough not to be dwarfed by participants on horseback. They'd positioned it so that it framed the waterfall beyond. If a wedding venue had ever been more beautiful than this, Anastasia couldn't imagine how.

Someone, no doubt Travis, had hauled in a compact sound system. The moment the women appeared, harp music filled the canyon. Harp music. Anastasia would never have thought of it, but the sound was perfect, as if angels hovered overhead blessing this ceremony.

The guests arranged themselves in a row in front of the trellis with a pathway in the middle. As the wedding march began, Charmaine straightened in the saddle and rode down the path to take her place to the left of the arch. Anastasia followed and spared a glance for the tall man on Cinder to the right of the groom on Storm Cloud.

Mac looked gorgeous in his Western-style tux, as she'd known he would. He smiled at her, and her heart stumbled. What was she doing, leaving such a man?

Throughout the ceremony, which made her cry, she thought of Mac and all that he'd done. If she could be two people, one part of her would stay with Mac and the other half would work for Kathryn Abernathy in L.A. But she was only one person, and her choice was clear.

After the ceremony she rode out with Mac. "You look great," he murmured, "as if you'd been born riding a horse."

"You're exaggerating, but thank you." The sound of his voice made her heart pound.

"I'm not. You've claimed your birthright. I hope you keep riding. It might not be easy, living in California, but—"

"I'll keep riding. I want to do it for myself, but I also want to keep it up as a tribute to you."

"Nah, I don't need a tribute."

"You do, Mac. You really do. I—"

Travis took that moment to organize the troops and get everyone lined up to head back. Although technically Anastasia should have been either ahead of or behind Mac, the order got scrambled. She didn't come face-to-face with him again until they'd returned to town and were gathered at Sadie's.

The reception was informal enough that they could have avoided dancing with each other, but suddenly he was there, pulling her out onto the floor. *One dance, and then we'll kiss good-bye.* And oh, what a dance it was.

They'd been great partners before they'd become lovers, but now the communication between them was complete, as if they were connected by an invisible wire that telegraphed their movements. She'd never felt so alive as they spun and circled. They cleared the floor as clapping and whistling filled her ears.

But the music ended, and Mac drew her over to a corner of the room, away from the crowd. They were both breathing hard and he paused before trying to speak. He cupped her face in both hands. "Knowing you has been one of the highlights of my life."

"Don't say it like that. You make it sound as if we'll never see each other again. We will. I'll be back for visits."

He smiled. "But essentially you'll be gone, as you

should be. I want that for you. I want all your dreams to come true." Then he kissed her softly, almost reverently.

When she tried to pull him into a more intimate embrace, he stepped away and shook his head. "I'll never forget you, Anastasia Bickford."

Then the party crowd closed in and they were separated. He never asked her to dance again that night. It was over.

Winters were milder in Southern California than they were in the Texas Panhandle. Anastasia had known that intellectually, but with Thanksgiving only a week away, she missed the threat of snow. Walking to work from the bus stop, she passed a group of tourists. They were all wearing shorts and T-shirts in the middle of November. Weird.

But she'd eventually get used to the climate and she loved her job. Working in the film industry had inspired her in ways she'd never have imagined. Everyone was friendly and she often went out for drinks or a meal with her new buddies.

But there were also evenings when she took the bus home to her little apartment and found herself dragging out her portfolio and looking through her old sketches. Inevitably she ended up with pictures of Mac lined up along the cushions of her couch.

Although she'd tried like hell not to miss him, she still did. He might be impatient with her if he knew how much she still longed to be in his arms at night. Yet that was a hopeless fantasy. Her work was here and he would hate living in the middle of a big city.

Georgie had called her the previous night to ask if she could make it home for Thanksgiving. No trail rides had been scheduled for that weekend, and the town had decided to have a community dinner at Sadie's so they could celebrate the revival of Bickford. Anastasia had told Georgie she'd think about it.

The plane fare would be outrageous at this late date, but she had the money. Her hesitation was all about Mac. Much as she wanted to see everyone, including him, it was bound to be awkward. Maybe she'd wait until Christmas, after they'd both had more time to get over each other.

That decision made, she walked into her little cubicle and found on her computer a Post-it from Kathryn, who wanted to see her first thing this morning. She left her messenger bag on the desk and headed off to Kathryn's lavish office. The receptionist buzzed her in immediately.

Glancing up from her computer, Kathryn smiled. "Hey, there. How are you?"

"I'm good, really good. Those sketches you wanted should be done in—"

"I'm not worried about the sketches. You always meet your deadlines. Have a seat. I wanted to ask about something else."

"Sure." Anastasia treasured the easy relationship she had with Kathryn. They'd bonded from the beginning and that connection had only grown stronger.

"When I first met you, I was struck by the sparkle in your eyes and lately I don't see it so much. Are we working you too hard?"

"Heavens, no. I love it here."

"I'm glad, but I can't shake the feeling that something's not right in your world. I realize I'm getting personal, but I miss that sparkle."

Anastasia stared at her as she wrestled with her thoughts. Kathryn was more perceptive than she'd given her credit for. Talking about the issue wouldn't change anything, but if Kathryn had picked up on it, then she deserved an explanation.

"I left someone in Texas I really care about." She paused to take a deep breath. "But we agreed it had to end. I'm not quite over him, I guess. I'm working on it."

Compassion shone in Kathryn's eyes. "There's no chance he'd move here?"

"None. He'd be miserable in L.A. He's bought a cute little house in Bickford, and that's where he belongs. He's a cowboy and he needs the wide-open spaces."

"And you love him."

"Yes."

"And he loves you enough to let you go so that you can follow your dream."

"Yes." Anastasia's throat hurt but she was not going to break down in Kathryn's office.

"Do you realize how rare that is?"

She swallowed. "Kind of."

"Anastasia, you're a special person and it sounds as if you've found another special person who loves you. Why are you working so hard to get over him?"

"Because we can't be together!" Maybe Kathryn wasn't so perceptive, after all.

"Of course you can. You're so creative that I'm amazed you haven't applied that creativity to this situation. I can help by freeing up your schedule. Pack more hours into four days so you can take three off and fly back to be with him. Some projects you might even be able to work on remotely from Bickford."

"I could?"

"Absolutely. You have an incredible work ethic so I know you'll get the projects finished. You'll spend a lot on airfare, but what's money for, anyway?"

Anastasia sat in stunned silence as the possibilities unfolded like a flower in her mind. She could be with Mac. *She could be with Mac.*

"Oh, Anastasia. Your sparkle is back."

CHAPTER 27

Something was going on. Mac wasn't sure what, but Georgie and Vince were involved in whatever it was and they weren't talking. He had a bad feeling that they planned to embarrass him with some kind of speech of gratitude during the Thanksgiving celebration at Sadie's.

Hell, he knew they were grateful for his help in teaching Anastasia to ride. They'd told him so about a million times. But maybe that wasn't enough for them and they'd make some public announcement proclaiming him a prince among men or some such hogwash.

The possibility nearly made him consider not going, but he didn't want to miss the fun. Ida had come up with the idea of this feast in honor of the town's economic recovery and she was paying for all the food. She'd also asked Mac and Travis to sit on either side of her and treat her like a queen. They were both looking forward to that.

Ida deserved his best outfit, so he'd worn his black Western shirt, his best jeans, and the black hat he saved for special occasions like this one. Inevitably she'd make outrageous comments about how handsome he looked, but he'd just about learned how to handle her compliments without blushing.

Smiling as he thought about sharing this dinner with Ida and the rest of the town, he walked into Sadie's, glanced around, and nearly passed out. Anastasia stood in the far corner talking to Georgie and Vince. Adrenaline sent his heart into overdrive.

Damn it, they should have warned him. If that's what they'd been so secretive about, he didn't appreciate it. Anastasia must have been in on the surprise, too.

She'd spotted him and was coming over. He had half a mind to leave, but then he'd look like he couldn't handle seeing her. He'd be seen as a coward. So he stood his ground, but his nerves were stretched tighter than a rope on a wild horse.

At least she seemed to be in the same condition. She didn't smile or anything. "Let's go outside."

"Good idea." He was amazed he'd been able to speak. He held the door for her and breathed in her scent as she walked past. It made him light-headed, and he had to concentrate as he put one foot in front of the other.

She led him around to the side of the building, the same place they'd had their big argument. Turning back toward him, she took a deep breath. "I love you."

"So what?" Suddenly angry, he had no control of his words. "I love you, too! Which means nothing if we can't . . ." He trailed off because she was smiling. That made no sense.

"But we can."

"You're not quitting. I've had reports from Georgie. She told me you're crazy about that job. I don't care if you love me. That job is perfect for you, and I—"

"I'm not quitting. But Kathryn came up with this idea, a flexible schedule so I can be here a lot. Pretty much, half the time. You work weekends, so I will, too. Midweek, I can be here for three days, sometimes longer."

He blinked. Then he scrubbed both hands over his

face. This moment felt real, but it was way too good to be true. "Say that again."

"I'll be flying back here on a regular basis, so I can—"

"Won't that cost a lot of money?"

"It will, but I don't care. I love you. Being with you is what's important. I don't spend all the money I make, anyway. I might as well use it for airfare."

"I'm so afraid I'm dreaming this."

"I don't blame you." She stepped closer. "I've had several days to think about it and I'm only just now starting to believe it's possible."

"Why didn't you call me and tell me about this conversation with Kathryn?"

"I considered it, but I decided it would be way better if I told you in person, because then . . . but maybe I should have . . ."

He got it. "Because then we could do this." He drew her into his arms. "And this." Tipping back his hat, he lowered his mouth to hers. Her warm lips and total surrender convinced him this wasn't a dream. He was rocketed back to that moment in the canyon when she'd kissed him this way, all the while telling him without words that she loved him.

He'd known then no one would ever take her place in his heart. He'd accepted the truth of that and had vowed to live with it, no matter how painful it might be. Now he wouldn't have to give her up.

This kiss had been a long time in the making, and he wasn't in the mood to end it anytime soon. She seemed as eager to continue as he was. So when someone tapped him on the shoulder, he motioned them away.

Whoever it was apparently couldn't take a hint. Instead there was much throat clearing and then another tap on his shoulder, harder this time.

It had better not be Travis. Mac reluctantly raised his head and turned toward the intruder.

Ida stood there smiling at him. "Does this mean you won't be sitting next to me at dinner?"

"Yes, ma'am, I'm afraid it does."

"Well, good! It's about damn time you two figured this out. I told you she had a crush on you!"

Anastasia smiled. "And you were right."

"I'll just go on inside and tell everyone you're smooching out here and not to wait dinner." She turned to leave.

Anastasia glanced up at him. "We can go in if you'd rather not have her make that announcement."

"Oh, no, I want her to make it. I'm proud to be out here smooching with you. But if you want to go in . . ."

"Not on your life, cowboy. Smooching with you is my favorite thing to do."

He lifted his eyebrows. "Really?"

"Okay, second favorite. But if we end up doing my favorite thing, we'll miss dinner and I think we should attend. It's an important celebration."

"It is, but I wouldn't want to make a liar out of Ida Harrington. Come here." And he recaptured the sweetest mouth he'd ever had the privilege to kiss.

Read on to catch up on the first book
in Vicki Lewis Thompson's Sexy Texans series,

CRAZY FOR THE COWBOY

Available from Signet Eclipse.

"Somebody should take a paintbrush to Sadie's left nipple." Vince Durant studied the six-by-ten mural on the far wall of Sadie's Saloon as he sipped his beer. "It's chipped."

A well-endowed nude reclined on a red velvet piece of Victorian furniture that he thought was called a fainting couch. Rumor had it that a local woman named Sadie had posed for the mural, but because the painting was more than a century old, the rumor was unconfirmed.

"Sadie's not the only thing needing a little TLC around here." Ike Plunkett was still behind the bar, which was reassuring.

Vince remembered Ike from four years ago, and although the bartender's hair was a little thinner and his glasses a little thicker, he looked virtually the same. That couldn't be said for the town of Bickford, though. Except for the general store and this historic hotel, the place was pretty much dead.

Come to think of it, he'd seen no evidence that anyone else was staying at the hotel besides him and the two friends who hadn't arrived yet. Even more troubling, the saloon was deserted, and that wasn't normal for a Friday afternoon. At the end of the day, cowboys in the Texas Panhandle enjoyed sipping a cold one. "I never realized how much the town depended on the Double J."

"I don't think any of us did until it was gone."

"You'd think by now somebody would have reopened it." Vince wouldn't mind working there again. Turned out he was good at wrangling greenhorns.

"Can't." Ike used a bar rag to wipe down the whiskey bottles lined up beneath an ornate mirror behind the bar. "Somebody torched it, probably for the insurance, and the land's tied up in a big legal hassle."

"Sorry to hear that." Vince polished off his beer and signaled for another. He was thirsty after the long drive from Fort Worth.

"Not half as sorry as we are."

"No, probably not." But he *was* sorry, and disappointed, too. He'd talked his buddies Mac Foster and Travis Langdon into having a reunion, figuring they could party in Bickford like they had during the three years they'd all worked for the Double J Guest Ranch. "I don't suppose you have live music this weekend?"

"We haven't had a band in here for a long time. Can't afford to pay 'em."

"That's depressing."

"Tell me about it."

"Oh, well. At least you have beer." Vince lifted his bottle in the direction of the mural. "And Sadie! After a few of these, I might decide to repaint her nipple myself."

The street door opened with the squeak of an unoiled hinge and Vince turned to see if Mac or Travis had come straight into the saloon instead of stopping by the hotel desk to check in like he had.

His smile of welcome faltered when Georgina Bickford walked through the door. He took some comfort in noticing that she seemed as disoriented by his presence as he was by hers. That made no sense, really. It wasn't like they had a history, although he'd tried his damnedest to create one.

His fabled charm hadn't worked on her and she'd never gone out with him. Maybe that was why he'd thought of her so often since then. She was the one girl he'd never been able to impress.

She didn't look particularly impressed to see him now, either. "Hello, Vince."

"Hello, Georgie." He remembered that cool voice of hers, but at least she hadn't forgotten his name. After four years, that said something. He wasn't convinced it said something positive, though. A name could stick in a person's mind for both good reasons and bad.

"I'm surprised to see you here." She approached slowly, as if he had yellow caution tape draped around his barstool. "Just passing through?"

"Not exactly." He thumbed back his hat so he could see her better. She'd gotten prettier, but she'd always been great to look at, with her big brown eyes and honey-colored hair. When he'd first started working at the Double J, he'd asked around and had learned that she'd left college to run the general store after her dad died. He'd tried to be friendly, but she'd never given him the time of day.

She frowned. "If you're looking for work, there's not much to be had, I'm afraid."

"So I gather." He hesitated. Oh, what the hell? "Can I buy you a drink?"

"No, thank you."

Shot down again, damn it.

"Georgie's first drink is always on the house." Ike sent a glance of compassion Vince's way as he placed a glass of red wine on the bar. "All of the council members get one free drink per day. Bickford Hotel policy. It's the least we can do when they have such a thankless job."

"You're on the town council?" Then he wished he hadn't sounded so surprised. "I mean, I'm sure you're well-qualified and all. I just . . ."

She appeared to take pity on him. "It's okay. I'm the youngest member, but I also run the second biggest revenue producer in town, so it's logical for me to be on the council." She smiled. "It wasn't a tough race. No one ran against me."

Hey, a smile. Progress.

"They wouldn't have dared run against you," Ike said. "What can I get you from the kitchen?"

"Does Henry have any barbecued pork back there?"

"I believe he does."

"Then a barbecued pork sandwich would be great. Thanks, Ike."

The bartender glanced at Vince. "Want to order some food? We still have Henry Blaylock cooking for us. Don't know if you remember, but he's terrific."

"I do remember Henry's food. Good stuff. But I'll wait for Mac and Travis to get here before I order."

"Fair enough." Ike opened the hinged section of the bar and walked back toward the kitchen.

"Mac and Travis?" Georgie picked up her wineglass but remained standing beside the bar instead of hopping up on a stool. "The same Mac and Travis who used to work for the Double J?"

"You have a good memory." She hadn't dated those old boys, either. Vince, Mac, and Travis had been the cutups of the group, and Georgie didn't approve of cutups. She'd made that clear soon after they'd met, and he doubted that she'd changed.

She took a sip of her wine. "Are you having some kind of Double J reunion?"

"In a way, but it's just the three of us."

Her brown eyes lit with curiosity. "And you're meeting here, in Bickford?"

"That's the plan." He liked her haircut, which was a little shorter than he remembered. It used to hang past her shoulders, but now it was chin length. The new cut made her look more sophisticated. Sexier.

"Why meet here?"

He shrugged. "It's where we used to hang out, but I didn't realize the place had gone . . . uh, that it's not the same."

"If you were about to say it's gone to hell in a handbasket, you'd be on target. If you want to have a fun time, y'all might want to head somewhere else. Go on up to Amarillo, maybe."

"It'll be okay." He didn't remember her being quite so curvy the last time he'd seen her. She filled out the Bickford General Store's hunter-green T-shirt, although he was careful not to be caught ogling. He'd noticed that her jeans fit mighty nice, too. Not that it made any difference whether she was a knockout or not. She hadn't changed regarding him. She showed no interest whatsoever.

"I can't imagine what you'll find to do around here," she said. "Sadie's doesn't heat up like it used to on the weekend. Anastasia and I might be the last two single women under thirty in Bickford."

"What about Charmaine?" Seven years ago, when he was a new hire at the Double J, Georgie's stepsisters had been too young to go out dancing at Sadie's, but Charmaine, the older one, had snuck in one time and Georgie had marched her back home.

"She's working in Dallas. She'd party with you if she could, but she isn't here, and Anastasia's not into that. Besides, even if she was, there's no live music anymore."

"Yeah, Ike said it wasn't in the budget. No worries. I haven't seen Mac and Travis since we left the Double J. Maybe it's better this way. We can drink beer and catch up."

"For the entire weekend?" She sounded skeptical.

"Well, no. We'll do that at night, but during the day we'll head out and round up the Ghost. Ike says he's still—"

"You most certainly will not!" She set her wineglass down with a sharp *click* and faced him, sparks of anger in her eyes. "Don't y'all dare go out there and harass that poor horse for your own amusement!"

He blinked in confusion. The dappled gray stallion and his small band of wild horses used to be fair game, a challenge for the cowboys who worked at the Double J. Vince and his buddies hadn't succeeded in roping him, mostly because they'd never been able to devote an entire weekend to the project. Now they could.

But Georgie was obviously ready to rip him a new one on the subject of the wild stallion. "There is no reason on God's green earth why you should go after him! He's not hurting anything, especially now that so few horses live in the area. Back when the Double J was in operation, I admit he tried to raid the corral a couple of times, but those days are over. There are four horses boarded at Ed's stable, and they're all geldings. No mares. The Ghost leaves us alone and we leave him alone!"

"But—"

"Is that why you decided to rendezvous here? To go after that stallion?"

"Partly, yeah. We always talked about capturing him, but we never did. Now seems as good a time as any."

Her eyes glittered in defiance. "You won't find him."

"Oh, I think we will. We have two whole days to look."

Ike returned from the kitchen, and Georgie wheeled

on him. "Did you tell Vince that the Ghost was still out there?"

Ike shrugged. "He asked. I wasn't going to lie to the man."

"Are you aware that Vince and his two cohorts are heading out on some macho quest to rope him?"

"I didn't know that." Ike looked at Vince. "You might want to reconsider. Georgie takes a special interest in those wild horses."

Crap. First he'd discovered that the town was deader than a doornail, and now Georgie Bickford was raining all over his wild-horse roundup. Maybe she was right and they should take this party elsewhere, but he'd craved the small-town experience and he wouldn't get that in Amarillo or Lubbock.

Mac and Travis chose that moment to walk into the saloon. They'd shared a ride here because they both worked at a ranch outside Midland. They sauntered in with wide grins as if they owned the place. Vince left his barstool and went over to greet them. Much joking around and backslapping followed. Vince couldn't believe how happy he was to see those old boys. Until they arrived, he'd been outnumbered.

Mac and Travis tipped their hats and said hello to Georgie, who replied without smiling.

"So where is everybody?" Mac glanced around. "Hey, Georgie. What's happened to this place?"

"We're experiencing an economic downturn." Georgie's jaw tightened. "I suggest you three mosey on to a place that's more suited to your needs."

"Nah, we don't need to do that," Travis said. "I assume Sadie's still serves beer."

"We do," Ike said.

"Then we're in business." Travis walked over to the

bar and shook hands with Ike. "Good to see you. I'll have a longneck, like always."

"And I'll take my usual draft." Mac sat on a stool next to him.

"Coming up." Ike looked nervous, but he busied himself getting the beer.

Georgie cleared her throat. "I understand y'all are planning to round up the Ghost this weekend."

Mac nodded. "Yes, ma'am, we sure are. Isn't that right, Vince?"

For a split second Vince considered telling Mac there'd been a change of plans. Then his rebellious streak surfaced. By God, he'd organized this adventure and he'd see it through. There was no law against chasing after that horse. He met Georgie's flinty gaze. "That's right, Mac."

Georgie's mouth thinned. "Over my dead body."

Vince admired her spirit. He always had. But he couldn't let her get the upper hand.

"Don't go sacrificing yourself like that, darlin'."

She balled her hands into fists. "Do *not* call me—"

"I promise we won't hurt those horses one tiny bit." He turned to his partners in crime. "Isn't that right, boys?"